THE ONE
I WANT

THE ONE I WANT

NANCY WARREN

BRAVA

KENSINGTON PUBLISHING CORP.
http://www.kensingtonbooks.com

BRAVA BOOKS are published by

Kensington Publishing Corp.
850 Third Avenue
New York, NY 10022

ISBN-13: 978-0-7582-1045-6
ISBN-10: 0-7582-1045-0

First Kensington Trade Paperback Printing: May 2008
10 9 8 7 6 5 4 3 2 1

Printed in the United States of America

THE ONE
I WANT

Chapter 1

"I'm not going to make it," Chloe Flynt moaned into the phone, each word dripping with despair and drama. "I'm so bored."

She was supposed to be in her oil-painting class, but she couldn't summon the enthusiasm. Apart from "Study of the Nude Male", she wasn't having nearly the fun she'd hoped for. She glanced out the window of her bedroom in the villa. The golden Umbrian hills reclined under the sun as though they were enjoying a siesta.

That was the trouble with this place. It was too relaxed. Slow meals, slow pace of life. No decent shopping for miles. Oh, the sixteenth century villa was certainly lovely, but she rather fancied that when she'd bolted from London and her broken engagement, she'd have been better off heading to Milan or Rome. Or better yet, Paris. Someplace where there was some life.

Apart from the rather dishy Tuscan chef who loved nothing more than to tempt her fickle palate, she wasn't really enjoying her newly chosen career as a painter.

"Of course you're bored," her friend Nicky said in the nasal drawl that made her sound like Keira Knightley with a head cold. "Perhaps it was a little soon after breaking off your engagement to be deciding on a career."

"I haven't any talent for painting, anyway," Chloe said,

staring dismally out of her window to the garden overlooking the vineyard where eight easels were set up and seven painters were dabbing at canvases with various levels of success. Her own abandoned effort was shockingly bad; even from here she could see that the ocher had been a mistake.

Hearing from Nicky about all the fun that was going on at home in London, without her, only worsened her boredom.

"I can't stand it," she said suddenly. "I'm going to have to quit."

There was annoying laughter at the other end. "Of course you are, silly. We've had bets on how long you'd last. I lost my ten quid last Thursday. If you make it through the end of the week, Gerald Barton-Hinks wins the pool."

They were placing bets on how soon she'd quit? Really it ought to inspire her to stay through to the end of the course, four weeks from now, just to show them all she could do it.

She contemplated this option for a minute, then thought, *Sod it, I'm not staying here another month for anything.* Besides, it was cheering to know that everyone at home missed her so much, they were making book on when she'd return. "Who wins the pool if I quit today?" she asked.

"I think it's Jack."

Her older and extremely annoying brother, Jack was extremely, annoyingly happy with his American chef-girlfriend. "Perfect. Maybe if he makes a profit he won't be so shirty with me for throwing more of Daddy's money down the drain."

"Are we talking about the same Jack? Your brother Jack? He adores you."

"He's horrible," she said, pouting. How unkind he'd been when she had to cancel her wedding at the last minute.

"He's not horrible. He thinks you should settle down and stop acting irrationally, that's all."

"My engagement was recently broken," she reminded Nicky. "I think I'm entitled to act irrationally."

Another laugh answered her. "That might have worked

the first time. You even managed it pretty well the second time, but Chlo, three broken engagements in a row, well, it's getting to be a bad habit."

Chloe sighed, twisting the bracelet with the intertwining Cs around her wrist. "I know. It's just that I've got such awful taste in men. Anyway, I'm done with men. I'm going to have a career instead. But what am I going to do? If I don't become a painter, which I can tell you isn't bloody likely, what sort of job would I like? Because I'm going to have to work, you know. Daddy says that's it. This is my last chance."

"Ouch. Nasty. But then you can always bring your dad around, you know you can."

It was true enough, but lately Daddy had been very glum and had taken to turning out all the lights at home to save on the electric.

"Still, couldn't you manage four more weeks?" Nicky asked.

Chloe glanced out the window again. She saw that the painters were taking a break, stretching their pleasantly tired painting arms, no doubt. She noted that they all gathered around her easel and Giorgio, their teacher, was pointing with his brush at her canvas, which elicited a riotous burst of laughter from the group.

She shook her head violently, and said, "No, I can't stay another minute." To emphasize her decision, she dragged out the matched set of Louis Vuitton luggage that her first almost husband had bought her and, holding the phone against her ear with her shoulder, managed to wrestle the larger of the cases onto the bed.

"Right, then," said Nicky, who was her best friend for a reason. "If you can't stay, you can't."

"It's lovely having someone who truly understands me. I tell you what, call in half a dozen of our friends—the ones with posh jobs. We'll have an emergency summit meeting when I get back." She was beginning to feel excited. She missed her friends, and someone was bound to know of some glamorous, high-paying job she could do.

"An emergency summit meeting? Like at the U.N.?"

"With better food, better drink, and much better-looking delegates."

Nicky was obviously flicking through her appointment diary, Chloe could hear the pages turning. "I'll see what I can do."

"Great. We can have the emergency summit right after my surprise welcome home party."

Happiness began to well inside Chloe like tears. She grabbed her own appointment book. "I'll get a flight out tomorrow. Let's say Friday for the surprise party. And Saturday morning . . . No, that won't work. Not after Friday night . . . better make it Sunday brunch. We'll meet for my career planning emergency session then."

"But—"

"Must go. Feeling better for talking to you. Bye."

Chloe's surprise party was crowded with young, smart Londoners. But, of course, parties she and her friends arranged always were. She'd told Nicky that she wanted only six strategic thinkers at the top-secret Sunday brunch to plan her career. But then as she wandered among her friends, she thought how sensible Rupert Hardwich was and invited him. Toward the end of the night, she noticed Gerald Barton-Hinks standing with a group. He was something to do with property development. Probably he'd have lots of leads for jobs. She rather fancied zipping around London showing flats, or whatever estate agents did. She strolled over and said, "Hello, Gerry. Look, this is very hush-hush, but you must come for Sunday brunch to a top-secret emergency summit meeting about my career."

"You've already asked me, my sweet," he said, sounding rather amused about something.

"Oh, did I?" Then, since he was standing with two other people she knew, she felt it was only polite to invite them as well. But it turned out she already had.

"Oh, well," she said, sipping a glass of champagne that was

far from her first. "Not to worry. Many heads are better than one."

"Or is it too many cooks who spoil the broth?" Gerald asked.

"I was never much good at cooking," she told him. "I went to Paris to learn, you know, but I had no idea we'd spend the first week peeling vegetables and deboning things." She shuddered in memory.

Gerald gave her that indulgent smile men had been giving her ever since Daddy experienced her first temper tantrum at the age of two. "How long did you last?"

"I could concoct you a soup that would make you weep, and hors d'oeuvres that would have you sighing in pleasure." She looked at his mouth. "And I could certainly amuse your bouche."

He laughed, then gave her a quick kiss. "You are hopeless, you know that, don't you?"

She pouted. It was a trademark pout, one she'd practiced in the mirror during most of her early teen years. "Main courses are boring. And dessert is fattening."

"Life isn't a series of appetizers, Chlo. Someday you'll learn."

But Chloe thought she could live very well on champagne and caviar, and never stray into the boiled beef of life. She hoped very much that the experts guiding her into her new career would provide her with a champagne and caviar sort of job.

Of course, since she'd been rather freer with the invites than she'd intended, there was quite a crowd at Nicky's brunch. In fact, it was more of a party than a serious gathering, but Chloe was nothing if not a party girl. She'd never met a problem that wasn't better put off for another day while laughter, good friends, and good eats and drinks took over today.

At last, however, when more bottles of champagne had been consumed than was strictly necessary, Gerald stood on one of Nicky's tubular steel sixties-style chairs she'd bought when she redecorated her Knightsbridge flat after watching *Factory Girl.* "Right, I suggest we bring this meeting to order."

After the giggling and stupid jokes died down, he said, "We are all gathered here to help Chloe find a proper job. Any ideas?"

After a long silence, Miranda Peppertree, who did something in banking and had become rather boring, said, "What experience do you have? What are your qualifications?"

"Well . . ." She'd given this some thought, not wanting to come to the summit unprepared. "I'm very good at shopping. I could be a personal shopper."

"Not bad," said Gerald, as though Chloe wouldn't notice that Miranda had rolled her gaze and gone back to picking at a bit of smoked salmon on her plate. "Bit of a crowded field, though."

"And would it be as much fun, do you think, shopping for other people?" Nicky asked. At least Nicky was thinking clearly.

"Oh, good point. I'd probably forget and keep buying things for myself."

There were a few more suggestions, but most jobs sounded bloody boring, and Chloe didn't like the sound of any position that included the words *entry level*. She saw herself more as a penthouse girl than a street-level girl.

"Too bad you didn't simply marry one of those rich blokes who were crazy enough to want to marry you," Gerald said at last.

There was a sudden hoarse laugh from Nicky. "The only thing you're really good at is breaking up with people."

"That's not true."

"It is. And so creatively."

"Well, one likes to be original." She thought of some of her breakups and had to admit she did have flair.

"You even helped me break up with that awful prat from Wales. The one who insisted on quoting Shakespeare when he'd had too much to drink. Do you remember?"

"Of course I do. We wrote him a sonnet. Quite a good one, as I recall."

Nicky snorted. "It started, 'Shall I compare thee to a bale of hay.'"

"He loved horses and farming."

"And was blockish and irritating."

"Why don't you do that, Chlo? Help people break up bad relationships?"

"But you can't make a job out of helping people break up with other people," Miranda said.

"Why not? We send out our laundry, pay other people to manage our finances, deliver our groceries, cook our food, fix our cars. Why not pay an expert to break up with someone for you?" Nicky argued. Of course, Nicky was the laziest girl in London, but still.

"And if you could do it without the other person ending up really hurt, maybe you could earn a bonus."

"Yes, right. It could be a tailor-made breakup, which, let's face it, most of yours are," Gerald said, sounding enthusiastic, for Gerald.

"Expand the concept a bit. People could hire you to break up really obnoxious couples that all their friends know won't work."

"Ooh, like Henrietta and Jeremy?"

Everyone laughed, including Jeremy.

"But . . . so many people already know me here," Chloe said, immediately seeing the flaw in this excellent plan.

"Oh, you can't run your business here, love," Nicky said.

Chloe felt some of her excitement dim. She glanced around at the flat crowded with her friends. "Leave London?"

"Not London, darling. England."

"But where would I go?"

Jeremy said, "You'll have to move to America. They'll love you over there. Very entrepreneurial people, the Americans."

"Go to America?" For some reason, she'd never been.

"It would give you a new start."

She thought for a panicked moment about leaving every-thing familiar, and then, just as suddenly, excitement began to build. "America. Of course!"

It was the perfect answer. There was more scope for her talents there. She'd always wanted to go shopping on Rodeo Drive and lots of her friends loved New York. And if those television shows were any indication, Americans could use her help sorting out their love lives.

"I'd be a real businesswoman with my own company."

"How much can you charge? To break people up, I mean?" Nicky wanted to know.

Silence reigned for a moment, then Chloe said, "I'll call some matchmaking agencies. And then I'll charge double their rates."

"Double?"

"Of course. As we all know, it's a lot easier to get into a bad relationship than it is to get out."

Gerald laughed aloud. "You know, I really believe you'll do brilliantly in America with this company of yours."

"My company," she repeated, not without pride. Then a puzzled frown knitted her brow. "But what would I call it?" she asked the assembled experts.

Gerald raised his glass. "To Chloe Flynt, The Breakup Artist."

Chapter 2

Really, when Chloe thought about it, England was a small island. Too small for her talents. America beckoned, big, sprawling, lovely America with its cowboys and fast food, its freeways and film stars. Chloe felt that she'd finished messing about with her life; she was absolutely done with ancient, draughty castles and men who disappointed one.

She longed for some big, burly cattleman with a very large hat to throw her over his shoulder and call her his little woman. Naturally, she'd have to groom him a bit and hint that outside the bedroom she liked very much to be treated like a princess.

No. She was leaving her past behind her and moving on. Look how it had worked for Fergie?

Chloe wasn't one to waste time once she'd decided on a course of action, but as usual in her life, the men were trying to spoil her fun. Daddy wasn't pleased. "No, poppet. I warned you, when you broke off your engagement and traipsed off to France to paint, that I wouldn't fund any more of these ridiculous ideas. You're going to have to settle down and act sensibly."

She was so stunned that Daddy had said "No" that she couldn't quite take in the rest. "It was Italy, Daddy," she said. "I painted in Italy."

He looked annoyed with her, but she'd bring him round.

She always could. But after half an hour of the sprightly chatter that usually had him chuckling and bending to her will, he had barely smiled.

"Really, Nigel, you'll have to tell her," Mummy said, sipping her third scotch.

"Tell me what?"

"It's the money, sweetheart. We can't afford you anymore."

"Can't afford me? But—but, I'm your daughter."

"You're twenty-seven, Chloe. Time you were on your own. We'd so hoped the marriage to the ski racer would work and he could take you off our hands."

"I'm sorry I'm such a burden," she said, feeling huffy on the outside, but underneath feeling a quiver of fear. Mummy and Daddy were the port in any storm. The one place where she always felt safe.

"Of course you're not a burden," Daddy said, glaring at his wife. "And we're not poor, love, we've simply got to retrench."

Mother rose and tottered to the drinks trolley.

"What about my credit cards?" she asked, horrified.

Her father looked ill, and for the first time she worried about him. He looked so old and worn out. She experienced a twinge of guilt.

"I'll pay them up once more. But that will be the last time."

"Don't worry, Daddy," she said, feeling like Hayley Mills in *Pollyanna*. "Once I get my new company started in America, I'll be sending money home."

She managed to get her first chuckle out of her father. "Of course you will, pet. Of course you will."

She left her home after the weekend, quite worried.

All right. She had hoped to borrow some start-up money from her parents to fund her new venture, but obviously that wasn't going to work.

Luckily, the Italian ski racer she'd been recently engaged to hadn't wanted the vulgar diamond he'd given her for an engagement ring. The thing was the size of a small alp and brought in a satisfyingly large amount of cash when she got her brother, Jack, to take care of a private sale for her.

Six weeks later, Chloe was on her way to Austin, Texas.

Jack, who was very annoying but also quite sensible in a way she never would be, and whose advice was usually right, warned her away from Manhattan. "The shopping and parties will do you in in a fortnight," he'd warned. "And this time you're on your own."

Then it turned out that Rachel, his girlfriend and a fabulous chef, had lived in L.A. and didn't think it was quite right for Chloe either. It was her friend Gerald who, once more, stepped into the breach.

"There's a man I know in Austin, Texas, who owns some property. He's a decent fellow and he'd look after you. Why not start there? I've already talked to him, and he has a house for rent that's much more reasonable than what you'd pay in Manhattan or L.A."

Chloe wasn't nearly as stupid as she sometimes pretended to be and she knew that Jack had immediately called Gerald to try and steer her somewhere safe. Instead of annoying her, the thought that these people cared about her made her happy. Besides, something about Texas appealed to her. Maybe it was from having watched all those reruns of *Dallas* and *Dynasty* when she was a child, but she quite liked the notion of living somewhere so over the top.

She'd waffled a bit over Austin, but then she saw the picture of the house. It was a proper house with a pretty garden and three bedrooms so she could have her office at home.

Texas. Cowboys and oil wells, ranches, and land barons. She imagined being surrounded by the scenery and men of *Brokeback Mountain* except, of course, they'd be straight men.

Within a ridiculously short amount of time, she had everything organized. Jack had helped her sort out a visa. She had

business cards printed and had placed ads in all the important papers. She even had a Web site.

Her ads were simple.

> *The Breakup Artist*
> *Breaking up is hard to do. We can help. Ex-*
> *perienced, professional, creative. We do the dirty*
> *work and do our best to make sure there are no*
> *hard feelings afterward.*
> *Discretion assured.*

Chloe had enough money for about six months if she were
careful. Of course, by that time her business would be estab-
lished. Perhaps then she'd expand into bigger cities, she
thought, filled with the optimism with which she threw herself into every new venture.

So it was with a light heart that she stepped out of a cab
onto a charmingly suburban street in Austin. She was to pick
up her key at the house next door to the one she would oc-
cupy. All very simple.

She looked around, ready to be pleased with America. The
street was lined with some kind of tree she'd never seen before. The houses were neat, mostly brick, and with well-kept
gardens, the sort of home where a person might raise a family. In fact, now she looked again, she saw some kind of playground in one of the backyards. Once the cab driver had
unloaded all her luggage for her, she walked next door and
knocked.

So far the people she'd seen in this country, at the airport
and on the street, had been disappointingly average. Then the
door opened.

She found herself confronting a long, lean, muscular man
with world-weary hazel eyes, a tangle of dark brown hair,
and a jaw whose toughness was softened not at all by the
shadow of stubble. She knew she'd found Texas.

Or heaven.

"Good afternoon," she said. "I'm Chloe Flynt. I've taken the house next door."

He blinked down at her and she felt his focus sharpen, which usually happened when men looked at her. It wasn't that she courted male attention exactly, more that she would have missed it if it stopped.

She glanced up at him, way up, from under her lashes. She wasn't particularly short at five feet five inches, but next to this man she felt tiny.

"Gerald's friend. Right." He stood there, all masculine and delicious in a T-shirt that showed off lovely muscles and low-riding jeans. "I thought you'd be older."

She smiled at him, and next to her pout her smile was her deadliest weapon. "Well, one day I will be."

What the bloody hell had Gerry said about her?

"I'm Matthew Tanner."

She held out her hand since it didn't look as though he was going to. She was pleased to find his grip was warm, firm, and manly. Yes, she thought, he might make an interesting neighbor.

"I need you to fill out some tenant forms." He glanced at her again. "But you look pretty tired. Here's the key. Get yourself settled and we can do the paperwork tomorrow. Everything's hooked up and ready for you."

Tired? She looked tired? And Gerald had made her sound old? Right. The first thing she was doing after a good long sleep was sorting the closest day spa.

"Thank you so much," she said, accepting the key. She turned and put a little extra something into her walk just to let him know she was neither too old nor too young, but just right. And she was certainly not tired.

She hauled her luggage into her new home next door and proceeded to set up house. She loved the place the second she entered it.

The hardwood floors were warm and welcoming. To the left of the entry hall was a cozy living room with basic furniture. All very clean and durable. She'd have to do something to pretty it up. Some throws and pillows and things, she thought. She peeked through and behind the living room was a dining area and bright kitchen with a big window and a door leading out to a back garden with a patio. Of course, some tubs of flowers would brighten up the patio in no time. There was even a gas barbecue tucked to one side.

She ran upstairs and thought how pretty the big front bedroom was. Rather masculine, but at least there was bedding. Something else Gerald had arranged for her. Bless him. Her bedroom boasted an ensuite bath with shower.

There were two other bedrooms, one of which was already set up as an office. Excellent. She peeked into the third bedroom thinking it could be a guest room if any of her friends popped over for a visit. And there was another big bathroom. Again, quite utilitarian, but nothing she wouldn't soon have prettied up.

Tomorrow she'd worry about groceries. Tonight she was happy she'd packed the absolute essentials. A tin of tea by Taylors of Harrowgate and a box of Cadbury's Milk Tray.

With the tea made and her essentials unpacked, she set up her laptop in the spare room, where she was delighted to find an old oak desk. Since the house came furnished, she'd imagined having to store a spare bed and buy a desk, so the fact that there was already a desk here and wireless Internet convinced her she'd made a good choice.

Her luck continued to hang about in the stratosphere when she found in her in-box, among farewell and good luck posts from her friends, a message from her first potential client.

"Can you help? I can't get rid of my girlfriend. I keep trying to break up with her, but she's not getting the message."

She shook her head. How people could make heavy work of the simplest things. She e-mailed him back and made an appointment for the following day. Then she went to bed and thought about her first job as the owner of her own company.

Her strategy would depend both on the man and what he told her of the woman, but already she was playing with ideas. She could reenact the dramatic breakup she'd managed for Martin Willowbrook when he'd been stalked by that woman he'd met at Oxford. That had been simple and effective. But where would she borrow a baby?

Chapter 3

Matthew wandered past his front door, yawning, fantasizing about the first strong, black cup of coffee of the day when he noticed a fat envelope on the mat inside his front door.

He stood there for a moment regarding it, eyes unconsciously narrowing. It wasn't part of the regular mail delivery. He'd locked up just after midnight and the envelope hadn't been there then. He glanced at his watch and wondered who had dropped off a fat piece of mail in the past seven hours and whether he should be alarmed.

As usual, curiosity was stronger than caution. He picked up the envelope. The name *Chloe* was handwritten on the front. The envelope was soft, the flap tucked in but not sealed. A man with strong moral fiber and a healthy conscience would walk right next door and push the envelope through the correct mail slot.

He pulled out the tucked flap and peeked inside, where he found a wad of cash. And a note.

> *Chloe,*
> *Thanks so much. Didn't want this on my credit card for obvious reasons. Everything worked out great. I'd use you again.*
> *Allan.*

He counted the money, then stood there chewing his upper lip with an unpleasant feeling that both he and his London acquaintance Gerald had been snowed. He shoved the money back and walked outside into the cool of morning. Lights were on in a few of his neighbors' windows, and Horace Black across the street and two down was backing his new truck down the driveway.

Up and down the street signs of life, but in his new neighbor's house nothing. She'd been here for two weeks, and while she seemed like a good tenant, she came and went at strange hours. He had a bad feeling he now knew why.

He strode next door and knocked on her front door, perhaps a little more aggressively than necessary.

He'd been conned, and he didn't like being conned.

Probably he should go back to his house and drink some coffee, give himself a chance to cool down and little Miss "I'll use your services again" time to wake up. But he didn't feel like doing the sensible thing.

He gave it a minute, then banged again, holding the bell with his finger at the same time.

After an age and a half, the front door opened. Chloe Flynt stood there, her black hair soft and tousled in the sexiest case of bed head he'd ever seen. Her eyes were the most amazing purplish blue, and they gazed at him in the vaguely unfocused way of someone who's not totally awake yet. He had no idea what—if anything—she was wearing since everything from the neck down was behind the door.

"You should have asked who it was before opening the door," he snarled.

"I looked out the bedroom window," she said on a yawn. "I could see you." Almost as though his sharp advice to be cautious had the opposite effect, she straightened and opened the door fully.

He'd checked her out, the way a single man in his prime always checks women out. He'd sensed a very nice body was packaged in the trendy clothes she wore. But he'd had no idea.

She wasn't a tall woman, but she was exquisite. She wore teeny-tiny girl boxer shorts with the Union Jack stamped all over them and a little white T-shirt with "Rule Britannia" printed across the chest. Her legs were shapely; her breasts, small and perfect. Even the tiny strip of skin between the end of her shirt and the beginning of the shorts fascinated him. So white, so smooth.

His gaze returned to her eyes and he found them fully awake now and regarding him with a certain amused speculation. Damn it, she'd knocked him on his ass and she knew it.

"Don't tell me, your bra has the queen on one cup and Prince Charles on the other."

She glanced down at her outfit as though she'd forgotten what she was wearing. "A going-away present from a friend."

The sun was against his back, already warm. To his right he heard a bee sounding like it was snoring in the Texas lilac bush he'd planted last year.

"Did you come over to check that my pajamas are patriotic?" she asked.

He realized he was staring and felt stupid, which annoyed him even more. "I came to deliver some mail which came to me by mistake."

He held out the envelope.

"Thank you." She put out her hand, but he didn't relinquish the envelope.

"What's going on, Chloe?"

Her eyebrows rose in an incredibly snooty fashion, as though she might call her palace guards to come and have him shot. "I beg your pardon?"

"Somebody stuffs a thousand bucks in cash in my mail slot in the middle of the night, it makes me curious."

"A thousand dollars?" she exclaimed, sounding delighted. "He must have added a tip. How sweet."

For an instant he was distracted by the thought of what her services were and what she'd done to deserve such a big tip.

A jovial male voice called out, "Mornin', Matt, ma'am." Chloe's hand waved in greeting and Matt turned to see Chuck Dawson and most of his car pool waving as his van drove by. He moved his body to block Chloe from view, though he wondered why he bothered, since she didn't seem at all worried about waving her flag to whoever went by.

"Maybe we could discuss this inside," he said.

"Discuss what? You're bringing me my mail. Thank you." She held out her hand again, flat palmed.

"Where did the money come from?"

"None of your business."

He shifted and as he did he saw a white convertible turn into the road, one he recognized all too well.

"Shit," he muttered, then stepped forward so fast, his neighbor squeaked when he bumped her with his body, pushing her inside the house and shutting the door fast behind them.

"How dare you. Leave this house instantly," she demanded, small and fiery.

He ducked away from the window and made a dash for the kitchen.

"Are you a lunatic?" that crisp English voice trilled.

"Quiet. She'll hear you." He was in the kitchen, jamming his butt onto a kitchen chair that put him out of window range of his own house next door.

"Who will hear me? Matthew, what on earth—"

"Brittany."

She followed him into the kitchen and looked down at him. "And who is Brittany?"

"My girlfriend."

She looked at him like he was a few cattle short of a herd, but she didn't say a word, for which he was ridiculously grateful. Explaining Brittany was complicated. Getting more so every day. She was perfect for him in every way. Sweet, cute, sexy, nice, and the kind of woman who would make a wonderful mom. So why was he, a grown man who should be getting on with his life, hiding in the kitchen of a neighbor who was probably a criminal?

Chloe left him sitting at the oak kitchen table he'd refinished himself, his fingers tapping the edge of the money-stuffed envelope.

Without a word she started making coffee. Then she walked out of the kitchen and back toward the front of the house.

"What are you doing?" he whisper-yelled.

"Don't you want to know what she's doing?"

"I already know." He could picture Brittany now. "She's walking up to the front door. And she's got a plate of muffins in her hand."

Chloe turned back to him. "Coffee cake. She's very pretty."

"I know." There was no more commentary from the front room but Chloe didn't come back either. He was such an asshole. "She's writing a note now, isn't she?"

"You're very good."

Chloe returned to the kitchen, and a minute later he heard a car drive away.

Her eyes widened and her eyebrows rose in a question. "Cream and sugar?"

He blinked at her. "Unless your Y chromosome is still asleep, you're dying to know what that was about."

"Of course I am. But everyone's entitled to their privacy, Matthew." She sent a significant glance toward the package in his hand.

He picked up the envelope and tapped it against the tabletop. "The cases aren't the same at all. When you filled out the tenant form, you said you had your own business."

"And I do."

"I figured it was a hair salon or dress store or something."

"How sexist of you."

She poured coffee into white mugs as elegant as swans, which she must have purchased since he didn't recognize them. He realized he'd never answered her question about how he liked his coffee when she poured milk into a pitcher that matched the mugs and placed it and a bowl of sugar on the table in front of him with a couple of spoons that gleamed with newness.

He slurped some milk into his coffee. "You're right. I shouldn't have made assumptions." He glanced up. "So, what kind of business are you in?"

"I'm not at liberty to say."

He tapped his spoon against the lip of the mug, then, irritated by the sound he was making, put down the spoon and sipped the coffee. It was good. Strong and rich and he took another hit. Across the table Chloe watched him with her purple-blue aristocrat's eyes over the rim of her own mug.

The envelope of money was between them, along with a silence thicker than brick. Finally, he blurted, "Look, I'm an ex-cop. You can't stay here if you're a hooker."

Her eyes widened—whether because he'd accused her of being a hooker or because he was an ex-cop, he wasn't sure.

"So you're not only sexist, you're vulgar, offensive, and unimaginative as well." She put the cup down on the table and it clicked like the period at the end of a sentence.

"Look, I'm just—"

"Isn't a thousand dollars rather a lot to pay a prostitute?"

He shrugged, suddenly uncomfortable with the direction he'd taken the conversation. Maybe he should have thought of other reasons a person might have cash dropped off in the middle of the night. "Depends on the service."

"I see. If I was paying one thousand dollars for sex, I'd want it gift-wrapped in a Tiffany's box."

"Well." He cleared his throat. "It's, uh, usually the men who pay."

3tm

"And what would you pay a thousand dollars for?" she asked him.

He glanced up and for some damn reason heat shot through him. Maybe it was the look in her eye, or the thought of that alluring little body naked and wrapped around him, but lust sucker-punched him. "I never pay for sex," he managed to snap.

"I see."

Then he pushed the envelope toward her. "Quit yankin' my chain, Chloe. What kind of business are you in where clients pay cash and you keep the weirdest damned hours of any businessperson I ever knew."

"I didn't realize you were monitoring my movements."

How did she do this? That cool, snooty, *My country has princesses and yours doesn't* voice infuriated and aroused him at the same time. It wasn't Brittany he should be hiding from, he realized, it was his neighbor.

"What kind of business?—it's all I'm asking."

She tilted her head to the side so she was looking sideways and up at him. "I run a private detective agency," she said.

He didn't laugh, but it was a close run thing. "Do you now?"

"Certainly. Women make excellent detectives. They know how to be subtle," she said with a tiny smile that showed off even, white teeth and managed to insinuate that he was about as subtle as a charging bull.

He thought about asking for her business card, but then her obvious lie would be out in the open, and he didn't want to end the most interesting conversation he'd had in weeks. "Do you have any specialties?"

"Specialties?"

"Areas of private investigation that you specialize in."

"Oh, I see. No, I run a full-service agency."

He was about to ask another question when she forestalled him.

"Shall we go and get the cake off your front porch to have with our coffee? I think your girlfriend has left."

Shit. Brittany. He was going to have to do something about her, and he had no idea what.

"Her name's Brittany. We had a fight."

"Her fault? So she's bringing you a peace offering."

He shook his head. "My fault. I was an asshole."

"Oh dear. Poor Brittany. Is she one of those doormat women who are sorry even when a fight is not their fault?"

"No, Brittany believes in talking things out. She brought the whatever it was to be civilized. But I already know it's my fault and I need to apologize."

"I see."

"We're probably going to get married, Brittany and me," he heard himself say, but the words came out stiff and arthritic, which was pretty much how his whole body felt when he contemplated his future. However, marriage was what everyone expected—his family, his friends, Brittany.

"Which is why you're hiding from her at first light instead of apologizing and getting on with things."

"It's complicated."

"Oh, please don't think I'm critical. It's the sort of thing I do myself when I'm engaged."

He was momentarily diverted from his own troubles. "You'd have hidden in my house if your boyfriend drove by?"

She looked at him, but he thought she was really looking back over her own behavior. "No," she said. "I think I'd have kissed you long and hard in your own doorway in full view of my fiancé."

Clearly, he wasn't the only one on the block with commitment problems. And the picture she'd put in his head definitely wasn't helping.

"Why?"

"Years of expensive therapy hasn't helped me understand my own behavior." She put her head to one side as though that would help her sift through her thoughts. "I think I want a man to want me enough to fight for me."

"And do they?"

She wrinkled her nose. "No, they are always terribly brave and noble, or pretend they don't notice whatever dreadful thing I've done until eventually we have a flaming great row and it's over."

He got up and walked toward her. "You've been in England too long. Here in Texas, we do things differently." He imagined how he'd feel if Chloe were his and he found her making out with some other guy. "Brave" and "noble" were not the first words that sprang to mind.

"Good." She seemed pleased by the notion of fights springing up over her. What a head case.

"No man wants his woman making out with another guy."

She shrugged. "I like drama."

Suddenly he found himself grinning. "Must be a drawback in the private investigation business."

She had a way of looking at a man that was both mischievous and tempting. "That remains to be seen."

He took his empty coffee mug to the sink. She sure kept the place neat. The sink shone and the counters were spotless.

"Matthew?"

"Mmm?"

"What about you?"

"I think drama's for the movies."

God, even her laugh was sexy. It was light and flirtatious, like a flower scent you'd smell once and never forget. "I meant for your job. You said you were an ex-cop."

"I'm in real estate now."

"In what capacity?"

He shrugged. "This and that. I buy places. Fix them up, then sell them or rent them."

He didn't turn around but it didn't matter; she asked anyway, "Why aren't you a cop anymore?"

He turned. "Long story. I've got stuff to do and you've got a business to run. I'll see you around."

"Yes, all right. See you around," she said, but she kept looking at him with a speculative expression that made him want to run.

Chapter 4

Chloe watched the long, tall Texan walk out her door as though he owned it. He did, of course, but she strongly suspected that lazy confidence went with him through every doorway. There was something decidedly appealing about a man who looked this good at an ungodly hour of the morning.

"Oh, no, you don't," she warned herself even as she moved to the window so she could watch him amble, slow as a sexy drawl, back to his own house. She did not have time for a love affair, particularly not a love affair with a man who was also her neighbor and her landlord. Two black marks that, naturally, only made him more appealing to her. Even though she knew it was the lure of the forbidden, she couldn't stop herself from licking her lips.

Was it her imagination or was there the tiniest hitch in his step? Not quite a limp, but not a perfectly smooth gait either. Eduardo, one of her former fiancés, had suffered a nasty skiing accident in the Italian alps, and after his knee surgery he'd walked that way when the weather was wet or he'd been overdoing his workouts. She doubted her Texan had suffered a skiing accident. Something to do with his work, no doubt. He'd certainly become huffy when she asked why he'd left the police force. She bet the two were related.

Interesting. Not her business, but that never stopped her.

He bent and picked up the coffee cake off his front porch, read the note, and turned to scan the empty street as though he were looking for the woman he'd hidden from earlier.

Chloe went back into the kitchen and added fresh coffee to her mug. It was clear from her brief glimpse of that sweet-looking girl with all that blond hair and the rather anxious look on her face that she was all wrong for Matthew. That girl was a nurturer through and through. She'd be a nurse, or a nursery school teacher.

She ran upstairs to shower and get ready for the day, much earlier than she'd planned. While the water rained down on her, a story began to form. She bet that Matthew had met Brittany when he was injured. Of course. He'd be hurting, wounded, and the nurturer in Brittany would respond. If he'd left the force because of that knee, he'd have been drawn to a giving woman like Brittany with her coffee cakes and her "Let's talk about it" mentality. But now that he was back on his feet, he'd reverted to an independent man. And since he was no doubt grateful to Brittany for being there when he needed her, he'd have no idea how to get out of a romance that was clearly hopeless.

Poor, dear man.

However, it was a good day. She had a thousand dollars in hand.

Once she had her makeup done and her underwear on, she went to her office.

She flipped on her laptop computer for the day's schedule, which was empty but for a manicure at 2:00 P.M. which she'd booked because a businesswoman should always look well groomed.

Besides, no one knew better than Chloe, who'd spent a good portion of her life in salons of various kinds, that the salon was a hotbed of relationship gossip. Men might tell the bartender their troubles, but women spilled their guts to their stylist, manicurist, or massage therapist. The world of beauty and personal pampering was a thriving market for her services.

She'd always thought of marketing as what Mummy's housekeeper Martha did when she'd drive to town to do the food shopping, but now that she was in business for herself, she was rapidly making the connection between marketing efforts and paying clients. If she wanted more of the latter, she was going to have to do more of the former. Since she did her marketing in person at places she liked to spend time anyway, the activity hadn't become a chore.

Chloe slipped on a black linen sundress, Miu Miu sandals—her green suede ones with the gold-tipped stiletto heels—and gathered a big straw bag that she'd decided was more approachable and chic than a briefcase, a bottle of water to drink, and an aerosol of Evian to keep her skin hydrated in the Texas heat.

Then she slipped on the Chanel sunglasses that always made her feel like Audrey Hepburn and headed off in her rental car, only having to be reminded once by the toot of a car horn that here in America people drove on the opposite side of the road.

Her first destination for the day was the mall, that most American of institutions and one she loved to bits. Inside, it was cool with air conditioning and a double decker of delicious shops awaited. Sadly, she didn't have the time or the money for shopping, but she allowed herself a few minutes of window browsing while she gave herself a pep talk. Today she would acquire three new clients, she decided, and make sure she handed out at least a dozen business cards. She'd try to place stacks of her brochures where those in unhappy relationships would be most likely to see them.

Her advert was in newspapers in San Antonio, Dallas, and Houston, as well as in the Austin paper. Her Web site was live. She had, as her brilliant marketing-genius friend Anthony had decreed, three levels of marketing—print, Internet, and direct person-to-person selling. And she hoped like mad that it would pay off and quickly. Before she ran out of money or got bored. Of the two fates, she dreaded the second most.

With a tiny sigh in the direction of Neiman Marcus, she headed for the food court where she bought herself a cup of coffee, sat at one of the round plastic tables, and settled back to observe.

She took a survey of the morning coffee drinkers and sticky-bun eaters, some obviously fueling up for a morning's shopping, some grabbing a quick snack on a work break, and those who were at leisure. She'd doubted there'd be any potential clients in a shopping center food court, but after spending a few minutes regarding a young couple talking earnestly, she moved closer, choosing a table where she had a clear view of the pair, was close enough to hear a bit of what was said, but not so close as to inhibit them or, even worse, cause them to leave. Though, frankly, she doubted they'd have noticed if she posed herself, naked, at the next table; they were that wrapped up in their conversation.

She drew today's newspaper out of her bag, propped it in front of her so she'd appear occupied if the intense couple should glance her way, and proceeded to watch human drama. Chloe never understood the appeal of reality shows on telly—the ones that played out in life were always so much more entertaining.

The pair were both early twenties. He wore a department store suit and an unimaginative striped tie. He had brown hair and glasses—the kind of Clark Kent who, sadly, has no alter ego superpower. The young woman had long dark hair clipped back off her face, large dark eyes, and a full-lipped mouth. Her clothing suggested a lot more personality than her companion's. She wore a soft, peasanty blouse, in yellow and blue, a tight black skirt, and high-heeled sandals. A tattoo of a tiny dragon hovered over her ankle.

They were both leaning forward, so intent on each other that their coffees sat in front of them untouched.

"On a stakeout?" The male voice behind her startled her so much that she slopped coffee onto her newspaper. She turned to glare, having already recognized the voice of her very annoying neighbor.

"What are you doing here?"

"I was in the neighborhood."

She sighed as he walked around in front of her. "You're going to be one of those annoying men, aren't you?"

"What annoying men?"

"The ones who follow me around and make fools of themselves."

He looked a bit stunned. Well, no man liked to be told he was making a fool of himself, and normally she'd have been gentler about letting him down, but she had a busy schedule to keep.

"You actually think I'm following you because I'm—I'm—"

He ran out of words, so she helped him out. "Besotted?" She'd seen the male interest in his eyes when he looked at her, something that happened to her so often, it registered only when she felt a return sizzle.

"I told you, I have a girlfriend. We're probably getting married."

"You barged into my house at an ungodly hour of the morning, hid from your girlfriend, and now you're following me. What am I supposed to think?"

"Try this. That I didn't believe your story this morning. I'm trying to figure out what you're doing."

She wasn't entirely sure she believed him, but he didn't really fit the profile of her usual besotted bloke. Assuming he really did want to know what her business was, she could tell him, and then he'd go away. But somehow she knew he'd make fun of her, and she wasn't in the mood for mockery.

Besides, action spoke much louder than words. She planned to use her actions like a bullhorn in his direction. That would wipe the smirk off his face.

He sat across from her without permission. She considered

making an issue of it, but that would only draw attention; so instead, she handed him a section of her paper and pretended to read her own.

The paper rustled as he spread out the pages. "Sports?" he said. "How sexist." Remembering their earlier conversation in her kitchen, she found herself smiling.

She leaned toward him. "I'm having a quick coffee before work, that's all."

"Why are you watching those two?" He didn't incline his head, he merely cut his eyes to the table she'd been observing. Damn.

"I like people-watching," she said.

"What's so interesting about them? They're talking about how great last night was and when they can do it again."

She shook her head. "No, that conversation has nothing to do with sex. They're more emotional. That relationship's on the rocks."

"And they come to a shopping mall food court for a heart-to-heart?" He reached for her coffee without asking and took a sip. He grimaced. "Too much sugar."

"Then get your own coffee," she said, taking hers back.

"I'm blending in with your cover," he explained, sounding serious and looking anything but. "We'll let those two and anyone else watching think we're too busy talking about our great sex life to have any attention to spare."

"We don't have a great sex life," she snapped, then immediately realized her mistake in answering when she saw his smile dawn, slow and sexy.

"You don't know that." He didn't say "yet," couldn't of course with Brittany busy making coffee cakes and planning a lavish wedding, no doubt with far too many frills. Still, the attraction was as undeniable as the heat waiting outside to slap her when she left the relative coolness of the air-conditioned shopping center.

Damn, damn, damn. She did not have time for this. Even as the thought passed through her mind, she found herself tingling with the thrill of attraction. He was so long and tall and sexy, so down to earth, and she was so tired of European playboys.

To avoid the issue of attraction, she ignored his provocation and answered his earlier question.

"Those two are here because it's convenient for them. Close to work for both." She didn't have to look back at the pair to visualize them in her mind and make a reasonable guess.

"He's an assistant manager at one of the shops in the mall, and she's—in the junior's clothing section at Penney's."

"You know them?"

"No, I'm guessing."

He shook his head. "He's a junior banker. She's a florist."

"A florist?"

He shrugged. "She likes color. Texture. I'm guessing flowers. And that is definitely a sex thing they're talking about."

She shook her head. "A breakup."

"Twenty bucks says I'm right."

"Twenty doesn't sound very sure. Fifty." Of course, she shouldn't be gambling. She should be hoarding her resources until she got her company firmly up and running, but the thousand dollars had gone to her head. Besides, something about playing games with Matthew—any kind of games—was exciting.

"You're on."

Now they were both focused on the adjacent table, so they both witnessed the young man take a diamond ring out of his pocket and offer it to the girl.

"Damn," said Matt. "We were both wrong. They're getting engaged. What do you give the chances of that marriage? Getting engaged in a mall."

"No," she said, satisfaction sluicing through her. "He's giving her back the ring. It was in his pocket, not a box. And she's not at all sure she wants it back." Instead of placing it on her ring finger, the man had offered it on the palm of his hand, like a supplication. After a long moment, where more than fifty dollars seemed in the balance, the woman reached over and picked up the ring. She slipped the reasonably sized rock on her wedding ring finger, but Chloe could see she was uncertain. The young woman turned the sparkly ring around a few times on her finger. Clark Kent watched her as eagerly as a puppy watches his empty bowl at mealtime.

"Not bad," Matt said beside her in a low voice.

"Not bad? Bloody brilliant detective work. Now do you believe that I am a private eye?"

The tanned skin around his eyes crinkled as he smiled. "Not hardly."

"But you will pay me fifty dollars."

During the time it took Chloe to finish her coffee, she became completely convinced that the couple beside her were making a mistake. The young man rose and leaned over the table to kiss his fiancée. As he walked away, the girl looked after him, a frown marring her prettiness.

"Follow him," she said to Matthew, who blinked and looked after the departing suit.

"Why?"

"It would give you something better to do than following me, that's why. Besides, I don't like the look of him."

"What's wrong with him?"

"Tough to explain, really, but I have good instincts."

"You're a case and a half, Chloe. And if you want my advice, you'll leave that girl in peace."

She beamed at him, giving him her best smile. "Advice is such a fascinating thing, isn't it? Everybody always trying to give it away and nobody ever wanting it."

He rose, to a deliciously tall height, pulled out his wallet, and slapped three bills on the table. "Good-bye, Chloe."

Two twenties and a ten. Classy. She liked a man who paid his bills.

She collected her winnings and waved him off, anxious to see the back of him before that girl moved. She hadn't, she was still staring at the diamond on her hand as though it might bite her if she moved quickly.

Chloe leaned forward and assumed an excited tone. "Congratulations."

"Hmm?" The girl looked up and her big brown eyes were troubled. *Bingo,* Chloe thought. She was never wrong about who belonged with whom. Well, almost never. With the extraordinary exception of herself and the men she chose.

Since the girl seemed too stunned to move, Chloe slid from her own table and took the seat across from her, the one recently vacated by the young man.

"I couldn't help but notice—frankly, jewelry always catches my attention. Did you just get engaged?"

The girl nodded slowly, looking far from deliciously pink with bridal delight. "Well, we got reengaged, I guess you'd say."

"Ooh, I do love a good romance." She put her chin in her palm and prepared to listen. "Tell all."

"I don't even know you."

"Of course you don't. How rude of me. I'm Chloe." She held out her hand and the girl shook it, albeit rather reluctantly.

"I should probably . . ."

"Sometimes I find it easier to tell a stranger my troubles. Odd, isn't it? Mummy and Daddy always think they know best for me, of course, and frankly I think I shock them. I've got an older brother, Jack, who says I'm spoilt. He's right, of course, but that's not the point. Sometimes a girl needs to talk. The urge to unburden oneself is easier satisfied with a stranger."

The girl gave up and sighed deeply. "I guess you're right. It's not like my family would understand."

"When is the wedding?"

"I don't know. I don't want to get married, not yet; but Derek really loves me, and maybe my friends are right and I should just do this, you know?"

Chloe knew all about friends and family trying to push one into marriage.

"But do you love him?"

"I don't think so."

"Then why on earth would your friends want you to marry him?"

"Because I have lousy, rotten taste in guys, and at least this one has a regular job, no tattoos, and he won't get drunk and try and hit on other women all the time."

"Is that what your last boyfriend did?"

"Pretty much all my old boyfriends."

Chloe thought for a minute. "But you have a tattoo. I couldn't help but notice. I like it."

"Derek wants me to get it lasered off. He thinks it looks cheap."

"My dear girl—what is your name, by the way?"

"Oh, sorry, Stephanie."

"Well, Stephanie, you cannot possibly marry a man you do not love and who wants to change you. It's hopeless."

To Chloe's alarm, Stephanie's eyes suddenly filled. "I know it's hopeless. I'm hopeless."

Chloe pulled out her pack of tissues with tiaras printed on them and offered the pack. "Of course you're not hopeless. You're simply a little confused. It happens to all of us." She glanced at the ring. "At least he has nice taste in jewelry."

Stephanie dabbed at her eyes. "He's the assistant manager at the jewelry store in the mall. We got forty percent off on my ring."

"I wonder if I could be of service."

"I doubt it."

Undaunted by the negative tone, Chloe pulled out one of her cards and slid it across the table. Stephanie picked it up and read it with a puzzled frown. "I don't get it. You're a matchmaking service."

"Oh, no. Quite the opposite. I end bad relationships. In complete confidence, of course. I do the dirty work so you don't have to."

For a second, Stephanie's eyes lit up; then they dimmed as

suddenly. "I don't make much money, and I have nothing saved. I couldn't pay you."

"Ah," Chloe said. The hard-nosed businesswoman in her knew she should walk away. She couldn't afford to take on free cases when she didn't have many that paid. However, she also felt very strongly that Stephanie shouldn't marry a self-important twit in a bad suit.

She had a brilliant idea. People called her impulsive, but the thing with impulses is that if you don't grab on to them in the moment, they pass. "I know, why don't you come and work for me?"

"I thought you wanted me to hire you."

"Well, that would be preferable, of course. But since you don't have any money and you obviously need a change, it seems obvious to me that I shall have to give you a job."

"In your match-breaking company?"

"Exactly."

"What would I do?"

"I need a secretary. Receptionist. Someone to answer the phone when I'm away from the office and to do"—she stopped to think for a moment—"all the jobs I don't like doing."

"Oh."

"Can you type?"

She received a look of astonishment. "How do you think I MSN all my friends?"

"Right. Of course. Good." She was really warming up to her idea. When she'd woken this morning she'd had no idea she needed an assistant; now she could see it was critical to her future. "You'll know all the places where I should be advertising my services." She smiled, full of excitement. "Our services. You can screen the customers, make up files, do the billing." She screwed up her face. "I hate boring things like paperwork. When can you start?"

The bright face dimmed. "I can't."

Chapter 5

"No," Stephanie said, looking down at that ring as though it contained a genie and three wishes. "No, I couldn't. I have to marry Derek. You don't understand. He's perfect for me. My family says so, my friends say so. I know he is."

Chloe felt a chord of sympathy chime through her in response. "God, yes, I know exactly what you mean."

She looked up. "You do?"

"Every time I got engaged it was to a man who was perfect for me."

The girl in front of her blinked slowly. "Every time?"

"Mmm. I've been engaged three times. But everybody was wrong. None of those men was right for me."

"I bet you never had your wedding stationery already ordered."

Chloe chuckled. "The last time, I had the estate booked, the catering paid for, the prettiest dress," she sighed. "It did give me a pang not to wear that dress. It was antique silk with rows of tiny pearls on the bodice. Really lovely. Anyway, it caused the most fearful row when I canceled."

"What about"—she threw up her hands—"everything?"

"Oh, well, it worked out rather well in the end. The Earl of Ponsford, whose estate we'd booked for the wedding, took the spot himself and married a darling girl. An American, actually. So nothing went to waste, you see. Well, except the dress. I gave it to charity. I like to think some poor girl was able to wear a really smashing dress because of me." She beamed suddenly. "So, you see, there's nothing that can't be undone. One simply needs resolution."

For a moment the girl bit her lip and looked hopeful. Then she shook her head. "No, I can't do it."

"All right." She wasn't about to beg. "Still, if you change your mind about the job, or know of anyone who might need my services, do let me know." Impulsively, she leaned forward and put a hand over the girl's newly beringed one. "Good luck."

Stephanie watched the English girl walk away. She walked quickly, as though she had a lot to do and no time to waste, but there was also something about that walk—Steph would guess she'd been a model if she were taller. She was gorgeous. Like a perfume ad come to life—elegant and expensive looking. But there was something that was almost childlike about her. Imagine offering a job to a total stranger.

She picked up the card, tapped it against her palm, put it back down on the tabletop, rose, and walked away. She didn't even make it to the edge of the food court before quickly turning tail and retrieving the card. She might know someone, after all, who could use the services of the Englishwoman who wanted to break up relationships for a living.

She stood there, the ring weighing down her hand like a diamond anchor, holding her in place. That was good, she reminded herself, marriage was steadying. Good.

She had about twenty minutes before her shift started. She'd go look at china, she decided, start getting ideas for the gift registry.

She walked to the rail of the gallery level of the shopping center and gazed down. There was a lone man riding the up escalator. He wore jeans that were ripped at the knee, obviously from impact rather than design. His leather boots were scruffy and worn, as was he. His hair was a too-long dark brown streaked with blond, which made her think the guy worked outside in the sun without a hat. His face was weather-beaten, careless stubble shadowed his face. He wore a battered leather jacket open over a black T-shirt, and from his hand swung a black motorcycle helmet.

He glanced up as though he felt her watching him and the dark Latino brown of his eyes saw right inside of her. The impact thudded into her chest and she knew he'd felt it too. He had a poet's eyes, she thought, which was ridiculous. What would a poet's eyes be doing in a thug's body? Those eyes held on to hers, practically speaking to her of hidden things, secret things, that made her body long instinctively for his. He was coming closer, floating up on a mechanical staircase. Soon they'd be level and she had the craziest idea that she'd be lost. With a gasp, she blinked and turned away.

What was she doing? She'd been engaged for four minutes and she was making eyes at one of her usual no-good types. She had to get a grip.

She walked quickly toward the department store, trying to ignore the awful itching that started deep in her belly where she could never scratch it.

She knew what this was. She understood it, recognized it, could control it.

She breathed slowly, and while her mind told her to use the card she always carried in her wallet and make the emergency call, her feet didn't falter on their way to the store.

By the time she got into the department store her heart was doing a bump and grind in her chest and she felt like there were hot embers in the pit of her stomach.

When she entered the store she immediately began to settle. This was her place. She loved shopping, she loved everything about it. The smell of new goods, the colors exploding everywhere, the fresh fashions, trendy shoes, the purses, scarves, oh, those darling earrings, and the watches. So many watches.

Her mother could use a new watch. Her mother, who'd

had so little all her life, and who was so happy that Stephanie was breaking her bad pattern and marrying a nice, steady man who didn't drink, who would be there for her.

Thinking of her mother's delight in a new watch filled her with contentment. The green leather strap was nice. Snazzy. And the face was big, with easy-to-read numbers. But she knew her mother would want something more practical, a watch that would match many outfits.

She browsed through several, liked the one with the cream leather band the best, but maybe the gold and silver would be more versatile. Her elbow nudged a Timex so it fell to the floor. She bent to retrieve it, and when she rose again she returned two watches to the display. The one with the cream leather band was safely in her bag.

The thrill that coursed through her was close to sexual, and the deep itch inside her began to dissipate. She headed over to the scarves and then had the uncomfortable feeling that she was being watched. A casual glance over the Italian silk scarf she was inspecting showed that the scruffy biker guy from the escalator was checking her out.

Her breath caught. Now that he was closer his impact on her was even stronger.

He'd followed her.

His espresso eyes seemed to see all the way into her, where she didn't want anyone seeing.

Had he noticed her slipping the watch into her bag? A badass like that—and he had badass written all over him—would think a little shoplifting was pretty juvie stuff, and it was. She lifted her chin at him. So what?

She drifted from scarves to earrings, from earrings to sunglasses. She slipped on a pair of huge Jackie O dark glasses, and as she pretended to check out her reflection, she checked out the guy. He was still there. Not following her exactly, but not leaving her vicinity either.

Now she felt the thrill of the chase, the danger of playing cat and mouse with a very large, feral, scruffy wildcat.

From the sunglasses, she moved to the makeup counter. He drifted to the men's watches, always keeping her within sight.

She spritzed a little cologne on her wrist and was shocked at how cold it felt against her overheated skin. She browsed, vaguely wondering what pop singers, clothing designers, or novelists were supposed to know about blending scents.

A salesclerk asked if she needed help, and with a polite smile, she shook her head and moved away. The Latino guy seemed absorbed in women's purses. She was delighted to see that he was getting a lot more suspicious glances from the store clerks than she, with her neat clothing, accorded.

There was something intoxicating about this unspoken game she and motorcycle guy were playing, but she did have to get to work. She hesitated. She was pretty sure he was more interested in hitting on her than in whether she'd paid for the items in her bag. But she wasn't completely sure. For all she knew he could be a new brand of store detective, one she'd never come across before.

She tried a tester of lip gloss, decided it was too pink and reached into her bag for a tissue to wipe off the residue. When she left the area, there was a watch with a cream leather band wedged between two bottles of lavender bath oil.

She felt all the frustration of an addict denied her fix as she stalked out of the department store knowing that on top of not getting her mother that watch, she was going to be late for work.

She moved as fast as she could, feeling the heat burn within her. Her heels clacked on the ceramic tile as she hurried.

"Good decision," a deep, lazy voice with only the tiniest Spanish accent said behind her.

Startled, she turned and found motorcycle boy at her heel. She didn't bother playing innocent. She knew he wouldn't fall for it and she didn't feel like playing any more games. She scowled at him. "You wouldn't know a good decision if it bit you in the ass."

He chuckled, falling into step with her and making the pace seem slow and easy. His teeth were very white in the tanned face. "Where are you off to in such a hurry?"

She glanced at him. She couldn't help herself. She had to know. "Are you a security guard?"

When he shook his head, that mess of hair swung. "No."

"Then why were you following me?"

His gaze seared through her when their eyes met. "You know why."

Her gaze dropped to the tiled floor. The heat between them was amazing. She'd never known anything like it. Yes, she knew why he'd followed her.

"I could give you a lift."

Her body, her wretched, weak body, always drawn to the man who was so bad for her, wanted to crawl on the back of his motorcycle and let him take her anywhere. Everywhere. But the semblance of good sense she'd worked so hard to cultivate dragged her back from the brink.

"No thanks."

"Okay." He looked at her as though memorizing her features. "Take it easy." And he headed down on the very escalator she'd watched him ascend on a quarter of an hour ago.

She stopped and breathed, holding on to the faint smell of leather and danger that clung to him. Then she dug out her wallet with hands that weren't quite steady. She was already late for work, one more minute wouldn't make a difference. And this was a call that might save her, once more, from ruining her life.

She clutched the business card to her even though she'd memorized the number long ago. And then she made the call.

Rafael Escobar didn't like puzzles. Puzzles could get a man killed. That *chica* with the wide eyes and great walk was a puzzle. As was his behavior. What had made him follow her into the store like that?

He felt like smacking himself upside the head. He knew

why he'd followed her even as he didn't want to know. He'd picked distress signals coming off her like cries from a sinking ship. When he caught her eyeing him on the escalator, he'd first noticed her brightness, the colorful clothes, the sexy attitude.

Her eyes were the eyes of a dreamer, and when he looked into them he saw sex. It was crazy, but he'd felt instant chemistry, a powerful mix of heat and lust that could burn a man to cinders. But then he'd seen the Mayday flares shooting out of them.

When would he ever learn? Wounded birds weren't for him. He'd had enough, enough of doves with broken wings. He couldn't fix them all, and every time he failed a little piece of him died.

He could tell himself to act differently next time. He still saw a wounded bird and he wanted to run to the rescue. He hadn't fallen for one in a long time. Why this one? Why now?

Stupido.

His helmet brushed his thigh as he walked out into the blazing sunshine of the shopping center parking lot, squinting while he dug out his sunglasses. Once his eyes were shaded he could see his buddy waiting, none too patiently, by a truck so clean it suggested its owner didn't have enough to do, which in Rafe's opinion was exactly the problem.

Because he could see impatience in the man's every line, he slowed his pace, taking the time to admire a truly excellent BMW Motorad, K1200 R. He pictured himself flying down the highway, leaning into curves. In a flash he pictured that sweet-eyed woman, still wearing her skirt, because what the hell, in fantasy nobody had to wear biking leathers. She was in her skirt, her long legs tucked around his, the dragon tattoo he'd noted on her ankle flashing green in the sun.

Shaking his head at his own foolishness, he kept walking to where Matt Tanner was standing, leaning against his too-clean truck, arms crossed over his chest. "Well?"

"I didn't see any English chick."

"She was talking to the long-haired gal with a small tattoo on her ankle."

Rafe nodded. "Her, I saw. But she was alone."

"In the food court?"

"No, I followed her into a department store. She never hooked up with any Englishwoman." She'd also shoplifted, which he kept to himself for reasons he didn't entirely understand. She'd thought better of it, so she hadn't in fact stolen anything, which made him feel okay about his silence.

"Hmm."

"What's up with the British chick? You know something you should be sharing with an old buddy who is still on the force?"

Matt shook his head. "No, nothing like that. She's my tenant, new to the States, and has a bad habit of getting involved in things that aren't her business."

Rafe recalled the aborted shoplifting attempt and felt a frown pull his mouth in tight. "You're sure we're not talking illegal activities here?"

"Not unless being nosy, interfering, and bossy is illegal."

He snorted. "Should be."

"You said it."

Because of his training and the kind of work he did, Rafe's eyes were never still. Even as he hung out in the parking lot his gaze was sweeping the vicinity for possible trouble. His eyes narrowed behind the glasses. There she was, his latest wounded dove, emerging from a mall exit to the east of where he and Matt stood. She walked quickly, as though she were late for something. She'd seemed like she was in a big hurry when he left her, so how had she come out of the mall so much later than he had? Had she hit another store the minute his back was turned?

He wasn't even on duty, and petty shoplifting wasn't exactly his area, but it irked the hell out of him to think that she'd gone and done such a stupid thing right after he'd confronted her.

"I gotta go," he said.

If Tanner was surprised at the abrupt departure he didn't let on. "Yeah, see you later. And thanks."

"No problem," he said over his shoulder. He was already on the move.

Rafe followed the woman on foot. He liked the way she walked in her heels, with that sway to her hips and the little flash of blue from her ankle. Her hair swung from side to side, a long, rippling curtain. She might be a petty shoplifter, but it didn't erase the fact that he had a serious weakness for long hair. Hell, from the second their gazes had connected he'd been hooked.

She walked into a bank without a clue she'd been followed. He didn't enter but took up a position on the street corner where he could see inside. To his surprise, she walked through the employees-only doorway and into the back.

Sure enough, within five minutes, she was back out front and settling herself into one of the tellers' chairs.

He wondered, with an uneasy feeling in his gut, what a thief was doing working in a bank.

Chapter 6

Deborah Beaumont didn't have time for sex. Not this morning. She had case files to review before she saw her patients today, and she had to pick up her new eyeglasses. However, Jordan Errington, her partner in work and life, was running his hand up and down her front in his usual signal and she realized it had been a long time since they'd made love.

So she obliged, raising her shoulders so he could slip the cotton nightgown off her body, making encouraging sounds when he rubbed her breasts and when his hand slid south, parting her thighs for him. After he'd caressed her a little bit, enough that she did have a mild buzz on, he asked, "Are you ready?"

He always asked. It was sweet and thoughtful, but sometimes she wished he'd just get on with it.

"Yes," she whispered. When he entered her, she began to move in tandem with him.

She stroked his back while she wondered whether the Petersons would have done their homework this week. If they hadn't bothered, yet again, she was going to have to suggest a different therapist. Some people didn't seem to realize that a successful marriage required effort.

When she sensed from Jordan's quickened movements and harsh breathing that he was approaching climax, she gave a theatrical shudder and a soft cry. He immediately followed with his own shudder and grunting sigh. Normally, of course, she wasn't an advocate of faking orgasm, but she didn't have the time or the enthusiasm right now, nor did she want to discuss her feelings, which was definitely the downside of being romantically involved with a fellow therapist.

Not that they'd had time to discuss much of anything lately with their busy practice and their book coming out. When Jordan gave her a kiss on the cheek and rolled off her, he headed for the main bathroom in her townhouse, leaving her the ensuite. She dashed into the shower, trying to make up the extra minutes of her day she'd sacrificed for keeping her own relationship running smoothly.

She and Jordan kept separate homes and, even though they worked side by side, rarely drove in to their downtown office together. She had her glasses to pick up, and his appointments might end at a different time from hers, so even though they were linked personally and professionally, they both respected each other's independence. One day she suspected they'd move in together, but for now this system worked.

The first thing she did once she reached the office was to slip on her new reading glasses and gaze lovingly at the copy of her book *Perfect Communication, Perfect Love* the way she'd view her own child.

The guidebook she'd coauthored with Jordan was the culmination of years of work as a counselor. She tried, in her practice and in her life, to find the order in life's chaos. Systems that made sense.

Deborah craved order the way a different woman might crave food. She didn't need her degrees in psychology to tell her that growing up in chaos had undermined her sense of security in self and family, and so she had compensated by creating rules and guidelines. It would have been one woman's coping mechanism if she hadn't found those same rules successful in helping her patients cope with their problems. Especially in the area of interpersonal communications.

And while she was helping her patients make sense of their lives and relationships, she'd met Jordan. Sweet, reliable Jordan whom she'd met while teaching the Transtheoretical Model of Change to other therapists. She had noticed him right away. His hair was reddish brown, and he had an intellectual face and the calmest blue eyes she'd ever seen. No turbulence tossed in their depths; looking at him was like gazing at a glassy lake, calm and clear. She somehow knew, just from a glimpse at him, that he was one of those people born with the secret of living calmly in a chaotic world.

They were a perfect match. The order she strived so consistently to maintain in her own life was effortless in his. She'd first felt their perfection working together, when she hired him, and then as a couple when they'd moved slowly but inevitably into intimacy.

A feeling of calm stole over her every time she looked at the book with their two names on the jacket.

Everything was fine. Her system worked.

She noticed a fingerprint on the dust jacket of her book, and, using the dusting cloth she kept in her bottom drawer, she carefully rubbed the surface back to a perfect gloss.

Her intercom buzzed; she checked her schedule. "The Petersons are here," Carly said.

"Thank you." They were right on time. She appreciated punctuality in clients.

She rose and crossed the soft blue carpet, chosen for its soothing color, and opened the door. Heinrik Peterson sat stiff, his body facing away from his wife's, thumbs busy with his BlackBerry. Janine Peterson sat beside her husband reading a magazine.

"Janine and Heinrik," she called out, "please come in."

They walked into her office, not even glancing at each other. Heinrik stood back and waited for his wife to enter first, but he did it without eye contact.

Deborah wasn't getting a good feeling about this. They

took their seats in the seating area she'd designed to look like a living room. Gentle lighting, neutral-colored armchairs. A glass and marble table.

She sank into a chair across from them with her notebook. She smiled. Mrs. Peterson smiled back at her. Heinrik wore the expression of a man who had to be somewhere ten minutes ago and didn't have time for this.

"How did we do this week?" She glanced between them. "Heinrik? Would you begin?"

He stared at the glass table. "Not good."

Silence.

"You remember your assignment from last week?"

He shifted irritably. "Yeah, yeah. Write down something about Janine that bugs me." He shrugged. "There are so many things, I didn't know where to start."

Making a note to talk later about why he belittled his wife, she said, "Let's see what you wrote on your work sheet."

She'd designed the binder system herself. The folder kept pages neat and uncreased, and she had instructions and questions that could be modified for each particular client. Task sheets with nice, long areas for self-expression.

"I didn't have time to fill out the form."

If he thought a divorce wasn't going to be a big waste of his precious time, he was fooling himself, she thought, but of course didn't allow her frustration to show.

"All right. Perhaps next week you'll have a little more time."

Mrs. Peterson, like most of her female clients, was more communicative. She opened her binder without prompting and Deborah could see her neat, looping writing covered the page.

"You asked us to choose one minor area of conflict to focus on. I chose how he never helps with the dishes."

"Huh," said Heinrik.

"Go on, Janine."

"I did exactly what you said. I waited until we had a relaxed time with not a lot going on and—"

"Relaxed, how can I be relaxed with you nagging all the time?"

The words went through Deb like tiny arrows. Puncture, puncture, puncture . . . She'd heard those words, and that tone, so many times in her life. Her father yelling at her mother. Her mother yelling at her father. Her siblings adding their loud voices to the mix.

"Heinrik?"

"What?" His face was red and his shoulders up around his ears with tension.

"Do you think that's helpful?"

"I'm here, aren't I?"

"Showing up isn't enough. You have not been using your book. I cannot help you if you won't use the book."

He tried to interrupt, but she stopped him with a hand in the air, rather like a kindergarten teacher, which was at about the right emotional level. "Do not interrupt me. I am suspending your session. It's pointless to continue with counseling or with me"—she stopped to drill him with her gaze—"until you are willing to do the work."

He went even redder in the face, but what did he expect? He lived in emotional disorder and he'd remain in that state until he did the work.

"I suggest you go home and think about whether you want to continue with me. If you decide you do, then please fill out the workbook as I asked you and phone my office to book your next appointment. Or I could help you find a therapist who might be more suitable for you."

Then she rose. "I'm sorry, Janine," she said, feeling that she'd let this nice woman down. The one who was willing to do whatever it took to save her marriage.

"It's not your fault." They both glanced at the man stalking toward the door.

"Good day." The farewell sounded formal and old-fashioned, which was fine by her. Polite behavior was governed by rules too.

The Petersons shuffled out and she thought she might use the remaining time in their slot to get ahead on some reports when her intercom buzzed. Carly's voice came through a little tinny. "Stephanie Baxter is on the phone for you."

Stephanie wasn't scheduled to see her for weeks. They'd finished regular therapy after Stephanie made such good progress that Deborah had dropped her sessions to four a year simply for maintenance. A call from her between regular sessions could only be bad news. "Thanks. Put her through."

"I need to see you right away," said the shaky voice on the phone.

"Where are you?"

"At the mall."

Deb's heart sank. Stephanie and mall equaled trouble.

"How soon can you get here?"

"I have to go to work."

"Okay. Come when your shift ends. I'll wait for you." She and Jordan had planned to have dinner together, but she suspected she'd be too busy helping a client in crisis.

"I almost took it." Stephanie's hands shook. "I almost took the watch. It was in my bag. I would have—" She gazed at Deborah with naked appeal. "I would have."

"But you didn't."

"He stopped me."

"Who?"

Her eyes fluttered closed and she put her shaking hands over them. "This guy. I don't know who he was. He was following me around the store, watching me."

"A store detective?"

She shook her head. "I don't think so. I didn't stay around to find out."

"Okay. Let's go back to the moment outside, in the mall,

when you first started having the urge. What was going on?"
Shoplifting was an addiction, like drugs or alcohol, Deborah
believed, but in Stephanie's case it was also a cry for help.
Her psyche's way of clanging a fire bell.

"I took back the ring from Derek. We got reengaged."

"So, you'd broken off the engagement? I didn't know that."
The careful neutrality of her voice was deliberately soothing.
She made a note on her pad with one fluid motion. No wonder Stephanie was in crisis if she was trying to dump the most
stable influence in her life.

"Yeah. Yes. We had a fight and I gave him the ring back."

"I see. What was the fight about?"

"It's dumb."

Silence.

"If it was enough to break your engagement over, it couldn't
have been dumb to you."

Stephanie stared at the floor. "I guess. It was about my
mother. He thinks she's too demanding of me. Too clingy."

"I see. What do you think about that?"

Her body stiffened and Deborah watched her hands clasp
each other tightly, as though meeting for the first time. "I
don't know. My mom's never had it easy, you know?"

"Yes, I do. You've told me before about your father's
drinking and jail time."

"He wasn't much of a dad, but he tried. Mom's so happy
that I found Derek. She thinks he's the best thing that ever
happened to me, so to have him talk about her like that, and
to tell me that I need to create more distance between us."
She shrugged. "I guess I lost it."

"What made you reconsider?"

"He says he loves me and he's sorry. He never meant to
hurt me. And all my friends tell me he's the best thing that
ever happened to me." She glanced up and her eyes were
troubled. "I haven't had great luck with guys."

You're not kidding. Deborah mentally went over the list of
winners Stephanie had fallen for. There was the drug addict,

the guy who thought keeping Austin weird was his personal one-man mission, the mechanic who turned out to be running a chop shop, the amateur boxer who practiced on his girlfriend when he was frustrated. No, Stephanie could not be said to have sterling taste in men.

"He's just so different. That's what attracted me to him in the first place. I decided I was finished with losers and creeps, and when I met Derek it was like a sign. He wears a suit and tie to work, he doesn't drink, he never borrows money off me."

Hardly a list of qualities in the perfect husband; still, for Stephanie, it was a big step forward.

"Why do you think you got that urge to shoplift right after you got engaged again?" Deborah asked quietly.

"I don't know. I don't know. This woman had been sitting beside us at the food court—"

"You got engaged at the food court?" She never interrupted a client, and she heard some strange things, but getting engaged at the food court was about as wretched a story as she could ever imagine having to tell one's grandchildren.

"Well, reengaged. The first time it was at a fancy restaurant and the waiter served the ring on a silver platter." She mimed a dome with her hand. "You know, one of those with the round lids you lift off?"

"How original."

"Yeah, it was sort of embarrassing because everybody in the restaurant started clapping, and the waiter popped a bottle of champagne, and . . . I never said yes."

"But you said yes this morning."

There was a pause. "Not really. I don't think he asked me a question."

Controlling fiancé, or just a nervous one?

"Then this woman at the next table came over to my table to congratulate me after Derek left. I was pretty stunned. I guess I wasn't acting very happy. She said I shouldn't marry him. And she offered me a job."

"A complete stranger told you not to get married?"

Stephanie nodded.

"And offered you a job doing what?"

"Secretary at this agency she owns."

"What sort of agency?"

"I don't know. She breaks up relationships for money."

Deb was starting to get a headache. "What?"

"It's what she said. She's like the opposite of a match-maker."

"I don't believe it."

"Here's her card," Stephanie said, digging the white rec-tangle out of her bag.

She handed it to Deborah, who read it carefully, pursed her lips with annoyance, and placed it on the glass-topped coffee table.

"Chloe Flynt sounds like a very destructive person."

Stephanie gazed at her in mild astonishment. "You always tell me not to make snap judgments about people."

Something tight pulled from beneath Deborah's scalp, like a fine wire. *Don't argue,* she wanted to snap. Instead, she re-peated to herself her mantra: *calm, cool, collected.* The three Cs that kept her functioning.

"Normally, I wouldn't judge someone based on a business card, you're right." What was it about this particular card that made her arteries vibrate, as though she could actually feel her blood pressure rising? She picked up the card and studied it for clues as to why something so frivolous and be-neath her notice should make her react this way.

"This woman has no letters after her name. No degree, no designation whatsoever. What training does she have for this work?"

"Do you need training to break up relationships?"

"You need the sense to stay out of other people's busi-ness," she snapped.

Stephanie didn't argue, simply looked at her with those big brown eyes. She didn't need to speak, it was obvious what she was thinking. Deborah made her living getting involved in other people's business. It was unlike her to get so rattled over something so trivial. She made a note to herself to consult with Jordan. "Why would she want to hire you? A perfect stranger?"

"Well, first she wanted me to hire her to break up the engagement, but I told her I, um, wasn't interested. So then she asked if I'd like to come and work for her."

"And what did you say?"

"I turned her down."

A puff of breath she hadn't known she was holding released in a sigh. "I'm very glad you did that. This woman does not sound like a good influence for you."

There it was again, thought Stephanie. One more person telling her what or who was a good influence, or a good boyfriend or mother or husband. When was she allowed to make her own decisions?

Then she recalled all the creeps who'd used her since her first boyfriend in high school and accepted that most everybody knew better what was good for her than she knew herself.

"All right, Stephanie," Deborah said. "Would it be fair to say you're confused right now?"

"Oh, yeah."

"Do you think your confusion caused you to relapse to behavior you know is counterproductive?"

"I guess."

"Get out your binder. Why don't you try doing one of our pro and con lists? What is good about marrying Derek? What are the negatives?"

"Okay," Stephanie replied, sounding anything but excited at the prospect. An increasingly familiar spurt of irritation gurgled up into Deborah's throat, scalding words she wanted to blurt out and couldn't. *Pull yourself together, you stupid twit. You've wasted years of your young life on losers. Here's a decent guy, finally, and you want to break up and go on a shoplifting spree? Marry him, settle down. Have some kids. Quit wasting my time.*

She didn't say that. She never said what she was thinking. Instead, she smiled her calm, cool smile, reached for one of her copyrighted pro and con lists, and passed it to her client along with a fresh pen.

"I don't know what to put first."

We've done about twelve of these. How hard is it? "Well, why don't we start with a positive, like we usually do?"

Chapter 7

Chloe returned home late that afternoon with a pleasant feeling of accomplishment. She had brochures and cards in quite a number of salons, as well as a really nice manicure.

If she spread out all her own cosmetic needs, she hoped she'd be able to support all the spas and salons that carried her promotional materials. She was also toying with the idea of some sort of commission, or gift, for other professionals who steered business her way. She'd have to talk to Gerald about that, she decided, stopping to make a note.

She'd almost reached her front door when, with a sudden shake of the head, she changed direction and crossed the lawn to her neighbor's house where she rapped on the front door.

She could hear music inside, and she waited. She had to rap a second time before the door opened. Matthew was dripping wet, a thick blue towel wrapped around his waist. Chloe tried not to notice that his torso was mouthwateringly buff. Muscles where a woman liked to find muscle, nice lean middle, exactly the correct amount of chest hair, wet and dark. "What?"

"You were in the shower, I see."

"That detective business must be doing real well with those skills of yours." His eyelashes were clumped together with water, and she'd never noticed the amount of green in his hazel eyes.

Her own spurt of lust made her snappish. "You took long enough to answer the door; could you not have grabbed a robe?"

Amusement gleamed in the depths of his eyes, along with the sexual awareness that flashed between them more than it should have. He glanced down at his rather delicious self and then at her. "Is this bothering you?"

Realizing she was in danger of letting him know exactly how much his half naked body was bothering her—and therefore playing intolerably into his already Texas-sized ego—she rolled her gaze, and said, "Please. A hand towel would have done the job."

Instead of looking horribly offended, his eyes crinkled.

"What can I do for you?"

Oh, she felt like pulling on the all-too-accessible knot, throwing the blue towel to the floor and showing him exactly what he could do for her. However, she was here for work, and besides, the coffee-cake-baking Brittany was between them, which meant that shagging him on the living room floor was probably not a great idea just at the moment. Sad, really.

The towel left his knees bare and she noticed a nasty-looking network of scars over his left knee.

"I wonder if you followed that tedious young man?"

For a moment she thought he wasn't going to answer her. His eyes lost their amusement and hardened. "It's generally not a real good idea to go around following strange men."

She smiled at him. "I know. That's why I asked you to do it. Did you?"

He nodded briefly.

"And?"

"You'd better come in."

"Ooh, good. That must mean it's juicy."

"It means I need to put some clothes on, and then you and I are going to have a little talk."

She stepped inside a house that was very similar to hers, only larger. "Have a seat," he told her, pointing into the living room. "I'll be right back."

She paused in the doorway to watch him pound up the stairs, enjoying the sight of a muscular back sparkling with water drops, a bottom that was deliciously round and firm, and long, hard-muscled legs. All right, so she couldn't touch. Didn't mean she couldn't look.

Once he was out of sight, she ignored his suggestion to sit and gave herself a tour of his downstairs. It was surprisingly tidy, almost as tidy as she herself liked to keep things. He'd refinished all the inside doors to a satiny, dark wood. There were bookshelves on either side of a stone fireplace, stuffed with an enticing assortment of books. Lots of construction and home handyman books, and novels of a range that surprised her, from literary authors to gory thrillers. The rest were science books.

She'd planned to speed around the entire downstairs, but his books had stalled her for too long, and he dressed faster than anyone she knew. Likely he'd hurried because he didn't trust her, she thought with a slight smile as she heard his footsteps pounding down the stairs. His furniture included rather chunky, mission-style pieces that were lovely but also comfortable, she found, when she finally sat.

He emerged still damp of hair and bare of foot, but with everything in between covered by jeans and a dark green polo shirt.

"So? Where did he go? That young man you followed?" she asked quickly, determined to forestall the talk he wanted to have with her until she had the info she'd wanted.

Matthew took the chair opposite to hers. "He went to work. He's got a job in a jewelry store in the mall." Not terribly surprising since Stephanie had told her about his job, and this was absolutely none of her business since the newly engaged woman had turned down her offer; still, for some reason, she couldn't quite let it go. "I don't trust him. I don't think he's good for Stephanie."

"The girl in the food court?"

She nodded.

He still looked far too serious. "Look, Chloe, I don't know what your game is, but it's got to stop. You can't hassle people in a public place and follow guys to work. That may be how you do things in England, but here in Texas you're going to find yourself in trouble."

She heard his words but ignored them, naturally. He didn't know that there was an important purpose behind her actions, and she didn't intend that he should know until she was good and ready to tell him.

What she did listen to was the subtext of what he was saying. She nodded her head in satisfaction. "You didn't trust him either."

"I didn't—" His lips firmed and she could have sworn he was counting in his head before his mouth opened again and he said, "You're not listening to me. You can't do this."

"Admit it, you enjoyed being a detective again."

"I did not—" He stopped, then glared at her once more. "How do you know I was a detective?"

How had she known? She puzzled over that as a drop of water trickled lazily down from his still-wet hair, down his neck to slide beneath the shirt, which she now knew covered a very broad, nicely tanned shoulder. "I didn't know. You seem like a detective."

The gleam of amusement was back and something about the way he looked at her had lust curling in her belly. "Being one yourself, you recognize the type."

She smiled at him. Eventually, of course, he'd find out exactly who she was and what she did, but she didn't want him finding out anytime soon. It would spoil all her fun. And, she realized with a shock, she was having fun. More than she'd had in ages. Part of it was this man she was so obviously driving crazy. One of her specialties.

"Where did you go while you had me tailing that guy?"

She shrugged. "I had some business to transact, and then I had a manicure. Which your fifty dollars paid for." She held up her hands as though he might not believe her. She'd resisted all the fun colors and stuck with a good old French manicure since it seemed more like what a businesswoman ought to sport.

"Nice," he said. Once more his eyes sobered. "Look, I know you're a long way from home and you don't know anyone here. I told Gerald I'd look out for you."

"That's very sweet, but—"

"All I'm trying to say is that I'm here. If you get stuck and need anything."

She was surprisingly touched by the gruff words. She tried not to think about the fact that she was thousands of miles away from everything and everyone familiar. "Thank you."

"Just stay on the right side of the law."

"Fair enough. I think—" She never had a chance to finish the sentence because her cell phone rang. "Excuse me," she said to Matthew. "This is probably business." In fact, it was most likely Nicky, bored, but surprisingly, it turned out that it was a business call.

"Is this The Breakup Artist?" asked a nervous-sounding man who was keeping his voice so low she could barely hear him.

"Yes, it is. How can I be of service, sir?"

"I have a problem."

"I see," she said. "What kind of problem?"

She waved good-bye to Matthew and then let herself out the front door and headed back to her own place.

"I need to end a relationship but the woman is my boss."

Sounded very efficient to Chloe to be able to chuck a job

and a romance all at once, but she was aware that everyone didn't share her love of drama, unemployment, and uncoupling.

"I see," she said, suitably grave. "That is a problem."

"Yes." The word was a sigh. "So, do you think you can do something? She can't know it's me wanting to end the relationship."

"You want to keep your job?"

"Yes, I like my job and I'm good at it."

"What kind of work do you do?"

There was a short pause. "Can I rely on your discretion?"

"Of course." She became mildly interested. Perhaps he was a spy, or a famous celebrity, or . . .

"You have to promise not to laugh."

"Certainly."

She entered her own home and ran lightly up the stairs.

"I'm a relationship counselor. My boss wrote a book and I helped her with it, so she made me a coauthor."

"What is the book called?"

"Perfect Communication, Perfect Love."

She didn't laugh, at least not aloud so he could hear her over the telephone, but she did have to put her hand over her mouth to stifle her reaction. This was either a practical joke, which, given the fact that the call wasn't from overseas, seemed unlikely, or this man was buggered.

"I see," she said at last. "Tell me about the relationship." By this time, she'd reached her office. While he talked, she Googled the title of the book and sure enough, found it listed. It was doing rather well too.

Oh, hello. Here was something interesting. She interrupted whatever the man was saying without ceremony. "It says here that the authors are appearing live on a chat show here in Austin."

"Yes, that's why I had to call you. I feel like such a fraud."

"Ooh, there's an idea. Tell you what." She was thinking fast, so many possibilities with a chat show. "We could have somebody show up in the audience, you know, a plant. And they could claim that the book's ruined their life, that it's a load of old rubbish and perhaps you could use the ensuing professional disaster to ease out of the affair."

There was a pause. "This is your solution?"

"Well, you've got to admit she'll never know you wanted to break up with her."

"Could you think of something that wouldn't destroy our careers and our business?"

"Sounds to me like your business might be better off without this book." She was skimming the reviews and it did sound like a load of old rubbish.

"Please, I'm desperate."

"All right. If you don't want to do the chat show, we'll have to get her to fall in love with someone else."

He laughed in amazement. "Deborah? You think Deborah would fall out of love?"

"Why not? You did."

"You don't understand."

"Then you'd better explain it to me. No, no, not now," she said when he began speaking. "In person. Meet me"—she flipped to her onscreen calendar, which Gerald had so cleverly sorted for her—"tonight. We'll meet for a drink."

"Somewhere quiet where no one will see us."

"I know, there's a lovely restaurant and bar at the Judge's Mansion on the Hill. Do you know it? Corner of Rio Grande and MLK."

"Near the university?"

"That's right."

"Okay."

"Seven-thirty?"

"Sure. How will I know you?"

"You won't. Carry a copy of your book. I'll find you."

When she arrived at the Judge's Mansion a few minutes past the appointed time, Chloe was pleased to see her newest customer. He glanced around nervously from one of the tables in the lounge area; a copy of the book lay on the table and pointed to the door. He had reddish brown hair and was what you'd call nice looking if he were going out with your best friend and you were trying to be generous. He had a chin that was neither strong nor weak, more irresolute, with pale blue eyes and the kind of skin that blushes easily. He was impeccably groomed, however. She'd never seen such a perfectly knotted tie or such shiny loafers.

She hadn't expected much, considering he was too timid to break up with a woman he no longer loved. He hadn't even ordered himself a drink; he was sitting there looking jumpy.

She slid into the chair across from him and said, "Hello. I'm Chloe."

He glanced around as though she might have brought his boss along, before saying, "Yes, hello. I'm Jordan."

Since Chloe believed that a meeting conducted at seven-thirty in a drinks lounge would go smoother with an actual drink in hand, she gestured to the sweet-looking young man polishing glasses behind the bar, who obligingly made his way to their table.

"Hi. What can I get you, folks?"

"I would like a champagne cocktail, please."

Her companion ordered a glass of red wine and she'd have bet anything he was thinking of the health benefits to his heart as he drank it.

"First, if you don't mind, I'd like to do a spot of marketing research. How did you hear about my company?"

"I found your business card in my partner's office."

She laughed aloud. "Are you sure she isn't as eager to break up with you as you are with her? Why else would she have my card?" Damn, she was good. A few days of dropping off brochures and cards at salons and fitness clubs and she was already reaping the rewards.

"No, not at all. One of her clients gave it to her. She showed me the card because she couldn't believe anyone would go around breaking up relationships for money."

"Well, that's like the pot calling the kettle black, isn't it?" She pointed at the book laying on the table. "She makes money to convince people they're in love. All I do is fix the mess."

He blinked pale blue eyes at her. "It's not really that easy. I mean—"

She waved a hand imperiously. "All right. We won't argue about the value of our respective professions." She sent him a reassuring smile. "Let's just say I'll particularly enjoy this job."

"You won't do anything terrible. I don't want her hurt."

"Of course not. We'll come up with something that makes sense all round. So, what's she like?"

"Deborah?"

Yes, boy genius. "Yes, Deborah."

"Well, she's kind of a neat freak. Nuts about order." He straightened the coaster in front of him. "She grew up in a dysfunctional family, very confrontational and argumentative. Completely disorganized and chaotic, so Deborah craves order. She needs it to function."

"Do you think that's why she was drawn to you? Because you are quiet and orderly and nonconfrontational?"

He pondered her words. "It's certainly a theory that could well prove sound."

"So you'll have to turn yourself into a mess."

"What?"

"It's basic. Whatever she likes about you, you must change. Be the opposite. I used to . . . that is, I had a client who used to laze in bed in the morning drinking tea and reading the paper. This woman was always up late at night, which suited the man. When she wanted to get out of the relationship, she simply began getting up ridiculously early and bustling about in the kitchen making a great deal of noise." She shuddered mentally recalling how awful it had been to wake up at six and then pretend to be capable of bustling at that hour.

"And did it work?"

"Like a charm. He was sleep deprived and miserable in no time. I imagine that if she's a neat freak, all you have to do is make sure to create disorder all over the place. She'll be running for the hills in no time."

"But I couldn't live that way." He touched the knot of his tie as though checking it was still perfect. "I'm a neat freak too. It's one of the things we have in common."

At the end of ten minutes, Chloe thought that Jordan and Deborah were the most boring couple she'd ever heard of and they had far too much in common. "Are you sure you want to chuck her? You two do seem perfect for each other."

He sighed deeply. "I know. I think maybe we're too much alike."

"Who have you fallen in love with?"

He blinked. "I never said—"

"Of course you didn't. Call it my female intuition." And the fact that he was so clearly the kind of man who wouldn't upset the status quo without a reason.

He sighed like a teenager with his first crush. "Her name is Pia. She's in fine arts at the university."

"Fine arts?"

"Yes, she's an artist." He sounded pretty enthusiastic. She guessed he'd thrown himself full on into this affair with a girl who was likely a fair bit younger. "She paints these huge murals, big bold splashes of paint, very abstract."

"Is she the orderly type?"

"No, not at all."

She nodded her head, satisfied. How could a man who talked as though he had about seven advanced degrees be so dim about what was under his nose? "I have a theory about order and chaos."

"Chaos theory? Like a physicist?"

Laughter trilled out of her. "No, silly. A theory about people. I think that order always looks for chaos and chaos responds to order. It's a basic theory of opposites attracting. Of course!" She tapped her nails on the shiny mahogany table between them. "I had it all wrong. Deborah won't be put off by you becoming disorderly. It will give her a purpose to try and fix you." She shook her head. "It's so simple. I'll set up a man as a client who will be such a mess that she'll be drawn to straighten him out." She chuckled.

"But I'm neat and she fell in love with me."

Chloe looked at him for a long moment. "Let me tell you another of my theories. Sometimes what we think we want and what we really want are two different things."

His expression told her that he thought his degrees—and something about his scholarly demeanor suggested he had several—and his work gave him a superior knowledge of human relationships. But there was a ping under her breastbone, as she'd related her thought-up-on-the-spot theory, that told her she was on to something.

Jordan had originally been attracted to Deborah's neatness and order, but he'd been wooed away by a woman who lived in a world of paint splotches and drop cloths. She'd never known an artist—and she'd not only briefly been a painter herself, but she'd modeled for two of London's hottest artists—who was a neatnik.

Perhaps Deborah also needed someone messy and chaotic to balance out her tidy tendencies and give her a purpose.

"If you can't change, we'll simply have to find someone else for Deborah to fall in love with."

His eyes widened slightly. It was the most animated expression she'd yet seen on him. "You think that's possible?"

Ah, yes, the male ego was no less fragile here than at home. Instead of snorting and saying, "Are you joking? She was stupid enough to fall in love with you, wasn't she?," Chloe reminded herself that she was a businesswoman and this man was obviously in a position to pay for her services. So she gave him her best Top Texas Businesswoman smile and said, "It won't be easy, of course, but try to remember that my team are professionals."

"You have a team?"

"Of course." She did, if she counted the receptionist she had yet to hire and the operatives she could see she was going to need. She couldn't break up all the relationships herself; she simply didn't have the time or energy. Yet another job she'd have to add to her expanding to-do list: hire more staff she couldn't afford. Oh, well. You had to invest in your business if you believed in it. She'd read that in a business magazine she'd picked up along with the latest copy of *Vogue*.

"When do you think you could, um, get this done?"

"Do you want the breakup to happen before the television program or after?"

"Oh, gee. Before, I guess. It seems more fair."

Personally, Chloe thought it was brutally unfair to break a woman's heart right before she had her fifteen minutes of fame on telly. Who wanted to appear on millions of television screens with heavy eyes and a red nose? However, since she was quite happy to pocket her fee earlier rather than later, she let him decide on the timing.

"Right. The television appearance is in two weeks, so I'll have to get started right away. Now, about my fees."

He looked a bit shocked at the price, but Chloe had spent too many years shopping on London's Oxford and Bond streets not to know that a marked-down item had no appeal. If you wanted top quality and hot fashion, you paid top price.

She fully intended this breakup to be both top quality and very fashionable.

She leaned forward and touched the tasteful blue cover of the book he'd brought along.

"So this is the book you'll be shilling on telly?" she said, pointing to the cover of *Perfect Communication, Perfect Love. Perfect load of bollocks.*

"That's the book we'll be talking about, yes."

"Excellent. I'll give it a read." At his look of surprise, she said, "It might give me some ideas about Deborah."

"Right. Yes, of course." His forehead creased in concern. "You will run everything by me before you act."

"Of course I will. Don't worry."

"All right." He drew out a checkbook and wrote the check for half of the amount she'd specified. She tucked it into the book as a bookmark and held out her hand to say good-bye.

Now all she had to do was find an attractive, disorganized man for a woman she'd never met to fall in love with so she'd then dump her partner.

Within two weeks.

Chapter 8

Stephanie sat at her teller's booth feeling the minutes drag across eternity like snails across a parched highway. Each unit of time seemed endless. Surely the clock was stuck. It couldn't be only two minutes since she'd last calculated that she had one hour and fifty-three minutes before her lunch break. Now she had one hour and fifty-one minutes.

Her head was aching and her eyes felt dry. She hadn't slept well; in fact, mostly she hadn't slept at all.

Her pro and con list was folded neatly in her purse, and she longed to leave her post and go and read it one more time, just to reassure herself that Derek was solidly winning the pro and con game.

"Next, please," she said, as an older woman hovered uncertainly in the line, waiting to be invited to visit the teller.

Stephanie manually deposited the pension check that could be electronically deposited into the woman's account. Mrs. Arles, like many older customers, didn't trust the paperless system. She liked to receive her check, walk it down to the bank, and have her passbook updated.

She withdrew one hundred dollars and Stephanie counted out five twenties by rote.

"Thank you, dear," the older woman said.

"You're welcome. Have a great day."

One hour and forty-nine minutes to go before she got a break.

"Next, plea—" She never finished the word since her tongue seemed to swell big enough to strangle her when the motorcycle guy she'd never imagined seeing again strolled up to her with that cocky walk of his. The gleaming black helmet brushed his thigh.

She swallowed, then gave him her most blank stare. "Can I help you?"

"Yes, you can." He let the words hang there for a moment, a moment that stretched. She noticed that his nose had a bump in it where it had obviously been broken. There was a scar bisecting one of his eyebrows and another beside his mouth, narrow, like an extra smile line.

His mouth was tough-guy firm, but his lips looked soft. Perfect for kissing. All of that she noticed while he settled in on his side of the counter as though he planned to stay all day. "I'd like to take some cash out." He handed over a bright blue debit card.

"You could use the banking machines over there," she said, pointing to the bank of instant tellers.

"I know. Truth is, I kind of like the personal touch." He emphasized the last two words so they stroked her skin. Her gaze flew to his and she found herself lured once more by the darkness of his eyes, by the wildness she saw within them. His gaze dropped slowly and deliberately to her chest. "Stephanie," he said, reading off her brass-colored badge. In his mouth, her name sounded like an endearment.

Her breath jerked in once. "Fine. I'll need to see some ID."

"I don't need ID when I use the banking machine."

"That's right. Because you have a PIN number. If you want to take cash out from a teller, we need photo ID."

He seemed reluctant, and for a moment, she thought he was going to turn away and quit harassing her; then he dug into his pocket and pulled out a black leather folder. He

flipped it open and a wave of heat flashed over her, quickly
followed by its icy opposite.

"You're a cop?" she said, her voice breathless and reedy.

"Yes, ma'am. I am."

She thought of how he'd watched her the other day at the
department store, how he'd taunted her as his eyes followed
her everywhere she went, knowing she'd slipped that watch
into her bag. She'd been so smug, felt so sure of herself. What
if she'd walked out of that store? She'd have ruined everything. Everything.

She gave him a withdrawal slip to sign and found her
hands were shaking. "What are you doing here?" she whispered urgently.

"Taking out some cash."

"No, I mean at this branch." She licked dry lips. "I mean . . .
I've never seen you in here before."

"Let's just say I'm keeping an eye on the place. The way
robbery is on the rise, you can't be too careful."

Her lips were rubber. No, too rigid for rubber. Molded plastic, as she tried to smile so it felt false and stuck and awful.

She counted out the money and then was so stressed, she
lost track, something she never did, and had to start over.
When she passed him his cash he pushed the wad into a
worn-looking brown leather wallet. "Thanks," he said. "I'll
see you around." The way he glanced at her felt menacing, as
though he were planning to watch her like a hawk until she
committed a crime.

By the time her lunch break arrived, she was ready to grab
her bag, run for the nearest Greyhound, and head out of town.
She wouldn't even care where. She'd get on the first bus and
ride it as far as it could take her. The burning itch in her stomach was acute; her skin felt hot and too tight for her body.

What if he reported her to the bank's brass? What if he
told them what he'd seen her do? Oh, God. He was a cop.
Rafael Escobar. She'd read his name on his badge, and she

knew his badge number since it was emblazoned on the back of her eyelids when she closed her eyes.

Sure, he hadn't seen her shoplift, because he'd stopped her in time. But one whiff of thievery in the bank—one hint of trouble—and she'd lose her job. All he had to do was snoop into her juvie record. It was supposed to be sealed, but she had a feeling that this guy would know how to get whatever information he wanted.

She couldn't let that happen. Fortunately, she was meeting Derek for lunch today. Since he'd decided they needed to save for the wedding, Derek had decreed they couldn't waste money on things like lunch out, which she supposed is how they came to get re-engaged at a shopping mall food court. That was as close as she was going to get to four-star restaurants for a while.

They were meeting on the corner and walking down by the river to eat their lunch. It was all very romantic, she supposed, unless you were the one making the sandwiches at six-thirty in the morning.

She walked quickly, her heels tap, tap, tapping as she walked mindlessly up Congress. Around her the lunch hour crowds milled, spilling out of big bank buildings, telecom towers, insurance offices. She ought to have blended in, but she felt as though she stuck out, as though she were wearing a neon sign around her neck that read, "Thief."

He knew where she worked. Was going to keep an eye on her. Her hand rose to her chest and she realized she was walking so fast, she was getting winded. Or maybe she was having a panic attack. *Slow down*, she told herself. *Breathe.*

Even if he didn't tell the management at the bank, he'd know. He'd always suspect. What if there was a robbery? He'd arrest her first, ask questions later.

The irony had her close to laughing in a nonfunny, mostly hysterical way. She'd pegged him as a lawbreaker himself, not a cop.

Derek was waiting on the corner, as they'd arranged. He kissed her and took her arm. He launched into a story about a customer and a big diamond purchase. She was glad he hadn't noticed that she was upset, but it would have been nice to have him ask her if she was okay. Her heart was still banging away and her breathing was far from normal.

They walked by a homeless guy with no legs sitting on an old sleeping bag. He had a harmonica beside him, but he wasn't playing it. An old black lab curled at his side. When Derek took a coin out of his pocket and tossed it into the guy's hat, she was astonished. "I've never seen you give money to street people before."

"It was an old golf token from the driving range. I found it in my pocket and needed to get rid of it."

"So you gave it to a homeless guy? Doesn't he have enough problems?"

"Hey, I work hard for my money. He should get off his ass and get a job."

"He has no legs," she whispered in a furious undertone.

"Cry me a river."

She slipped a hand down the strap of her purse. She wanted to grab some money and run back and drop it in the guy's hat. She wished she had the courage to defy Derek, but then he'd be furious and she really needed him in a good mood today.

They found a nice spot on the riverfront. It was hot, but there was shade under the trees. She laid out the blanket she'd packed and pulled out sandwiches, cookies, juice, and apples.

"What kind of cookies?"

"Oatmeal raisin."

"I like chocolate chip better." She bit her lip and didn't blurt out that she'd gotten up extra early to bake them. And a thank you would have been nice.

She let him get most of his ham sandwich eaten and listened to another work story. This one was about his ambitions, how he was planning to be store manager by Christmas. Which might mean moving.

It was the opening she was looking for.

"I'm thinking of making a change myself."

He glanced at her. "What kind of change?"

"I'm not very challenged in my job. I was thinking of looking for something else. Maybe in another field."

He glanced at her, his eyes hardening. "We've been through this," he said, speaking slowly as though she were too stupid to keep up with normally paced speech. "I showed you the calculations on my home accounting program. You can't screw around anymore, Stephanie. We're getting married. We need your money and your benefits. As soon as we're hitched, we'll get your checks deposited into my account."

"What?" This was unexpected and unwelcome news.

"I'll give you an allowance." He pulled her ponytail as though they were kids on a school playground. "That way you won't blow your money like you do now."

"An allowance?" Her throat was so dry, she couldn't swallow her sandwich.

"I'll have one too. We both get a small cash allowance and everything that's left over after the bills are paid goes toward a down payment on a house."

"But, I need—"

"You're going to stop giving money to your mom. You've got other responsibilities now."

He had it all planned out. If she lost her job, she'd muss up his careful plan. What if he found out about her problem? He couldn't see the bills for her therapy, of course, but how was she to pay them if she had no money of her own?

"I don't want my checks going into your account," she mumbled.

"Grow up, Stephanie. I'm the best thing that's ever happened to you and you know it. So does your mother. Do you know she thanked me after I gave you that ring?"

Stephanie remembered that Deborah had explained shop-lifting was an addiction. That's what this felt like, this desperate urge that was on her again, sharp and itching as it took her over. Except that, oddly, she didn't have the urge to steal jewelry. Right now she had the urge to give some back.

For the second time.

She glanced around at the other couples, the group of teens horsing around, the tourists. "You never asked me."

"Asked you what?"

"To marry you. You never even asked me."

"You've got my ring on your finger, haven't you? What the hell's your problem?"

"I can't do this." It was all so clear to her, clearer than the pro and con list. "I'm sorry, Derek. I want to be the kind of woman you want, but I'm not. I don't want a house right away. I don't want to give you my paycheck and make you lunch every day."

She tugged off the sparkling ring, dropped it in his lap, and scrambled to her feet. She didn't give him a chance to say anything. She needed to get out of there. She left the blanket, left her mostly uneaten lunch. She didn't like the look she saw on his face, it was too much like how her old boyfriend Bruce used to look at her right before he hit her.

Walking rapidly back to work, she passed the same homeless guy and defiantly dropped five bucks into his hat. *And screw you*, Derek, she thought, seeing the token glinting in the sun.

She was almost at the bank when she saw a cop car drive by. It was stupid of her to jump into a doorway. Cop cars drove around the downtown streets all the time. It might seem like it slowed when it drove past the bank, but that had to be her imagination.

Still, she dug out her cell phone and called the number she'd memorized yesterday.

The phone was picked up on the third ring. "Hallo? This is The Breakup Artist. Chloe speaking."

"Hi. Um. This is Stephanie Baxter."

"Yes?" The crisp voice left the question mark hanging; obviously the woman didn't remember Stephanie. She drew in a breath.

"We met at the food court yesterday. You, um, offered me a job."

"Oh, my goodness. Yes, of course. That Stephanie."

Which immediately made Steph wonder how many other Stephanies the Englishwoman could possibly know. "Right. That Stephanie."

There was a short pause. "Beastly hot today, isn't it?"

Steph glanced up at the sky, which was clear and blue. The weather was a balmy 78 degrees, according to the forecast she'd read in today's paper. If the Englishwoman thought this was beastly, just wait a month. "Yes, it is."

"May I ask why you're calling?"

"Oh, yeah. I mean, yes. It's about the job."

"The receptionist job?"

"That's right. Is it still available?"

"Well, as a matter of fact, I was just writing out an advert for the paper. It would be lovely to scratch one thing off my to do list."

Stephanie found herself smiling for the first time all day. "Great. Do you want me to come in for an interview?"

"No, I wouldn't have a clue what to ask you. Why don't you come on Monday and start work. We'll sort it out together."

"Monday. Oh, I have to give notice."

"Oh, of course," said the crisp voice on the other end of the phone, sounding disappointed. "Notice. I was so hoping you could start soon."

"Let me see what I can do. I'll explain that you really need me. It's not that busy at the bank, so I could probably get away early."

As though the sunshine had come out to dry up the rain, the disappointment vanished from Chloe's voice. "Oh, that would be fantastic."

"We didn't discuss salary."

"No, tedious business, isn't it. Money."

Not as tedious as not having any, but Steph didn't say that either. She simply made a mmm-hmmm sound.

"What are you being paid at the bank?"

Stephanie told her.

"Gosh, that's not much, considering you handle money all day long, is it?"

"No, it isn't," Stephanie said, heartily agreeing with her new boss for the first time.

"Well, since you're leaving a perfectly good job to come and work for me, how about I add ten percent to what you're earning with a bonus if you bring in any new clients."

"That would be great."

"Good. Monday then?"

"Awesome."

"The address is on my card. Do you still have it or do you need it again?"

"No, I have it." Locked in her memory along with a lot of other useless and not so useless trivia.

"Shall we say nine a.m.?"

"Okay." She pulled out the neatly folded sheet of pros and cons regarding marrying Derek and it felt like the paper was made out of cement. She crumpled it in her hand.

Briefly, Stephanie toyed with the idea of phoning Deborah before she irrevocably messed up everything by quitting her job.

Then she decided, Screw it. Maybe she was meant to be irrevocably messed up. As she passed a trash can, she dropped the pro and con list into it. There were dozens of reasons why she should marry Derek, but the single con canceled out everything else.

She didn't love him. And he was never going to make her happy.

During the last few minutes of her lunch hour she composed her resignation letter. She felt lighter than she had in months.

Wrecking her life had never felt so good.

Chapter 9

Chloe was so pleased with her excellent morning's work, and her first confirmed employee, that she headed for a day spa to celebrate.

Where else could a woman spend the afternoon and come away with a series of business leads, as well as a rejuvenated skin from a facial and a spectacular pedicure? She looked down at her Tequila Sunrise polished toes as she returned home. Perhaps she'd been too conservative with that French polish manicure. She wasn't a lawyer or a banker; why shouldn't she be as colorful as her business?

She walked up the path in her sandals and stopped midstep to admire her newly pedicured feet, smooth of skin and shiny of nail.

"Practicing counting to ten?" that deep and most annoying voice called to her from next door. She glanced up to see Matthew heading up his front path on foot. He was holding a bundle of twigs, as though he'd been gardening.

"No," she said, glad to have the opportunity to tackle him. "I'm looking at the exceptionally long grass in the front garden. It looks quite ragged, don't you agree?"

Matthew dumped the twigs in a neat pile and strode across his own neat and well-tended lawn to wade into her own overgrown and rather brown grass. He peered around. "Yep, it is."

"And do you think you could manage to mow it?" she inquired at her most imperious.

"Nope."

"I beg your pardon?" There was a look about him that said he could do pretty much anything he put his mind to. *Capable* was a word that aptly described him, she thought.

"Read your lease. Housework and gardening are the tenant's responsibility." He looked altogether too pleased to be giving her such ghastly news.

She glanced around at the scrubby grass and the weedy things in the flower bed. At home, she lived in a flat in town, and when she was at home with Mummy and Daddy, Old Mo came around every Saturday to do the gardening. She wished Old Mo wasn't so far away. Of all the things she was homesick for, she'd never imagined feeling such a keen wish to see the garden and the odd job man's homely visage.

"Is there a gardener one could hire?"

He was doing that thing again, laughing at her with his eyes, which was at one and the same time wildly intriguing and truly annoying. "Probably, somewhere, but I don't personally know any gardeners. Around here, folks mostly cut their own lawns."

"I am not from around here," she said loftily.

"That's obvious." He stared down at her from his delicious height. "Are you telling me you don't know how to run a lawnmower?"

"Of course I don't."

He didn't seem satisfied with the answer. If she wasn't careful, he was going to suggest she might like to learn. She sighed. "My mother was a lady," she explained.

He blinked at her. "Weren't most people's?"

She laughed. "No, a real lady. Lady Hester Thorpe."

"I don't recall you putting Lady Chloe on your lease agreement. Are you here incognito?"

"Certainly not."

He seemed quite interested in her all of a sudden, even

though she noted the crinkles around his eyes had deepened. "What did you do to lose the title?"

"I didn't do anything. It's not a hereditary title."

He looked at her through eyes narrowed against the sun, still twinkling. "So, you're saying you're not a lady?"

The heat encircling her didn't seem to be coming entirely from the endless sun streaming down from the sky. She shaded her eyes and looked up at him. "Under what circumstances might I persuade you to mow this lawn?"

His teeth were white and even as he flashed her his "Matthew McConaughey everything is bigger in Texas" grin. She had the distinct impression she now understood what a crocodile's prey's last moments must be like. "Can you cook?"

"I studied at Cordon Bleu in Paris," she said. "They teach gourmet cooking," she added in case he didn't know.

Fortunately, like most people, he didn't ask her exactly how long she'd remained in the course.

"Impressive."

"Thank you."

"I wouldn't have pictured you as the chef type."

"It was *Sabrina* that convinced me."

"Who is Sabrina?"

"The movie. Audrey Hepburn? She's the chauffeur's daughter and she goes off to Paris to learn how to cook. Of course, she ends up with both William Holden and Humphrey Bogart wanting her in the end."

"Interesting way to choose a career."

"Obviously it didn't work out in the long run. But I am a fabulous cook." Of soups and hors d'oeuvres.

"Tell you what. Since you're not a lady, and this is a democratic country anyway, I'll mow your lawn if you cook me dinner."

She would much rather cook than mow, but the main course was going to be a problem. "What about appetizers and drinks?"

He surveyed her yard and shook his head slowly. "That's a

big lawn, and I've got a big appetite." Why was it that the minute he mentioned his appetite her thoughts skittered away from food?

"Matthew, might I remind you that you are an engaged man?"

"You might do anything you damn well please. Let's say you'll cook dinner for three. I'll bring along a chaperone."

"Excellent." And that would give her a chance to get to know Brittany better. "Tomorrow night?"

"Works for me."

She nodded and continued on her way, her Tequila Sunrise toes twinkling up the path.

The afternoon was hot, sultry, and her calendar, while now holding a few appointments, wasn't exactly overflowing with business. She sighed. She wasn't overbooked for business or pleasure. In London, she'd have three or four events to pop in on. Parties, restaurant openings, first nights. Now that she was settled, she was going to have to do something about getting known in Austin social circles.

She calculated the time and decided to give Nicky a call. She had a sudden longing to hear someone speaking a language she understood.

Nicky's mobile rang three times. She was about to ring off when it was answered on a giggle. "Lo?"

"Nicky?"

"Chloe, darling!" There was noise and laughter in the background. Nicky was partying. Had been for some time by the sound of things. "It's Chloe," Nicky bellowed, presumably to whoever else was present.

She heard various people shouting "Hallo, Chloe" in various stages of drunkenness and felt a piercing pang of homesickness for all her friends.

"Tell everyone hello back," she said.

"So, when are you coming home?" Nicky asked her, her words slurring slightly.

"Coming home?"

"Oh, can you wait until tomorrow? I win the pool if you pack it in tomorrow."

"Pack it in? Nick, you're drunk. Have you forgotten that I've got a business to run?" And didn't she sound like a Fortune 500 company president.

A wheeze of horsey laughter greeted her. "I'm not so drunk that I don't know my best friend. You always quit."

"Not always."

"Yes, always. Schools, men, fashions . . . name me one thing you don't change every few months?"

At a thousand pounds a minute or at whatever long-distance mobile phone costs were, there was an extremely expensive pause. What had she ever stuck with?

Then she had it. With satisfaction, she announced, "My hair color."

Another snort of laughter greeted her statement. "Only because that artist threatened to kill himself because he said such a perfect black could not be reproduced by any colorist on earth." Nicky shouted the line with all the drama poor Dennis, the almost-forgotten artist, had used when he slashed the portrait of Chloe he'd been working on and then held the knife to his own throat, threatening to do himself in if she wouldn't marry him.

She'd have been frightened if he'd threatened himself with anything sharper than a palette knife. As it was, the story had made good telling, and Dennis's outburst had caused her to stick with the hair color nature had given her and art couldn't duplicate.

Chloe laughed too. How could she help it? Nicky and she went way back, and they knew each other too well to mess about.

"You really don't think I'm going to make it, do you?"

"Darling, you're like Peter Pan."

"A boy who flies?"

"No, silly. He never grows up. Jack says that's your problem. You've never grown up."

"Jack should mind his own bloody business." She tried to sound annoyed but was secretly rather pleased they were discussing her and laying bets on when she'd return. All her friends, and even her brother, missed her. She'd have to go home for a visit when she got enough money together.

"Give everyone my love. I miss you all."

"Wait, am I going to win the pool?"

She was certain the noise level dimmed in whatever smart club they were at. She pictured the lot of them leaning forward, desperate to hear whether she'd soon be back among them. The thought made her smile.

"Not this time."

As she rang off she realized that she'd now been in this country for more than a month and she had none of the usual itchy feet. That was good. Progress.

Her new career wasn't remotely boring since her creativity was constantly taxed. As in the case of her newest client. She had precious little time to get the coauthors of *Perfect Communication, Perfect Love* perfectly cocked up.

She decided to read Jordan's and his boss's book since Jordan was her priority client at the moment. She was very much hoping that this book would give her the secret to breaking up that romance before Perfect Love ever had its Perfect Communication on the telly.

She was hot, so she stripped down and changed into white shorts and a purple gauzy Stella McCartney top and jeweled sandals. She couldn't bear ball caps but understood that one must protect one's complexion from the withering heat, so she'd bought a plantation-style hat with a huge white brim. It made her feel like Scarlett O'Hara when she slipped it on. She tipped the brim to a rakish angle before donning big sunglasses and picking up the book. She stopped in the kitchen to fill a large glass with iced tea, an American invention she was beginning to enjoy very much, and her Evian spritzer.

Soon she was ensconced on her lounger, parked under a

shade tree, her face pleasantly misted, her tea at her side, and her book open on her lap.

"*Perfect Communication, Perfect Love,*" she read in the preface, "came about as the collaboration between two colleagues."

"Oh, right. Blah, bloody blah," Chloe muttered as she flicked past the front piece to Chapter One and began to read.

An annoying sound smote her ears. The irritating buzz of a small engine.

Really, just when she was trying to read quietly. She rose, thinking this was the first moment she'd had all day to be quiet; then a mower came into her line of vision from around the side of the house, dragging Matthew behind it. Bare-chested, yummy, superyummy Matthew.

She retreated once more to her lounger and proceeded to read, giving herself a mental reward for each page she finished with a peek at her most delicious gardener.

Chapter 10

Matthew wondered what the hell he was doing, playing gardener to Lady Chatterley over there in her lounger with her feet up and her novel open on her lap. Nice life.

He wondered if she really could cook. And if he did the weeding as well as cutting the lawn, if her skills stretched to breakfast.

Then his cell phone vibrated in his pocket, his call display telling him it was Brittany calling, and he pulled his gaze away from his neighbor. "Tanner," he said, because he always answered that way no matter who was calling.

"Hi, Matthew, it's me, Brittany." Just as he always identified himself, so did she even though she knew he had call display. Just one of those stupid things people do, he told himself, willing himself not to be irritated with the woman he was planning to marry. Someday.

"Hi, honey. You packing for the conference?"

She was heading out for a teacher's conference in San Antonio for three days. "The conference was postponed. The main presenter is sick with pneumonia so it was rescheduled."

"Too bad."

"It's fine. It gives me three days off, since I already have the time booked off, and you know what that means?"

Matthew didn't even want to speculate.

"It means that you and I can start our redecoration project."

A drop of sweat trickled down his temple under his ball cap and he swiped at it with the back of his hand. "What redecoration project?"

"You know. Your house."

"Since when are we redecorating my house?"

"Honey, don't you remember when I said that I thought your colors were too dark and you agreed?"

He didn't remember any such thing, but he knew he had a bad habit of not always listening too intently to everything she said.

"Right. But I didn't necessarily want to change everything right away." Or ever. His colors might be dark, but he was a guy. He was supposed to like dark colors.

He made a mental inventory of Brittany's decorating style and thought he might as well just kill himself now as be ridiculed to death when his buddies saw throw pillows and a collection of antique dolls in his house.

"Well, why don't we spend the day tomorrow looking at decorating stores and get an idea of what might work. You never know when things might change," she said softly. Once more he felt like a pig. She was right. They were an acknowledged couple, they got on well, were compatible in the sack, though he sometimes thought she tried too hard to please.

While his bride-to-be outlined an exciting day's events shopping for paint samples and fabric swatches, and more sweat dripped from his forehead, he stole a look at his tenant next door. She was laughing her head off at something in that novel of hers. Must be a pretty good comedy. Kind of like his life.

The thought stole through his mind, unbidden, that Chloe would never be the kind of woman who would try too hard to please. He had a pretty good idea that she was one of the demanding ones who took what she wanted from a man and gave as good as she got.

Her shorts, pretty damn short to begin with, had ridden up her thighs, and he had a vision of pale skin on legs that weren't long but were slim and shapely.

As though she felt his gaze, Chloe glanced up and the laughter died on her face. Whether she'd read his mind or not, he couldn't tell, but a zing of lust, hot and visceral, shot between them like a very bad idea.

At the same moment, they both averted their gazes. She to her book, he to the row of bushes, which needed pruning, at the side of her yard against the fence that bordered the road.

"And then tomorrow night," Brittany said, "maybe we could go out for dinner somewhere, just the two of us. We've both been so busy lately that we've hardly seen each other."

"I know. Dinner would be—oh, shit. I just remembered. I'm having dinner at Chloe's."

"Chloe's?"

"Yeah, my next door neighbor."

"You're having dinner with another woman?" She sounded surprised rather than jealous. But that was Brittany all over. She'd expect there was a reasonable explanation before jumping to conclusions.

"I'm doing some gardening for her so she invited us for dinner. I knew you'd be away, so I asked Rafe along. I can't really get out of it now, but why don't I tell her there'll be one more for dinner?"

"I don't want to impose."

"You won't be. I'll do some extra stuff for her, that should make it even."

"I suppose it is better with even numbers. More like a double date."

He chuckled to himself at the thought of the scruffy down-to-earth Rafe with the English princess. Should be an interesting evening.

"So, what about tomorrow?"

He could think of about six million things, including chopping off his toes with the weed whacker, that he'd rather do tomorrow, but he'd been less than stellar as a boyfriend to Brittany the last month, so he figured it was penance. "Yeah, okay. I'll pick you up at ten."

He ended the call and finished the lawn before walking over to tell Chloe the good news, that she now had a fourth for dinner.

She was chuckling again when he walked up and pulled out one of the patio chairs to sit down and cool off for a minute.

"Pretty funny book?"

She raised her head, looking like a movie star with the big hat and oversized sunglasses. "It's not meant to be."

She closed the book and showed him the title. He felt a jolt of pure nausea. *"Perfect Communication, Perfect Love.* What are you doing reading that crap?"

"It's for business, actually."

He opened his mouth and she forestalled him with a finger in the air. "So it's confidential, naturally."

It was funny, Chloe irritated him a hell of a lot more than Brittany ever did, but at least he didn't feel boredom creeping over him at the same time he wanted to grind his teeth.

With Chloe, it was pretty much only the dental problem.

She handed over the book. "You might want to give this a read. It might help you work things out with Brittany."

His eyes narrowed. "What makes you think I need help with Brittany?"

"Women's intuition." She rose. "You look hot. Would you like some iced tea?"

"Yeah, thanks."

He flicked through the book, which, from what he could see, was made up of rules to follow. For love. Like there weren't enough rules in life, a man needed more.

When Chloe returned with a huge glass of iced tea, he thanked her with a nod and downed half of it. He wiped his mouth with the back of his hand. "You were laughing when you read this."

"It's the most ridiculous nonsense," she said. She took the book back and flicked pages. "Listen to this."

> *"Conflict is a natural part of any relationship. Bad feelings can be destructive if you let them grow, leading to alienation or shouting matches. We recommend a regular session with your loved one. Imagine you're in our office; talk to each other about your issues, how it went this week. Always end by holding hands, looking each other in the eye, and saying, 'I love you.'"*

He loved the sound of her voice, so crisp and British, so different from what he was used to hearing. That's probably why she was so intriguing to him. She was different. She was an English rose in a field of Texas bluebonnets. That's all.

"Sounds like a load of crap to me."

"Exactly. I'm all in favor of a good row. Clears the air."

"Leads to some great sex too," Matthew remarked. "With all those emotions flying."

"My thoughts exactly." She seemed happy they viewed arguments the same way and he thought she'd say more, but suddenly she snapped the book shut and looked past him.

"The lawn looks lovely. Thank you for taking care of it so promptly."

He wasn't positive about what had made her suddenly treat him like the hired help, but he had an idea. He rose from the chair.

"You're welcome. I need to ask you a favor."

"Yes?"

"I need to bring one more person for dinner tomorrow night."

Her brows rose. "How many girlfriends do you have?"

His teeth wanted to grind again. "One. And she was supposed to be out of town. The chaperone I already invited is a buddy of mine."

"I see." She glanced at him. "You knew I was expecting Brittany. Why didn't you tell me you'd invited a man?"

He thought about it for a second, and decided to go for the truth. "There's something about you that just begs to be riled up."

She shot him a surprisingly understanding look. But then she'd spent her life riling other people up, he could just tell. Unfortunately, the list had his name on it. Currently, as far as he could tell, he had the top spot.

"So we're four for dinner. How cozy."

"Look, I feel bad about this. Why don't I bring over steaks and we can barbecue?"

She looked delighted and, he thought, a little relieved. "That's very nice of you. I'll prepare appetizers and salad and pick up something for dessert."

He rose. "And I'll keep taking care of the lawn for you."

Her surprise showed even behind the glasses. "What do you want in return? More dinners?"

"I'll call in the favor if I ever need any private detective work."

Instead of rising to the bait, she gave him a smile that was suspiciously smug. One he didn't trust at all. "I'm at your service," she said.

Chloe loved markets. She loved the smell of food, the vendors, the colors and textures of produce, and here, everything was so different. The displays seemed larger, the fruits bigger.

Of course, she hadn't brought many recipes, but the Internet was an amazing source of inspiration, and she knew her favorites by heart.

Two men, and if his friend was anything like Matthew, he'd be big and a man of simple tastes, she thought, immediately discarding the idea of frog legs, escargot, or anything with too many sauces. In the end she opted for fresh prawns in a coconut masala, and a salad with organic greens and her own special salad dressing in which the secret ingredient was champagne.

She bought cheerful sunflowers for the table, some pretty blue cloth napkins, and candles. A nice white wine for the appetizers and a hearty red for the steaks. Dessert, she decided, would be a selection of cheeses and fresh fruit.

When she returned home, she got to work. Singing along to the Dixie Chicks as she prepared the masala.

Her doorbell rang at precisely seven. Chloe ran lightly down the stairs, slipping the second diamond earring into her ear. How prompt.

She opened the door and suffered a slight shock. A disheveled-looking, thuggish type stood there, in a battered leather jacket, jeans that no designer had had a hand in, and scuffed boots. His hair was too long and he needed a shave. "Can I help you?" she asked, wishing she wasn't always so impulsive. She really ought to use her peephole in the door. Still, at least Matthew was next door. One good scream away.

The guy on her doorstep gave her a crooked grin as though he'd read her mind reasonably well. "I'm Rafe." Then he raised his hand and, instead of some deadly weapon, he held a wrapped bottle. "Matt's friend."

"Why thank you," she said, accepting the wine. "Come in."

She stepped back, and said, "Can I take your coat?" She noted the shiny black helmet. "And, um, your bike helmet?"

"Thanks." He handed her both and she put them in the hall closet, wishing Matthew would hurry up. She had plenty of social graces and ease, but there was something criminal and unnerving about the man behind her.

"I thought we'd start outside," she said, leading the way down the hall into the kitchen. "It's such a nice evening."

"Sounds good to me. It was nice of you to invite me. The kitchen smells great."

Well, at least he had manners, and a rather delightful

Antonio Banderas inflection to his tone. Though if she were casting a movie about him, she'd go with someone more sinister, but still dishy, like Benicio Del Toro.

She settled him on a patio chair on the table out back. "I can offer you wine, beer, or a margarita."

He sent her a white-toothed grin that suddenly lightened his face and made him seem much less sinister.

"I'll try your margarita. But I'm a tough judge."

"Oh dear. I've never made them before. I got the recipe off the Internet."

He looked seriously worried. "Did you use a mix?"

"Of course not. I never use mixes."

"Let me see." He rose, followed her into the kitchen, and pored over the recipe she'd printed off her computer.

She had the ingredients assembled on the counter alongside the recipe, and after he put the printout down, he picked up the tequila bottle and nodded his approval. "You buy good tequila."

"I wasn't sure. I just bought the most expensive kind they had in the shop."

His dark eyes gleamed. "That's how you pick stuff? By price?"

"No, not always. But it's not a bad method. You said yourself that's good tequila."

He rolled up the sleeves of his white shirt, washed two of the limes, and said, "You want one?"

"Thank you. I was thinking of making a pitcher of them."

She wasn't a bit surprised when he shook his head. "Margaritas should always be made fresh."

She chuckled. "I am officially putting you in charge of the cocktails." He was clearly one of those take-charge men, good in the kitchen and, she suspected, in bed. There was strong sensuality in him and, she guessed, he was the kind who'd take charge of a woman's pleasure before worrying about his own. She highly approved.

While he squeezed limes and she skewered huge bay shrimp, she said, "So, how do you know Matthew?"

"Through work."

"Real estate?"

"No, before that. We were on the force together." There was a slight pause. "He's a good cop," he said, with a trace of sadness.

"So, you're a police officer?"

He grinned that charming smile once more. "Surprises a lot of people."

"What branch are you in?"

"I do a little of this and that," he said evasively. And she nodded, thinking, *Undercover*. How exciting.

By the time Matthew and Brittany arrived, half an hour later, she and Rafe were fast friends. She would have thought they'd have nothing to talk about, but he was in his way a foreigner too. He could relate the things he'd found strange about Austin and Texas, and she could tell her stories.

"At least you can get Mexican food here," she said, thinking she'd passed many a Mexican restaurant. "I have yet to find a place that serves a decent cup of tea. Or a scone with proper Devon cream."

He grimaced. "Tex-Mex? Don't get me started."

Then Matthew strode into view, with that sweet-looking blonde beside him. Chloe rose. "Hello." She walked forward. "You must be Brittany? I'm Chloe."

"Hi, sorry we're late. We got held up at a fabric store."

There was a choking sound from Rafe. "Come again?"

"Nothing," Matthew said hastily. "I was helping Brittany with some things."

Chloe wondered what on earth Matthew had been doing in a fabric store, but at least that explained the tight look around his mouth and the pinched skin edging his eyes. He looked irritable, hot, and bored. But he held a tray of thick steaks, so at least he'd remembered those.

Brittany simply looked confused. Poor dear. She was holding a pie in her hands, which she handed over. Chloe beamed at her. "Pie. How clever of you."

Once Rafe had made two more of his super-excellent margaritas, there was a slight pause.

She turned to Brittany. "Why don't we let the men do whatever men do out here with the barbecue. Perhaps you could help me in the kitchen."

"Sure."

In fact, Chloe had already done most everything, but she wanted some time alone with Matthew's girlfriend. Matthew sent a worried glance her way, but she ignored him.

Brittany seemed like a nice woman. There had to be someone who would suit her better than Matthew. In fact, there must be dozens.

She glanced briefly at Rafe, obviously single, but one look at the scruffy bad boy and the blond cheerleader type had her shaking her head. As much as she believed in opposites attracting, one could only go so far.

In the kitchen, Brittany went immediately to the book *Perfect Communication, Perfect Love,* which Chloe had left on the counter. "Oh, you have this? How is it? I've heard it's wonderful. I have to get it." She glanced shyly at Chloe. "I think it might be good for Matthew and me."

The thought of Matthew being forced to listen to that twaddle almost made her feel sorry for him.

"I haven't finished reading it, but I have to say it seems a bit rule bound for my taste."

"I kind of like the idea of rules in life, don't you?"

"God, no. The only rule I follow is never to buy anything you have to line up for or order in advance. Otherwise, I prefer to wing it."

Chloe was dying to tell the other woman that it wasn't the rules that were her problem. It was the man.

In spite of the odd collection of personalities and the fact that they all knew each other and Chloe didn't know any of them, she still managed to be the life of the party. It was her talent. One of her many.

Her appetizers were spectacular, and as the evening progressed she found everyone loosening up, especially Matthew.

Over steaks—and she had to give her neighbor credit, the man could cook a steak to perfection, and salads—talk turned to when he and Rafe worked together. He was kidding his former partner about the mess he always left in the squad car and how nobody would ever work at his desk because it was such a disaster, when Chloe had her brilliant idea.

Bright lights, like those on Broadway, lit up inside her head.

Messy, disorganized, dressed like a gang member, Rafe, who was also intelligent, fiercely committed to justice, and attractive in an entirely unusual way, might just appeal to Deborah, who had her rules of engagement, rules of marriage, rules of love, and her engage-in-weekly-therapy-sessions-with-your-loved-one rule book.

At least, it was worth a shot.

But how would she convince him that he was exactly the man to inspire Deborah to throw her rule book away and embrace all the messiness of life?

Chapter 11

Once dinner was done, Matthew and Brittany got up to leave. "Thank you so much for a wonderful dinner," Brittany said.

"You're welcome. I enjoyed meeting you." And she had. She knew now, beyond the shadow of a doubt, that Brittany and Matthew were never going to make each other happy.

Of course, that was a pro bono case and right now she had to focus on the one paying her. Rafe rose to leave at the same time and she stopped him, saying, "I wonder if you could stay behind, Rafe. There's something I want to discuss with you."

Matthew flicked her a glance that was full of surprise and hostility. She blinked, then realized he was condemning her for what he obviously thought was a ploy to get his ex-partner in bed. She raised her brows to him and then shot a rather significant glance at the woman waiting patiently by his side.

Matt's jaw clenched, and with a curt "Night," he was gone, shutting the door behind him with unnecessary violence.

Rafe didn't say a word, simply looked at Chloe. His expression was, if anything, carefully expressionless.

She laughed. "Oh, don't worry. I don't want to seduce you."

He sat back down. "I am sorry to hear this, but it will save me a pounding from my buddy there."

"Matthew's a fool," she said.

"Seemed to spend more of the evening with his eyes on you than on that gal he's set to marry."

"Oh, he's not going to marry that sweet girl. It would be a disaster."

Rafe's eyes stayed steady on hers. She could see the cop in him now. "Matt tell you that?"

"Of course not. He doesn't know it himself yet." She took a deep breath, knowing she was going to have to tread carefully. "But I didn't ask you to stay to talk about Matthew." She twiddled with one of her earrings. "Rafe, I want you to do me a favor."

"Uh-huh."

"I run a rather unusual business."

"Yeah, Matthew seemed pretty bent out of shape by something you were doing."

"Matthew gets bent out of shape by pretty much everything I do," she said.

He didn't argue and she wondered how much Matthew had said about her. "Tell me about this business of yours."

"You have to promise not to tell Matthew anything about it."

"I can't promise anything if you're operating outside the law."

She giggled. "Oh dear. Is that what he thinks? Poor Matthew. No, of course I'm not a lawbreaker. I am the owner of The Breakup Artist."

"You're a makeup artist?"

"No, breakup. People pay me to end unsatisfactory relationships."

"You're kidding me."

"No, I'm not. You'd be surprised how many people want to end an affair and have no idea how to do it. I help them."

"What do you do? Deliver dead roses and slap faces?"

"Please, I have standards. Mainly, I try to end things in a way that's the least painful for all involved."

"What's wrong with these people that they can't do their own breaking up?"

"Oh, a multitude of reasons. Don't want to hurt their partner, don't want to do the dirty work. They've moved on and simply can't be bothered. Sometimes they try to get the other person to break up with them."

He sent her an odd look. Then glanced down at his hands. "You do this work alone?"

"I do have one employee," she said with a hint of pride. "Stephanie, my receptionist. She starts on Monday."

His glance shot up to meet hers, sharp and slightly alarming.

"Stephanie. I know a Stephanie who works at a bank."

"Isn't that a coincidence? My Stephanie works at a bank. But I offered her a job and she accepted."

"When was this?"

He seemed to be taking an awful lot of interest in things that had nothing to do with him. "I doubt it's the same person."

"Yeah, probably." He shifted. "So, what's the favor?"

Suddenly, she wasn't so certain she wanted to ask him for this favor. And yet, he was perfect, and if he said no, she'd be no worse off than she was now.

"I know this will seem odd, but I need someone very much like you, someone disorganized and chaotic, but also intelligent and attractive. I want you to make an appointment with a psychotherapist and get her to fall in love with you."

It seemed like ten minutes that Rafe sat there and stared at her without moving a muscle. Of course, it was probably no more than thirty seconds, but they were among the longest seconds of her life.

"How am I going to get some woman I don't even know to fall in love with me?"

"I suspect, for all your scruffiness, that you don't have much trouble in that department," she said sharply.

She was rewarded with one of his lightning grins, the ones that she'd hazarded her assumption on.

"What would be in it for me?"

She regarded him for a moment, her head to one side, considering. This was, of course, the sticking point. "I'm assuming you're single?"

"Uh-huh."

"I could break up an unsatisfactory relationship for you with no charge."

"I don't have any of those."

"Aren't you lucky." She stood in the hallway that Matthew had no doubt rebuilt in some clever fashion and she wondered what would appeal to this man in front of her. "Well, of course, the sessions with the counselor will be free. She's got an excellent reputation. Perhaps you have a problem you need help with?"

His gaze sharpened suddenly on her face. Oh, interesting. There was something. "I'm not into shrinks."

"Really? I love therapists. It's so lovely to be able to talk about oneself for hours without then feeling obliged to listen to the other person's problems. I look on therapy as a day at the spa for my psyche. Perhaps you'll learn something. Perhaps there's some small behavior pattern you have that you might like to modify."

Rafe had good manners and his *abuela,* who'd drummed them into him from the time he was old enough to sit at a table with the adults, would roll in her grave if he gave in to his inclination to grab his stuff out of the front closet and walk out.

Besides, he knew that this was the woman Matt had wanted him to tail from the food court, and that she'd been seen with Stephanie right before he appeared on the scene, by which time she'd vanished and so he'd followed Stephanie instead.

He was curious.

And worried. What was up with Stephanie that she'd leave a safe job at the bank to run off and work for this British wing nut?

An awful sense of guilt crawled up his spine. He'd gone into the bank deliberately to warn her that he was keeping his eye on her. He was trying to protect her. He hadn't wanted to scare her out of her nine-to-five routine, her livelihood, and her company pension plan.

Had he done that?

As much as he hated anything to do with shrinks, he'd sure like an excuse to keep an eye on Stephanie, and it seemed pretty likely that his Stephanie and Chloe's Stephanie were one and the same.

"I'll think about it," he said, walking purposefully to the front closet where she'd left his stuff.

She followed at a leisurely pace. "Thank you." She handed him a business card. He read it and shook his head. "I never heard of anyone who made money off breaking people up."

"What about divorce lawyers? They make a lot more money and cause a great deal more misery than I do. The thing you must remember, Rafe, is that a solid relationship is safe from anything I might do. By the time someone comes to me, the relationship is all but over. I merely ease the transition along and, if I do say so myself, make the breakup easier on the other party."

"By tricking someone like a therapist to fall in love with a guy like me who's only there to cause trouble?"

Chloe rolled her gaze. "Honestly, think it through. If a woman who is ethical and obsessed with orderly rules of relationships begins to get feelings for another man, she's not going to go after him. She's going to realize that there's a problem in her primary relationship. I've thought it all through. She'll never allow herself to get involved with a patient. You're safe. All I want you to do is go along and perhaps share with her some of your disorderly attributes."

"Like I said, I'll think about it." By this time he'd shrugged into his coat and was halfway to her front door, his helmet swinging at his side.

He strode down the path to where he'd left his bike and

rode off into the night. Even as he told himself not to be stupid, he passed the turn that would take him home and headed instead for the office.

He muttered a string of obscenities in Spanish even as he parked and headed into the precinct.

Because of the nature of his work, he was often there at odd hours, so nobody thought anything of his appearing at eleven o'clock at night to use the department computer and resources. He tried to convince himself he was doing the work he was paid for, and not using government property for personal reasons, but he didn't try very hard.

Instead, he worked swiftly. He knew her first name was Stephanie, who her employer was, and at which branch she was a teller. In a ridiculously short amount of time he had her full name, date of birth, home phone number, and address.

There'd been an engagement ring sparkling on her finger both times he'd seen her. Was it a live-in arrangement?

He figured he'd drive by her place, check to see if there were lights on, and take it from there.

Once more he headed off on his bike, this time riding to her address in south Austin where a string of blocklike apartment buildings stretched like boxcars.

She was in the second building, apartment 318. He glanced at his watch. Eleven-thirty. A lot of lights were shining in third-floor windows, but he had no idea which one was hers. Or if she was alone.

He walked to the front of the building, contemplated ringing her apartment, when a couple walked out of the front doors, the guy holding the open door politely for him to enter.

Of course, he should read the pair a lecture on safety and security, but instead he muttered thanks and entered the building.

He never took an elevator if he could help it, so he found the staircase and jogged up a couple of flights of stairs that smelled of stale air and some kind of bug repellant.

The third-floor corridor was dimly lit, and the carpet needed replacing. The walls were scuffed, but the place was clean enough. It would rent to transients, young people starting out like Stephanie, divorcées in transition, people new to the city. He found 318 and noted light under the door. He put his ear against it and heard voices. He was about to walk away when he realized the noise was from a TV.

Knowing it was crazy, he knocked on the door anyway.

There was a long pause, then a female voice said, without opening the door, "What do you want?"

At least somebody in this building knew the importance of security and safety precautions, he thought, even as it irritated him that she hadn't opened the door. Maybe the boyfriend was there. He said, "Police business." If the boyfriend was there he'd make up something. He hadn't survived undercover without being quick on his feet.

Once again there was a pause. He wondered if she'd open the door at all and figured she was pondering the same thing.

At last he heard the dead bolt slide; then she opened up the door a measly six inches.

She'd had a bath. That was the first thing he noticed. Her hair was wet, hanging in damp tendrils down the front of a white terry cloth robe, like the ones in hotels. He wondered if she'd swiped it.

He saw a tantalizing six-inch strip of soft, damp skin at the vee of her robe. Her calves, ankles, and feet were bare. She had cinnamon-colored nail polish on her toes and a funky silver toe ring.

She didn't say anything, simply regarded him from those eyes that drew him in with their hints of warmth and cold warring. He understood exactly how she felt, for he was at once thrumming with heat simply from being in her presence and filled with an icy anger that such a great woman was messing up her life.

"Are you alone?" he finally asked.

She moved her head to glance behind him. "Are you?"

"Yes."

Their gazes met and held. Wordlessly, she opened the door and he walked in, still wondering what the fuck he was doing.

The door shut slowly behind him and they stood there in a small hallway with beige carpeting and beige walls, and he thought how wrong the setting was for such a vibrant woman.

She turned, pulling the lapels of her robe tighter, and stalked into the small living area. She picked up her remote and cut off Conan O'Brien.

Silence surrounded them. He felt the heat in his blood that she stirred every time she was near. It was crazy. She was needy, wounded in some way he didn't yet understand, and a ring sparkled from her engagement finger. Then she turned and he realized he was wrong. Her hands were ringless.

"Where's your engagement ring?"

"I took it off."

He moved closer, he couldn't help himself. He wanted to smell the female scents of shampoo and flowery soaps and lotions. He wanted to be close enough to touch her. He saw the wariness in her eyes, but she didn't back away.

"Why? Why did you take off your ring?"

Her eyes heated and he could see her about to tell him to go to hell, when something shifted in her expression. He picked up sadness, confusion, saw the distress flares flash, and felt again that pull toward her that came from somewhere outside the physical realm. "We broke up."

"I'm glad," he said, because it was the simple truth.

"You don't even know him." She whispered the words, her lips barely moving. She had a beautiful mouth. Bare of any makeup, she looked young, fresh, voluptuous.

"I'm glad for me."

"What do you want?" Her voice was unsteady and he fought to remind himself he wasn't here to sample the nakedness under her robe.

"I didn't mean to scare you," he said.

She laughed, a jerky sound, and turned her head away. "You came to the bank and practically threatened me. Every time I turn around, there you are, watching me. Why would that scare me?"

"I'm trying to protect you."

Her head swung back, wet hair slapping her neck. "Protect me?" she shouted. "You've been stalking me, intimidating me, making me feel . . ."

"Feel what?" His voice came out husky.

"Guilty."

"I had to stop you."

She sat down suddenly on the couch, more as though her legs wouldn't hold her up than that she wanted to be seated, he thought. Her color was up. From embarrassment? Anger? Guilt?

"What were you thinking?" he asked, sitting beside her on the couch, but not too close. Realizing he was still holding his bike helmet, he reached to place it on the floor, then straightened and turned to face her. "Why would you steal cheap shit that could get you in trouble?"

"I used to have a problem," she said, "but I haven't for a long time. I don't even know what's the matter with me. I get this crazy urge and I can't stop myself."

"What if you'd been caught? You could have lost everything. Your job, this apartment, everything."

She returned his gaze. "Exactly." She slumped back and blew out a breath. Her robe parted and she didn't seem to notice. He tried to tell himself he didn't notice either.

"I've been going to therapy for years. It was part of my probation agreement when I got caught."

"You have a record?" How did she get a job in a bank with a shoplifting conviction? And how come it hadn't come up when he searched her?

She shook her head. "I was a juvie. Sixteen. No permanent record, but I had to go for therapy. My lawyer made an argument that I was under a lot of stress at the time. My parents were splitting up and I'd started hanging out with the wrong crowd." She shrugged, obviously uncomfortable. "You know how it is."

He nodded. "How come you haven't been caught again? Do you think your luck's going to hang in forever?" He was getting angry. She was so young, so bright. Why would she throw her life away for a bunch of crap stolen from a mall?

Her eyes were so big and so troubled when she turned to him. "You don't get it. I haven't. I call my therapist every time I get the urge. And she gets me in. It's always saved me."

"Not always," he reminded her.

"No, if you hadn't followed me around that store, I would have taken that watch." She rubbed her temples as though she had a headache brewing. "I snapped."

"What made you snap?"

Her smile was a little twisted. "Getting engaged."

A pulse beat in the hollow of her throat. He watched it, unable to look away. If he put his lips there he'd feel that pulse throbbing against his mouth. He wondered how her skin would taste. Ached to find out. "Must be the wrong man."

"No," she said sadly. "He was the right man. That's my problem, I'm always attracted to the wrong men."

"Always?"

She looked at him, and he felt the heat coming off her, coming off him. "Yeah," she said, and leaned over, putting her lips on his. And just like that, lust sucker-punched him.

He had his arms around her before he could even think about stopping himself, about restraint, brains, consequences, going down this fucking path again. Another wounded bird.

But with her curled against him, smelling of all those girl scents and the underlying woman scent of her, how could he think?

Why would he want to?

Their mouths were greedy for each other, crazy. They

kissed the way starving people might eat. His hands were in her hair, fisting in the still-damp strands.

She had her hands under the leather jacket he hadn't taken off, pushing it off his shoulders. He stopped to shrug the thing off, to help her yank his shirt over his head. It caught on the gold icon his grandmother had given him and he almost strangled as they dragged the shirt off in spite of the restriction.

She touched his naked chest, dipping her head to lick at him. He plunged under that robe, feeling for her, for her breasts that were round and plump and perfect. She moaned when he cupped her, nipped at him, and kept going south.

His blood was pounding, need driving him to take, to give.

Her hands were working at his belt, but his raging erection and the way he was sitting made everything too tight.

He pushed her hands away, not wanting to waste the time, and, half rising off the couch, dealt with the thing himself.

He kicked off his boots, dragged off his socks, and while she watched him with those amazing big brown eyes of hers, yanked his jeans and shorts off in one less-than-smooth move.

Her gaze traveled up and down, drinking him in, and he felt a tiny sizzle of embarrassment along with a need stronger than any he'd ever known.

Chapter 12

Stephanie thought she'd never seen a guy she wanted more. She loved the darkness of his skin, the tight, hard abs, and the glorious cock arrowing her way.

Rafe was the latest in a string of disastrous decisions. She understood that. Deborah had explained her self-destructive tendencies—her addiction to bad boys who would hurt her was like being hooked on crack or booze. She wanted to be stronger than this need. She'd tried to be, but she was going down.

His eyes were dark, liquid, heavy with wanting that matched her own. His breathing was ragged. He reached for her and she loved the play of muscles in his arms. He had a snake tattooed around his right bicep.

He reached for the belt of her robe, holding her gaze with his, and when he unwrapped her, she felt like a gift.

His gaze traveled down her naked body, and he made a sound that could only be satisfaction. She felt beautiful, irresistible, and so hot she was about to explode.

He kissed her again, kissed his way to her breasts where he spent a good amount of time, and she was hot and restless by the time he moved down her belly, not as athletic as his, but he didn't seem to mind.

Before she quite realized his intention, he was pushing her

thighs apart with his tough cop's hands and burying his face in her heat.

Surprise, shock, intense pleasure hit her in a big, swamping wave as he proceeded to use his tongue and lips to savor and torment her.

Her head dropped back against the arm of the couch and she gave herself over to the sensations rioting through her body. Shivering heat, little electric thrills. When he pushed a finger inside her and rubbed unerringly at her G-spot, she couldn't hold back the cry that shook her, as her body thrust and rocked against him, spilling over.

"I want you inside me," she said, feeling desperate to be filled.

"Condoms," he gasped.

It took her a minute to take in his meaning. "Bathroom. Cabinet," she gasped. "Hurry."

He sprinted to the bathroom, giving her the opportunity to enjoy the muscular round butt and the thighs of an athlete.

She heard the cabinet open. Something crashed to the counter. He cursed in Spanish, she noted, smiling to herself as, in his haste, he knocked something else over.

She'd deal with the mess later. All of the mess. For now she was willing to accept that she'd gone crazy. But at least this kind of craziness wouldn't get her arrested.

He brought the entire box with him, spilling them out in his haste. She could help him, but she didn't feel like it. With the edge taken off and the certainty that this guy might be terrible for her in every way, but that at least he'd be a great lover, she gave herself over to the moment.

Tomorrow she'd curse herself for her stupidity, not tonight.

He fumbled the condom on and there was something endearing about his clumsiness since he was so obviously one of those athletic, coordinated types who were rarely clumsy.

Once more he parted her thighs. Once more she opened for

him. This time he looked into her eyes. The intimacy was so shocking, she wanted to look away, but she didn't. Couldn't.

He entered her and she felt the slow slide of pleasure as her body took him in. Little pulses from her first orgasm sent tiny shocks through her.

Wanting to be closer, wanting more, she wrapped her legs around him and pulled him inside her even as he thrust deeper.

She came in a glorious rush and felt his body climax in tune with hers. He rolled them so that she was snuggled against him on the couch. She could hear the bang of his heart begin to slow, his harsh breathing even, and the heat of his skin fade to being warm.

She traced the snake that encircled his bicep. "Why a snake?"

"Trying to look tough. To fit in with some guys."

She nodded. She'd been pretty far off base. Even his bad stuff was a front for a good guy.

Mostly because she wanted excuses to touch him, she slipped her index finger under the gold chain so she could see his medallion. It was warm against her fingers, warm from his body. "And this?"

"Our Lady of Guadalupe. She's the patron saint of Mexico." His voice rumbled, low and intimate. "My birthday is December 12, the saint's day. I always thought the big celebration and the feast every year was for me." He grinned. "My grandmother told me I'd always be blessed, like the saint. She's the one who gave me this."

"It's beautiful," she said. "I wish I had a saint watching over me."

He kissed her shoulder. "We can share."

She drifted, feeling loose and warm and sleepy, thinking that Rafe's looking out for her was more satisfying than a gold coin around her neck.

*   *   *

"Babe." The low male voice brought Stephanie out of a deep, dreamless sleep. Her eyes were heavy when she opened them, and for a moment, she couldn't figure out where she was. Then she realized she was on her own couch in her own living room.

"Mmmm?" She pushed a hand up to get the tangle of hair out of her eyes.

Her housecoat lay over her like a blanket and Rafe was bending over her, fully dressed. Like a stranger again.

"I'm heading out," he said. "Make sure to lock up behind me."

"Yeah, sure."

She stumbled to her feet, holding the housecoat in front of her. He turned to head for her door and she scrambled her arms into the sleeves and rapidly belted the robe around her. She felt physically replete, heavily satisfied, and so emotionally screwed up that she wanted to cry.

At the door he turned to her and gave her a quick kiss. "See you," he said.

"Yeah, see you."

And then he walked out of her life, like so many had before him. And once more she felt her heart break a little bit.

As she slid the dead bolt home, she wondered if she was ever going to get her life to work. She flipped off the lights, walked to her bedroom, and crawled into bed. Her sheets felt cold and she shivered.

See you. He hadn't even asked for her phone number.

See you. As if.

Chloe was beginning to think she might actually have a career that she wasn't going to get bored with and chuck. Of course, it was in the early days yet, and her income wasn't quite keeping up with her expenses, but she was getting busier. More hits on the Web site, more e-mails, more phone calls of inquiry.

Some of the people who contacted her were a bit on the odd side. And she'd instinctively turned down a few people who seemed more interested in humiliating their partners or in exacting some sort of revenge than in a clean breakup.

That wasn't her purpose, and she quickly rejected anyone who wanted to use her service for unsavory purposes. Honestly, some people had no standards. Most, however, understood that a breakup was difficult enough and could be handled much more easily by an efficient third party.

Twice, she'd actually organized a meeting with the lovers and herself. One had ended in a reconciliation when it was clear that the woman who had hired Chloe to help her break up her romance was, in fact, mistaken in thinking her guy was having an affair.

He was playing tennis four nights a week, which Chloe thought was enough to have her dumping him for pure abandonment, but when he offered to take his girlfriend to his tennis club every night so she could see him play, and even suggested that he buy her tennis lessons for her upcoming birthday, all problems were magically resolved.

Whatever, as the Americans loved to say. Chloe pocketed her fee and even got a referral.

The second time she'd met her two sparring partners for dinner it wasn't so pleasant. In fact, she'd decided then and there she wasn't doing a dinner again. Still, by dint of making each of the parties stay silent for one full minute while letting the other speak, she was able to get them to agree that their relationship simply wasn't working. By the end of the meal, they'd been able to laugh at a shared memory and she thought that at least this couple might be able to move on with fond memories.

She was now heading out to the bank, rather pleased to have another check to deposit, when Matthew came out of his house right after she had emerged from her own.

"Good morning," she said, sounding as cheerful as she felt.

Matthew's answer was a single-note grunt.

"I thought the dinner last night went very well, didn't you?"

If it was possible, the scowl on his face grew heavier. "You seemed to be having a good time."

She looked at him, puzzled. "I thought we all had a good time."

"Some more than others," he mumbled.

She'd never been what one would call a patient woman. "My, you did get out on the wrong side of the bed this morning," she said, doing her best to sound like Julie Andrews in *Mary Poppins*. "Perhaps you need your happy pill."

"Looks like you got your happy pill last night."

"Is this pointless rudeness leading somewhere?"

"Not a damn place I can think of. I don't like you seducing my friends, is all."

"Seducing—" Her mouth opened so she could tell him exactly why she'd asked Rafe to stay behind last night; then she realized she couldn't without giving away the nature of her business, and that she was determined not to do until she was good and ready.

She bent her head to shift her bag and then looked up at Matthew provocatively from under her lashes. "I can assure you that no seducing was necessary," she said. Then, just to annoy him, she tossed out that most American of expressions, "Have a nice day."

When she got back from her errands, Matthew was, thankfully, nowhere to be seen. Instead, she found Brittany getting out of her car, loaded down with sample books of some sort. As she struggled to close the car door, one toppled to the sidewalk.

Chloe, as drawn by curiosity as Good Samaritanism, called out, "Let me help you with that," and walked up to scoop the dropped book off the pavement.

"Oh, thanks," said Brittany, holding her chin against the

pile of books she still held. "I should have taken them in two trips, but I'm too impatient."

"I'm exactly the same," Chloe agreed, helping herself to two more off the top of Brittany's load and walking behind her up the path to Matthew's house. "Redecorating?"

"We're getting some ideas, that's all. Matthew's colors are all so dark. I thought it might be nice to brighten the place a little."

Oh, you poor, sweet, misguided thing, Chloe thought. Not only were Matthew's color choices in keeping with his house, but any fool could see he was not a man who'd have any interest in color swatches and wallpaper sample books. She glanced at the closest cover and shuddered. Especially not anything found in a book called *Country Inspirations*.

She was going to have to move quickly, before this misguided woman had repapered Matthew's entire house in ducks and gingham, and he ended up murdering her in her bentwood bed.

She'd been so busy setting up her business and dealing with her actual paying clients that Chloe hadn't had much leisure to think about Brittany and Matthew, but clearly, based on the decorating demon now lodged in Brittany's psyche, she had to quicken her pace.

"I did a year at the Buckingham Institute, an interior design school in London. Perhaps I could be of assistance?"

"Oh, wow. In London?"

"Yes. I didn't do enough to get the degree, but I certainly learned the basics. I'd be happy to lend a hand."

"That would be great."

"Excellent. Why don't you call me later when you've had a chance to get some ideas and we can talk color palettes and so on."

"It's very nice of you. Oh, and thanks again for last night. I had a really good time."

"Me too. You know, I haven't had a chance to make any

real friends here. I do miss my girls." She thought of Nicky and Rachel and all of them.

"Oh, I can't imagine. Well, you'll have to come out with me and my girls. We'll show you how to have fun Texas style."

"Really? That would be super. Thanks."

"My pleasure."

They took the books inside and she put the books she'd brought in on the third step and headed for the front door.

"When Matthew's free, would you ask him to help me move a couple of heavy things in my house?"

"I sure will."

Ten minutes later, there was a pounding on Chloe's front door. She didn't even have to look out the bedroom window to know who it was.

She finished the e-mail she was composing to Jordan assuring him that she had matters well in hand to inspire Deborah to break up with him. She disregarded the fact that Rafe hadn't said yes, since she was an optimist at heart and had good reason to know that her persuasive powers were top-notch.

When the pounding on her door was joined by the persistent ringing of the bell, she got up and went downstairs.

She threw open the door. "I am trying to run a business here," she reminded her glowering neighbor who looked as though he'd love to be back on the force simply so he could go around brandishing a gun and arresting people.

He'd reduce crime in Austin simply by glaring at potential criminals.

"So am I. I hear you want furniture moved. There's nothing in your lease about moving furniture."

She gazed at him calmly. "Bite me," she said.

His jaw clamped as though he were preventing himself from doing exactly that. "I've got Brittany trying to turn my place into tutti-frutti central and you moving furniture. Can't you women ever leave anything alone?"

"Not if it needs improvement," she said, glancing significantly at him.

His eyes narrowed and he stalked by her. "What are you thinking of moving?"

"The bed out of the second bedroom. I've hired an assistant. I'm putting in a desk for her."

"An assistant. You hired an assistant."

"That's right," she said, walking ahead of him up the stairs.

His voice sounded a lot less stressed when he said, "A junior detective."

Her lips curved. "Exactly."

She fluttered around a little, trying to help him, but Matthew basically hefted the mattress up and carried it upstairs to the attic single-handedly. He did the same with the box spring and the headboard, and she couldn't help but enjoy the sight of his muscular build and the manly way he had of making nothing of what would for her have been a huge job.

"Where's the desk?" he asked her once the bed was all gone. He'd even offered to hike the dresser out of there, but since she couldn't afford much in the way of office furniture, she'd elected to keep it for supplies.

"It's in a box. In the kitchen. It needs putting together."

"Mmm-hmm." He looked down at her. "Want me to take a look?"

"It's not going to cost me another dinner, is it?"

"Coffee'll do."

She put on a fresh pot while he hauled the box upstairs. By the time the coffee was done and she carried a mug up to him, she found him on the floor, the pieces already unboxed and the Allen wrench, which she personally considered the most evil tool known to man, already at work.

He took the coffee with a grunt of thanks.

"Why aren't you helping Brittany with the decorating?"

He shot her an evil glance and went back to his furniture construction.

She watched him for a moment, enjoying his handiness, the way his biceps tightened and flexed as he worked, the shifting of muscles in his back.

"You do realize," she said to that very nice back, "that if you don't stop her you'll end up living in a gingham cottage?"

"Mind your own business."

She shook her head. "If you weren't a genius with furniture-in-a-box, I would definitely take offense," she said breezily and went back to her own office to catch up on some paperwork.

It was actually rather nice to listen to the shifting of furniture, the creaking of floor boards as he moved around. When he cursed, she smiled to herself. She was alone too much, she realized. She'd enjoy having someone to work with.

In a shorter time than she would have believed, he bellowed, "Where do you want this thing?"

She rose and went into the other room; she had him leave the desk in the middle, facing the door. Stephanie could move it wherever she liked, Chloe decided, since she didn't intend that clients would actually visit the office.

"Thank you, Matthew," she said, feeling sincerely grateful in spite of his rudeness earlier.

He seemed in no hurry to leave and picked up all the packaging, bundling it neatly.

"So, Rafe."

She glanced at him. "Yes?"

"He's a good guy."

"I would hope you'd think so since he's a friend of yours."

He shuffled a little, seeming uncomfortable but determined. She had an idea she knew where he was going with this but had no intention of helping him get there. Foolish man.

"Doesn't seem like your type."

She ducked her head to gather a piece of tape that had stuck to the oak baseboard Matthew had no doubt installed.

Probably after fashioning it from an oak tree he had personally grown and then felled. "You don't know my type."

Something electric sizzled between them when their gazes met. He stared at her for a second, then turned to go. "Yeah, I guess I don't."

Chapter 13

Stephanie put on a happy face that was more fake than a kid's Halloween mask and got herself to work. The branch manager had been so understanding, so eager to help her leave without working out a full notice that Stephanie got the distinct impression they weren't any sorrier to see her go than she was to be leaving.

That was good, of course, since it meant she could work for Chloe sooner, but it was also kind of a blow. At least they could have pretended that she was God's gift to the teller's wicket.

Oh well, at least Chloe would be happy. Stephanie was working through Friday, then had the weekend off before she started at her new job. And still the minutes crawled by. Toward lunchtime, there was a bit of a stir when a florist's delivery guy came into the branch with a vase containing a dozen long-stemmed pink roses and some pretty greenery.

How romantic. Of course, Steph would have gone for something colorful, like gerber daisies or huge, happy sunflowers. She wondered if it was someone's wedding anniversary. Everyone, from customers to the bank execs in the back, seemed to pause for a moment in suspense.

"Stephanie Baxter?" the guy asked in a Bronx accent, glancing around with his brows raised looking like he didn't have all day.

"I'm Stephanie," she said, and felt her heart start to pound. Rafe hadn't asked for her number last night; he'd waltzed out of her apartment with a peck on the lips and a "See you." Was this Rafe's way of telling her last night had meant something?

While the floral guy plonked the vase at her workstation and made her sign a delivery receipt, she felt giddy and girlish and giggly. "Do you mind?" she asked the woman who happened to be standing waiting to cash her paycheck.

She was middle-aged and overweight in a white blouse that had been washed too many times so it was yellowing. She stood there like her feet hurt, but for that second her eyes glowed too. "No, I don't mind. I've been married thirty-four years. The only flowers I see are the ones I grow in my own garden. Enjoy the romance while it lasts."

Stephanie felt so many gazes on her, with expectation, maybe envy, that her fingers fumbled when she opened the tiny little envelope.

Darling, it said. Oooh, he'd called her darling. She never would have pegged him for the darling type. Or the pink roses type.

She read the message; then she read it again before the truth sank in.

> *Darling.*
> *Please forgive me. We can make this work. I*
> *love you.*
> *Derek.*

Derek. She stuffed the little card back in its little envelope and turned back to her customer with a quick word of apology.

The woman's eyes rested on her face, which felt hot and itchy, like she was about to break out in a rash. "How did he screw up with flowers?"

"He didn't." She shook her head, wanting to tell somebody. Wanting to lay her head on this nice woman's bosom and sob her heart out. "It's the wrong guy, is all."

"Oh, honey. As my kids would say, 'That blows.'"

She sent her customer a quick smile. "Yeah."

Instead of confronting Derek, which she didn't have enough courage to do again, she e-mailed him on her lunch break. It was difficult to come up with the right words and it took her ages to word her simple message.

> Dear Derek.
> Thank you for the flowers. I wish you hadn't sent them, though. I'm not going to change my mind. I'm so sorry. Be happy.
> Stephanie.

She dragged herself home at the end of the day, exhausted. "Aren't you taking your flowers?" Elsbeth, the girl who worked beside her, asked.

"No. You want them?"

"Yeah, if you're sure." She bet nobody ever sent Elsbeth roses. She was exactly the sort of woman Derek would despise, which made her happy to think of those flowers going home with the colorless teller.

All she took was the little card in its little envelope, which she threw out in a city trash can so no prying eyes could see it.

Once home, she ate a bowl of Cheerios for dinner, a single-serving carton of peach yogurt for dessert, and flipped on the TV. It wasn't that she even wanted to watch TV, she just wanted an excuse to curl up on the couch.

Of course, she told herself not to be a moron and relive all the details of what had happened on that very couch last night, and of course she was that moron. She curled deeply into it with her robe tucked around her and imagined she caught the scent of Rafe even as she relived their encounter in every amazing detail.

When the phone rang, she was so deeply into her fantasy that she was certain it was Rafe, until she realized he didn't have her number because he hadn't asked for it. She ignored a couple of rings, then realized that Rafe had come here, to her apartment. He must have her number if he had her address. Being a cop, he must have access to all that stuff.

So she bounded across the room, stubbing her toe on the hair dryer she'd left plugged into the wall this morning.

"Hello?" she said, trying not to sound too eager.

"Steph, we need to talk."

Her stomach was like an elevator in freefall. If she'd ever had any doubts about her decision to call off her engagement to Derek, she didn't have them any longer.

"We already talked. I'm really, really sorry, but I can't marry you."

"But I love you. I have plans."

Always he talked about himself. He never seemed to worry about her feelings, or her plans. However, she'd hurt him and she knew that, so she tried to be understanding. "I don't think I'd be the right wife for you. You need someone more . . ." More what? Stable? Less inclined to shoplift when she was upset? Not so much of a slut? She settled on "More mature. I guess I'm not ready."

"You got cold feet. It can happen. Look, have lunch with me tomorrow. It's the least you can do."

She opened her mouth to agree, then stopped herself. If she went to lunch she'd do something stupid like let him stick that ring back on her finger and she couldn't. She just couldn't.

"Sorry. I'm busy for lunch tomorrow. Look, I have to go."

"Wait." His voice took on a different tone. Sharp. Accusing. "I'm coming by the bank. I have to see you."

"I quit my job. I'm leaving the bank."

"Are you crazy?"

"Probably."

"I'm serious. You need to see someone. You're quitting

your job? And thinking about leaving me? There's something wrong with you."

"Lucky you, then. You're getting rid of me."

"Is there someone else?"

His constant jealousy used to reassure her. She'd believed a man who was possessive wouldn't run around on her, but now she was beginning to think there was a darker side to him.

A kick of combined elation and pain smacked her. She knew that if she answered his question honestly it would forever be over with him. She was tempted to say yes, but the truth was, she'd had a one-night stand. Because she had feelings didn't mean the other party did.

"I have to go."

The receiver clicked in her ear as he hung up on her.

She closed her eyes and stood there, waiting for the regret to come. She was not surprised when it didn't. She'd always been good about hurting herself.

Then she picked up the receiver again, knowing there was another call she had to make and one she dreaded.

"Mom, hi. It's me, Stephanie."

In less than two minutes, she had exactly what she wanted. An invitation to dinner tomorrow night. She'd tell her mom in person about the split; then she'd stay overnight in her old room. For some reason, she craved her old room where she'd planned her big plans and dreamed her foolish dreams, before life got in the way.

Deborah did what she usually did when a client stumped her. She walked from her office to Jordan's. They'd both seen their last client of the day and he was tapping away at his computer, looking scholarly and earnest.

"Jordan?"

He started and blinked when he turned to her.

"Deborah, you startled me."

"I'm sorry. I can come back if you're busy."

"No, of course not. Come in."

"I want to talk to you about the Petersons. A couple I'm working with." She made a wry expression. "I'm not making much progress."

"Tell me about them."

He always did this. So calmly inviting her to share her load. So comforting. She settled into the chair across from his desk and marshaled her thoughts. "Heinrik's a workaholic. He's rarely home, all he ever thinks about or talks about is work, and his wife feels neglected and unappreciated."

Jordan made a sound like a snort. He never interrupted so she was surprised and glanced up, raising her reading glasses so she could look at him more clearly. "I'm sorry?"

"Nothing. Go on."

"I feel like I can't get through to them. Janine, the wife, is doing the work every week, but he's resisting. He won't do the work, refuses to acknowledge he's got a problem. Do you have any ideas?"

Jordan stared at her for a moment. Maybe it was the way the light hit him, but she thought his eyes didn't look as calm as they usually did. "Sometimes you can't fix people, even when you want to."

"We're not here to fix people," she argued. "We fix relationships."

"Sometimes I think it's the same thing. Heinrik's not going to change until he wants to change, and as hard as someone who loves him tries, it's not going to make a difference."

She nodded her head, thinking of Janine trying so hard and being ignored. One day Heinrik would wake up and his wife would be gone, she suspected, and then it would be too late.

"I wish there were a way we could hold up a mirror that would show people the destructive patterns they engage in that ruin their personal relationships."

"So do I, Deb. So do I."

She tapped her pen on her notepad. "I wonder if they'd be happier with another therapist. Would you be willing to give them a try?"

Jordan shook his head. "I think I'm done with lost causes."

She leaned forward in concern. "Have you had trouble with a client recently? I didn't realize. Do you want to talk about it?"

"No, it's okay. I think I've figured out how to resolve it." He turned off his computer. "I've got to head out. I've got dinner with an old school friend."

She nodded. "And I've got to get caught up on some paperwork. I'll see you tomorrow, then."

She leaned across the desk and kissed his cheek.

"Yes, see you tomorrow."

Chloe couldn't help but notice that her newly hired associate was not looking her best. In fact, Stephanie's eyes were heavy with tiredness and her smile seemed forced.

"You're not regretting the job already, are you?" she said the second she saw the younger woman's face.

Stephanie let out a startled laugh. "No, I haven't been sleeping too well. Excited about the new job, I guess."

"I tell you what, I'll work you so hard today, you'll sleep like a baby tonight," she said.

That earned her a reluctant grin. Oh dear, she thought.

Knowing she'd hear Stephanie's troubles soon enough, she set about showing her the brand-new desk and the files and things she'd bought on Saturday at Office Depot. She'd also splurged on a second computer, thus running her credit card a little higher than she'd like when the words "Neiman Marcus" were nowhere to be found on the statement.

She soon had Stephanie creating files for all the clients she had on the books, and it turned out that Stephanie knew how to use the simple bookkeeping program she'd bought and hadn't been able to work yet. By the time she went down to make the morning coffee, at eleven, she was congratulating herself on an excellent hire.

She was about to carry the tray upstairs, showing Stephanie what a truly modern employer she was, not only making the coffee herself, but serving it to her secretary, when the doorbell rang. Putting the tray down on a hall table, she opened the door to find Rafe standing on her doorstep.

She was delighted to see him, fairly certain her optimism about him had been well-founded. "I do hope this is good news?"

He nodded. "I thought about the favor. I'll do it."

"Fantastic." She beamed at him. "Come upstairs to my office and we'll talk. Do you want a coffee?"

"Sure."

He waited until she had a mug, and then surprised and delighted her by taking the tray out of her hands and carrying it up himself.

She was behind him as they reached the top of the stairs. She could see Stephanie through the open door. Her head was down and she was at the table by the window, but obviously she heard footsteps for she said, "Chloe, I was wondering about these files."

She turned, her hands full of files, and took a step forward. Then, before Chloe's bemused gaze, she went pink, then white, and dropped the files on the floor.

For a second there was no sound but that of the cardboard folders plopping on top of one another like a deck of playing cards being shuffled.

"Stephanie, are you all right?" She would have rushed straight in, but the bulky Rafe standing there with his tray was somehow in her way.

"Hi, Stephanie," he said, and there was a world of intimacy in that tone. He entered the second bedroom cum office and Chloe popped in behind him.

Chloe glanced sharply between them. Stephanie stood stock-still, her color still fluctuating between feverish pink and chalk white. Rafe looked exactly the same as he always did, but Chloe could feel the heat coming off him.

She didn't need a crystal ball to tell her that these two had slept together. How interesting. How very interesting.

Stephanie knelt to pick up the folders, saying "Hi" on her way down while her hair swung in front of her face hiding her expression.

Rafe took a step forward and then stopped himself as though he'd forgotten he was holding on to a tray of coffee mugs. He glanced around and put the thing down on top of Stephanie's desk. The silence was so thick you'd need a sledgehammer to crack through it.

"I didn't put in milk and sugar because I wasn't sure how you liked it," Chloe said, feeling very much like a gracious hostess smoothing over an awkward moment.

When no one said anything, she shrugged, stepped forward, helped herself to milk from the jug she'd prepared, and added half a spoon of sugar.

"When you've got yours, Rafe, would you come next door to my office?"

"Sure," he said, his eyes still trained on her secretary, who'd risen from the floor and was stacking the folders once more looking anywhere but at him.

Chloe walked next door, thinking she'd give them a moment. She heard the low tones of his voice, and a short, quiet burst from Stephanie; then Rafe walked into her office. He didn't have a coffee and she didn't bother remarking on his forgetfulness.

"Shut the door," she said.

He hesitated, then complied, before walking forward and sitting in the chair opposite her desk.

"How is it that you can take this time off work?" she asked him.

"I was working undercover and I've got a lot of comp time coming."

"Comp time?"

"You don't get paid overtime when you work undercover. Instead, you take compensatory time. Comp time. At time and a half, I've got a fair bit banked."

"And you want to spend your time helping me out?"

He sent her a cop stare. And it was a good one. But she'd stared down angry lovers, her brother, and on one never to be forgotten occasion, Princess Anne when she'd called her horse by the wrong name. Rafe didn't bother her a bit. Finally, he said, "You asked me to do you a favor, remember?"

"I did. However, you didn't seem too enthralled by the idea. Or by the compensation."

He shrugged. "Maybe I'll get you to break up a bad relationship for me sometime." He shifted on the chair. "So, tell me about the shrink."

She held up a hand. Not so fast. "Tell me about you and my secretary first."

"That's personal."

"So is the business of breaking up relationships. I don't want any messiness."

"No messiness."

"Right." She'd ask Stephanie. In her experience, it was always easier to get the goods from a woman than a man. "Here's Deborah Beaumont's book. I should warn you, the contents will make you positively queasy, but you'd better read it. What I want you to do is be as untidy, as hopelessly messed up as you can be."

He took the book and turned it over to read the back cover. "Why?"

"It's a theory I have that this poor woman, as you'll see from her book, is so hopelessly trapped by her systems that what she really wants is a terrible mess of a man to fall in love with and fix."

Rafe's shoulders went rigid. "I can't make a woman fall in love with me."

"Just go once and see what happens. Here's the address.

I've already made you an appointment for tomorrow." She
handed him her business card, on the back of which she'd
written both the address and time of his appointment.

"You did?"

"Yes, otherwise you'd have had to wait more than a week
to get in."

"But I might have turned you down."

"Then I would have cancelled the appointment," she said
sunnily. "But luckily you didn't turn me down."

"I should have. I'm getting a bad feeling in my gut about
this."

"Nonsense. You're helping two people to find happiness.
What could be better?"

"How can she find happiness with me? I don't want anything to do with a shrink."

"Sometimes escaping from the wrong person brings almost as much happiness as getting together with the right
person. At the very least, I'm hoping you'll make her rethink
her own relationship and see that it's not working."

"I don't know."

"Well, keep your appointment tomorrow. If it doesn't
work out, you don't have to go back."

He nodded. "All right."

"May I ask you one question?"

"You can ask."

"Does your sudden willingness to take this job have anything to do with Stephanie?"

He sent her one of those unreadable glances from his dark,
dark eyes. "What time's my appointment tomorrow?"

Recognizing a brick wall when she'd just bashed her head
against one, she sighed and shook her head. "Two o'clock."
He took her card and the book and turned toward the door,
the sexy mess of streaky hair straggling behind. Oh, yes, she
thought, if you wanted an absolute disaster of a sexpot,
Rafael Escobar was your man.

Chapter 14

Had that bastard stuck a GPS device on her? Stephanie wondered as she furiously returned her neatly labeled files into the new filing system.

But if he'd wanted to keep track of her so badly, could he not have called? Or repeated his late-night visit? Hot waves of anger washed over her as she admitted to herself that she'd changed her bed sheets, shaved her legs, and bought a new nightgown, then sat at home all weekend like some pathetic, lovesick moron.

Rafael Escobar hadn't called; he hadn't banged on her door late at night bringing his dangerous self into her apartment and her body. He'd humped her and dumped her.

He might carry a cop's badge, but he was still a badass. Her fatal weakness.

She was close to losing it when she realized she'd filed Doran under the Bs. Today was supposed to be a brand new start for her.

Yet another brand new start. How was it possible that this man was following her to her new job when he couldn't be bothered to follow her home?

Stephanie wouldn't put her ear to the wall, even though she was almost certain she could hear what Rafe and Chloe were saying if she did.

But she would not demean herself.

Fury bubbled inside her along with an awful pain, the kind that comes when you do something really stupid and you've got only yourself to blame. Maybe this was how people felt when they had gangrene and had to cut off an important part of their body before the rot killed everything. Maybe she had gangrene of the heart.

The conference wasn't long in Chloe's office. Well, why would it be?

When she'd first seen him walk up those stairs, she'd had a moment when her heart banged against her ribs and her spirits soared. He'd found her.

Somehow he'd found her.

But he hadn't rushed to take her in his arms as he did in her daydreams.

She replayed the scene, all the while hearing the murmur of voices in the other room. He'd said, "Hi, Stephanie."

Once Chloe had gone into her office and left them alone, she'd asked him, "What are you doing here?"

"I'm here to see Chloe." His face gave her no clue to what he was feeling. Or maybe it did and what he felt for her was nothing.

Would she never, ever learn?

She asked him if he'd known she'd be here, and he'd said, "Had a pretty good idea." And the gangrene spread a little more.

She heard the door to Chloe's office open, signaling that the meeting between her boss and Rafe was over. She grabbed up the phone and started talking. She had the appointment screen open on her computer and pretty much mimicked her dentist's receptionist when she made an appointment.

Rafe hovered a minute in her doorway while she said, "Thursday at nine?" And then, "Okay, how about Friday at eleven?" When he still hadn't left, she said, "Sure, I'd be happy to tell you a bit about our services." And she started reading aloud from the brochure.

She kept reading until she'd heard his footsteps fade. She

glanced around at the office she'd spent only a few hours in. She'd been so hopeful.

She was packing up her bag when Chloe came into her office.

"Is it lunchtime already?" How could she like the woman so much when she was such a twit?

"It's not lunchtime. I'm leaving. I'll save you the trouble of firing me."

Chloe blinked. Those big blue china doll eyes of hers closed and opened, but there was no other indication of emotion in her face. Well, maybe a trace of curiosity. "Why would I fire you?"

"Oh, come on. Rafe was in your office and I don't think he needs any help breaking up with anyone. He does a great job of that on his own."

"Rafe broke up with you? I knew you two had slept together. I can always tell. But I thought you were still engaged to that tedious jewelry shop clerk."

She flashed the ringless engagement hand and Chloe shrugged her fashion-model shoulders. "One had hoped. I am glad. The jewelry clerk struck me as a total fuckwit."

At any other time she'd have smiled. Chloe pronounced "clerk" so it rhymed with "lark," and "fuckwit" as two complete words. She was the only person Stephanie had ever met who cursed with perfect elocution. But Stephanie didn't feel like smiling. She felt like snarling.

"Rafe told you about me."

"Told me what? I do wish you'd sit down. Have some coffee. You haven't touched yours, and I made it specially."

"I'm a thief!" She yelled the words. Shouted them so that Rafe could hear them over the infernal noise of the motorcycle racing him away from her.

Chloe picked up one of the two untouched mugs of coffee on the tray and added milk. Then she glanced around the room. "What we need in here is a nice comfortable chair. This won't do. Come, bring your coffee and follow me."

Stephanie wondered which one of them was crazier as she picked up the second mug of coffee and followed her boss (for now) not into the other office, as she'd assumed, but into Chloe's bedroom.

"This is much nicer, isn't it? Though I haven't had time to really decorate it yet. Pull the chair closer to the bed and we'll have a proper chat."

Then she kicked off her gorgeous sandals, propped two pillows behind her, and curled her legs under. The bedding was all black and white but amazingly Chloe.

She pulled up the single chair, a department store type wingback, and sat down, feeling stupid and not knowing what to say now that she'd blurted out her problem.

Chloe didn't seem to share her reluctance. "Are you a jewel thief? I've always thought that would be so exciting." She paused to sip her coffee. "So long, of course, as one didn't get caught."

"A jewel thief. Not unless you count crappy costume jewelry." She stopped, feeling almost as embarrassed that she'd set her sights as low as she did about the actual stealing.

"Why don't you tell me about it?"

So she did. Told her about the thrill of danger, the possibility of getting caught, the way she'd be fine for ages and then this urge would take over her.

"Rafe didn't tell you?"

"No."

"God, I feel like an idiot."

"You shouldn't. I'm glad you told me."   .

"You've probably never stolen anything."

"Well, I get the same thrill of danger and getting caught from having sex in odd places and from the emotional drama of my love life. Does the trick. Darling, we all have our vices. We simply must learn to channel those energies so as not to end up in some horrible jail."

"But—you never checked my references. You're just start-

ing your business. Don't you think you should be more careful?"

Chloe took a sip of her coffee and appeared to think about
what Stephanie had said. "Are you planning to steal from
me?"

"No."

"Then we'll be all right."

She had the strangest feeling that Chloe got it. The "it"
she'd never successfully understood herself or been able to
explain to another person. How could it be that this woman
from a different world should understand her?

"May I make a suggestion?"

"Sure, I guess."

"Try having sex outside. I think you'll find it much more
fun. And you'd be far less likely to go to jail."

Stephanie felt a smile break out on her face.

"I would think Rafe could take you to some very interesting places." Chloe glanced up under her lashes. "On his
motorcycle."

"I don't think Rafe and I—" She couldn't even finish the
sentence. She didn't want to voice her fears.

She didn't have to. Chloe got it. Of course. "I saw him
look at you. He's a bit of a complicated man, as all the interesting ones are. But I would say he is smitten."

She snorted. "He's got a funny way of showing it."

"What exactly happened between you two?"

And suddenly, she had someone she could talk to who
wasn't a relative, who wasn't a friend who'd known her in
her wild, bad teen years, and who wasn't paid to counsel her.

She described the day they'd met, how he'd followed her
around that store, and she'd felt scared, excited, aroused, and
finally mad when she had to put that watch back.

"So you met him the same day you met me?"

"Yeah. Weird, huh?"

Chloe nodded. "Quite a coincidence. Or was it, I wonder?"

"What do you mean?"

"Nothing. Sorry, do go on. What happened next?"

So she told Chloe what she still hadn't been able to tell another soul. Not her girlfriends, who were going to be pissed that she'd broken up with Derek, and not her mom, who was brokenhearted that she'd broken up with Derek. Not anybody. It felt great to spill all that stuff and to the only woman in her life who didn't seem all that thrilled with Derek.

When she got to the part about Rafe coming to her apartment, she stalled, wondering what she was doing spilling her sex life to her boss on her first day of work. But Chloe wasn't like any boss Stephanie had ever had. She said, "And was he fabulous in bed?"

"We never made it to the bed," she said, and got warm just thinking about their escapades on the couch. "And, yeah, he was fabulous."

Chloe looked delighted. "I knew it. There are some men you can take one look at and know they'll be fantastic." She sighed. "And tell me, is his backside as amazing naked as it is in jeans?"

"Better. All of him is better."

Chloe picked up one of the pillows and hurled it at her. "You lucky girl!" she cried.

"I don't know. He hasn't called or come by again. I think he dumped me." She sighed. "The guy I'm crazy about doesn't want me, and the one I'm trying to break free from won't leave me alone."

"What do you mean?" Chloe looked a little worried and Stephanie wished she'd kept her mouth shut.

"Nothing bad. He sends me flowers, pushes gushy greeting cards under my door—"

"Oh, you don't mean the ones with dozens of overblown roses on the outside and equally overblown sentiment on the inside?"

"Yep, those kinds." She felt sort of sick even talking about them. "And I'm pretty sure he followed me to work today."

The concerned expression on Chloe's face deepened. "Oh dear."

She contemplated the room, which was tidy and feminine and restful. "Sometimes I wish I was a lesbian."

"And then a man like Rafe walks into your life."

"And out of it again so fast he's like a blur."

"I asked Rafe outright what was going on between the two of you and all he would say was that it was complicated. If he thought it was a one off, he wouldn't have called it complicated, would he?"

She shrugged. She'd learned early not to trust her own judgment about men. Unfortunately, she still followed it. She felt miserable, was certain she looked worse.

"Well," said Chloe brightly, "as Shakespeare said, ''Tis better to have loved and lost than never to have loved at all.'"

"Actually, that was Alfred Lord Tennyson."

"Really?"

"Yep, *In Memoriam,* written in 1850."

"I didn't know you were literary."

"We studied it in school. I remember weird stuff."

"How extraordinary. I wish you could remember where I left my house keys."

"Sorry. I only remember useless stuff. And it has to be written down."

"Do you have a photographic memory?"

She wished she'd never mentioned Tennyson. She should have kept her mouth shut. "Not really. Sort of, I guess."

"But that's wonderful. I think it could be really useful for our business."

"How?"

"I don't know. But I'm absolutely certain something good will come of it." She smiled and uncurled from the bed. "Well, you've cured me of misquoting poor Shakespeare. That's bound to be useful."

"So if Rafe didn't come here to tell you about me, what did he come here for?"

"Ah, yes. I'm not sure you're going to like it, actually."

Stephanie's heart sank. "He is here to break up with somebody." When they were going at it in her apartment he probably had another woman waiting at home for him. She'd never asked. Never even thought about it.

"No, quite the opposite." She snuggled deeper into the pillows. "I didn't know anything about the two of you, of course, but I've asked him to help me professionally."

"He's a cop. What's he going to do? Moonlight as an investigator?" That would be interesting. She wasn't quite so furious now that she knew he hadn't come to inform her employer of her little problem. If he was here to do some investigating, she might at least see him occasionally. It wasn't much, but it was something.

"Not exactly. He's going to make another woman interested in him, enough that she'll realize she's not in love with her current fiancé." Chloe ran her finger around the white circle on her bedspread.

"That is the stupidest, craziest idea I've ever heard." Except that he'd done exactly that to her. Ridden an escalator into her life and within days caused her to dump her fiancé. She wailed, "What if he falls for her?"

Chloe glanced up at her. "Then you'd better do what you're good at. Steal him back."

Chapter 15

Matthew needed some air. If he didn't get out of the house he was going to tell Brittany that cranberry in the bathroom did not make his heart sing. Any more than sage, or pumpernickel, or any of the other colors she was shoving at him—all of them based on foods he didn't like.

He felt like the walls were closing in on him. She never got mad. Even when he was being a pig. If she'd just yell at him once in a while, he'd have a chance. But she never did. So he tried to stifle his irritation and accept that if she was going to share his life, she had a right to choose colors. But did she have to be quite so nice? He was being smothered in niceness.

He left her drawing the living room furniture on graph paper, no doubt so she could change it all to pumpkin, quince, and seaweed colors, and then move everything around.

He claimed he had some garden work to do, figuring he'd sweat off some of his frustration.

Instead, his frustration level shot up like a geyser when he stepped outside and saw Rafe's motorcycle outside Chloe's place.

Cozy.

None of his business; Rafe and Chloe were both single, and if Rafe had lost his mind, he figured there wasn't much he could do about it. But the burn in his esophagus didn't abate. He pulled a muscle moving boulders around—the same pointless rearranging that was going on inside his house—but he needed something dirty and physical to do. He didn't bother thinking about why.

He was staggering a boulder from one cactus bed to the other when he heard a familiar voice say, "Need a hand?"

He shook his head, made it the rest of the way, and dropped the thing in the garden.

"I think you just obliterated a succulent," his old partner said.

"You're spending a lot of time in this neighborhood."

Rafe looked at him with steady eyes. "You got a problem with that?"

"Hell, yeah. That woman isn't half sane, and for all we know she's up to something illegal."

"You sure that's all that's bothering you?"

His hands were scraped raw, his T-shirt was sticking to him with sweat, his breathing was ragged from overexertion, and he felt like his bum leg was about to collapse beneath him. The thought of Chloe and Rafe together made him want to howl. "Yeah."

Rafe shook his head. "Stupido," he said, and turned away.

Now, Matt wasn't fluent in Spanish by a long shot, but you didn't have to be to translate that one. "Make sure it's me who's the stupid one and not you."

Rafe turned back to face him. Women had always gone for his slovenly partner, he remembered, cursing himself for being the one who'd introduced him to Chloe.

"She's not doing anything illegal," Rafe said.

"How do you know?"

"Because she told me about her business."

"What business is she in?"

Rafe had faced down some of the toughest criminals in Texas. He wasn't about to crumble because a guy had stopped gardening to give him a hard time. "I don't think she wants you to know, my friend."

Then, with a careless salute, Rafe sauntered to his motor-cycle and mounted it with fluid grace.

Matt scowled. "You wouldn't even have met her if it wasn't for me," he yelled, but his words were drowned by the roar of the bike.

Deborah slipped a super-strength painkiller in her mouth and swallowed it down with water. She stopped what she was doing to make a note in her headache diary. Headache diary. What was her life coming to when she had to keep a headache diary?

Her temples throbbed and she wanted nothing more than to pull the blinds in her office, turn off the lights, and curl up in her faux living room couch and sleep.

Of course, she'd do no such thing. She had patients to see and they didn't stop having problems simply because she had suddenly developed a nasty thing called *cluster headaches.*

Are you under more than usual stress? the doctor at the clinic had asked her. *Is something bothering you?*

Those were *her* questions. The ones she asked her patients in a more carefully phrased way.

But a person didn't suddenly develop cluster headaches— painful episodes that seemed to hit her almost daily. She'd agreed to keep a diary only when the MD had agreed to send her for testing for a physical cause. Not that she wanted to discover she had something awful like a brain tumor, but nei-ther did she want to believe there could be a psychological trigger to her head pain when everything in her life was going so well.

She resolutely put her own problems out of her mind and prepared herself for a new client.

Rafael Escobar.

She rubbed her temples with her fingertips and tried some deep breathing, but the throb had barely dulled when her re-ceptionist buzzed through to say that Mr. Escobar had arrived.

"Thank you," she said.

She rose and walked to the door. Opened it. Outside, her gaze was immediately drawn to the man who looked so out of place in her deliberately soothing, orderly office.

He was not soothing. And he most certainly wasn't orderly. In fact, the man was a mess.

He rose when she called his name and came toward her with guarded eyes and a reluctant gait. He didn't want to be here. Interesting. Who had made him come? An employer? Parent? Spouse or girlfriend?

Soon, she'd know. Usually the idea of fixing someone, especially someone so disorderly as Mr. Escobar, filled her with anticipation, but today she felt irritated that she was going to have to hear the boring problems of another screwup.

Shocked at her own thoughts, she put a smile on her face and, offering her hand, introduced herself. "I'm Deborah Beaumont," she told him.

"Rafe," he said.

When they got into her office she ushered him to the living room area. "Would you like coffee or tea?"

"No, thanks."

"Water?"

"I'm good."

"Fine." Why did she feel rattled? She picked up hostility and reluctance all the time and didn't react. Why today? Must be the headache. Or the fact that while most people's confessions in this office were surprisingly similar, she had a feeling this guy's secrets included things like where the bodies were buried.

They sat across from each other and she let silence fill the air. Some of her patients were so desperate for relief from their problems that they couldn't wait to unload them.

Silence lengthened.

Rafe was not one of the desperate ones.

She picked up her notebook.

"Do you have any questions before we begin?"

"Nope."

"Fine. Why don't you tell me why you're here?"

He dropped his gaze to the coffee table. A sure sign that what he was about to say was likely not the truth. "I'm not sleeping too good."

"I see."

She waited until he'd raised his gaze. "Any ideas as to why you're not sleeping?"

He shrugged. "I do a lot of night work. My schedule gets screwed up."

If his trouble was a sleep disorder he needed an MD, which he must know. He wasn't the first patient who had a problem he needed pried out of him.

"Why don't you sleep?"

"I told you. I work a crazy schedule."

"It says on your intake sheet that you're a police officer."

"That's right."

"Is there something about your work that's bothering you?"

"I've been a cop for eight years. Only had trouble sleeping recently."

"What's changed?"

He shifted on the leather couch.

She decided to take another tack. "Tell me about the rest of your life. What do you do when you're not a cop?"

"I eat. See my family. Hang out with my buddies. Go dirt biking."

"You're not married, I see. Any girlfriends?"

He glanced up, his eyes hot; then his gaze dropped to the table again. He crossed his arms and turned so his body was protected from her. But he must have studied at least as much body language as she had and she watched him deliberately turn his body forward and look up at her.

"Not really."

"Not really? What does that mean?"

"There's a woman. But it's pretty casual."

She made a note to come back later to this woman who was so casual.

"You get on well at work?"

"Yeah."

"Is there a case that's bothering you?"

"I can't talk about that."

She resisted the urge to tap her foot. If he wanted to waste his money, who was she to stop him? "Your family. How do you get on with your family?"

"They're great."

He'd slipped back into his defensive posture. She ought to continue with gentle questions. Use one of the techniques she'd learned, but she had a headache and it seemed to her that life was too short to give up hours to people who only wanted to waste her time.

She put down her notebook.

"Rafe," she said, "why are you really here?"

She felt for the first time that she had his full attention. Maybe he was as surprised as she was that she'd pretty much accused him of lying to her. She had the odd feeling that he respected her for her directness. "I read your book."

Okay, not exactly the answer she'd been looking for, but interesting.

And surprising.

"You did?"

"Yeah."

Nothing more was forthcoming, but he'd mentioned her book for a reason. "Was there a chapter you found particularly interesting?"

"Chapter eight."

She mentally scanned the table of contents. "Bad relationship choices."

"Yeah."

Good. This was progress.

"What bad relationship choices are you making, Rafe?"

He blew out a breath, the kind of breath he'd been holding for years. "Wounded doves."

"You have a Galahad Complex?"

"You're the shrink. You tell me." He snarled the words, but he wouldn't have brought this up if he didn't want to talk about it.

"Give me an example of one of your wounded doves," she said softly.

He shook his head.

Once more, she wondered who had made him come to her. Certainly this visit wasn't voluntary.

"Tell me about the first person you ever loved."

"My mama."

"What's she like?"

"A saint."

"You meant she's passed on?"

"No, she's the best person I know. She was planning to be a nun but"—his face suddenly lightened in a grin—"my dad came along and gave her other ideas."

She found herself smiling back at him. "How many brothers and sisters do you have?"

"Two brothers. Three sisters." He clasped his hands tight together. "Used to have four sisters."

"What happened?"

"Drugs. Drugs happened. Angel was my younger sister and she got into drugs and some bad shit. She died."

"And you couldn't save her."

He shook his head.

"How old were you?"

"Seventeen." His voice was husky. "She was fifteen."

"I'm sorry."

"Not your fault."

"Not yours either."

He glanced up then and now she knew they were where they needed to be. His gaze was intense and she could see the pain shimmering there, not wet like tears but hard like steel.

"I was the one who knew what was going on. I didn't say anything. I thought I could handle it. But I couldn't."

"And now you keep trying to save other women?"

"I guess."

"How did your mother react when your sister overdosed?"

The woman's words were matter of fact, but they banged into Rafe like nails into his flesh. *You were supposed to protect her,* his mother had screamed at him. And even though she'd later begged his forgiveness for her harsh words, he'd known they were true.

"I was born on December 12," he said. The shrink looked at him with the same polite expression she'd worn since he got in here. Of course, she wouldn't know. Even now he was surprised how often he forgot that what was part of his culture wasn't part of Texas.

"It's the day of Our Lady of Guadalupe." How to explain? "She's the patron saint of Mexico. To be born on that day is—" He shrugged, unable to explain. He saw his mother and his grandmother, smelled the incense in the church. "A most blessed event. My mother and grandmother wanted me to go for the priesthood." He was vaguely aware that his accent had thickened. If he didn't pull himself out of the past, he'd start speaking Spanish.

"And did you consider it?"

He nodded. "When I was a kid." And what a disaster that would have been.

"What happened?"

"Too much hate." He felt it welling inside him again as he went to that dark place in himself. She'd been so young. His special charge from the moment she was old enough to idolize him. "I found those guys that sold her the stuff. I nearly killed them."

He'd nearly been killed himself, but fury drove him, gave him strength unlike anything he'd ever known.

"Then I left and came here."

"And became a cop."

"That's right." He wished he hadn't come here today, hadn't agreed to this stupid session. He felt like shit, he didn't want to talk about this stuff. Why hadn't he told that English *chica* no?

"You're still dispensing justice and, I suppose, vengeance." The shrink had green eyes that were pale but looked like they didn't miss much, and red hair, also pale, tied back off her face.

"I do my job," he said tightly.

"And when you're not working, you rescue wounded doves."

He pretty much thought that summed it up. He wasn't stupid. He'd figured this out himself. Damn it. Why had he bothered coming here? Putting himself through this? She couldn't help him. No one could.

And as for falling in love with him, that was a laugh. Unless she was wounded, he wouldn't be interested. And unless he was some asshole with a bunch of degrees and an Armani wardrobe, he didn't think she'd be interested in him.

"What happens after you fix their wings?"

He gazed at her. Her eyes were clear and intelligent, but she kept rubbing her temple like she was in pain. "What always happens when a bird's wing is fixed? It flies away."

"Not always."

He didn't answer. He felt his body slouching into the chair. He resisted the urge to put his boots on her perfect glass tabletop.

She gave him a minute to answer, and when it was clear he wasn't going to, she pushed.

"What happens when they are healed but don't leave you?"

"Nothing happens."

"Do you leave them? Do you lose interest?"

"I don't know. Maybe."

"Tell me about this latest woman."

"She's messed up. I think I messed her up some more."

That calm, still voice was relentless. Like a dentist's drill. "What do you think you should do about that?"

"I don't know." All he knew was that he'd been reckless. He'd been trying to keep Stephanie on the straight and narrow, and instead he'd scared her so badly she'd quit her job. "Shit." He slumped farther into the couch. "I think I should stay away from her." Even as he said the words his body clamored, *No! She is hot, enticing, and so sweet. Making love to her had only whetted his appetite for more.*

But he wasn't helping her by getting involved with her. He would only hurt her.

At least if he did this favor for Chloe, he could still see Stephanie every time he went to the office.

It would be hell, but he could keep an eye on her and make sure Chloe didn't do anything crazy enough to get them both arrested.

He watched the shrink rub her temple once again. "Do you want to stop and take some aspirin or something?" he asked.

She smiled, and he thought the sudden lightening did her face a big favor. She looked at him for the first time, not as a patient, he thought, but as another person. "You are good at picking up when a woman's in pain."

Chapter 16

Stephanie came home and saw yet another envelope that had been pushed under her door. It was becoming an annoying daily habit, one that had started more than a week ago, before she started working for Chloe. She ought to throw them out unopened, but for some reason she felt compelled to read them.

She put down her bag, stepped out of her shoes, and walked to the galley kitchen to pour some water.

On the way she opened the envelope and pulled out the card. It was different from the usual. Very different. Instead of the usual painted floral bouquet, this was a plain white card. Derek had taken Chloe's brochure and cut it up into a bizarre collage that he'd pasted to the front of the card.

The words *The Breakup Artist* were underlined in heavy black ink. Inside, Derek had written, *This is all her fault.*

That was all. No pleas for a reunion, no offers for lunch or dinner, no promises about their wonderful life together.

A vague creepiness enveloped her. Somehow Derek was getting into her building, but she'd never given him a key to her apartment, thank goodness. Even so, she flipped on all the lights and walked through the place.

Then once she was certain she was alone, she picked up the phone and called Chloe.

When she described the card, her boss's reaction was immediate. "What a stupid thing to do. Those brochures were very expensive."

Stephanie shook her head. Trust Chloe to see things in a completely unexpected way. "I really don't think he's the type to do anything, but"—she shrugged helplessly—"you never know."

"Do you want to come and spend the night here? We can haul down the other bed from the attic. Nothing easier. We'll have a girls' night. Drink only things that are pink and watch movies that make us cry."

Stephanie laughed. "No, I'll be fine. I know lots of people in the building."

"I believe you also know a cop who makes house calls."

"I'm not that desperate."

"All right. Call if you change your mind and want to come over. I'll see you in the morning."

The ringing phone pulled Matt out of the deepest sleep he'd had in weeks. He woke on the first ring and was fully alert by the second. He noted the time was a little after two when he picked up and answered, "Tanner." He was out of bed and reaching for his jeans when he remembered he wasn't a cop anymore, which was also the same moment a breathy, female voice whispered, "Matthew?"

"Who is this?"

"It's Chloe." She was whispering and she sounded scared.

"What's up?"

"Have you got a gun?" It was a crazy question, at a crazy hour of the night, but he didn't call her on it. Not yet. He'd ensure her safety first, as he'd been trained to do. Then he'd yell.

"Yes. Why?"

"I think I might be in trouble."

His eyes rolled, even as he walked, naked, to the window and peered between the slats of the blinds out onto the darkened cul-de-sac. Before Chloe moved in, this had been a haven of peace and tranquility, exactly the place for a burned-out ex-cop who'd seen all the action he ever wanted to see in his life and who craved nothing more than peace and quiet. He felt like he could count on the fingers of one hand the minutes of peace he'd had since that English gal had moved in next door.

"I don't see anything in front of your house," he told her.

"No, I think he's trying to break in at the back."

He ran the length of the upstairs, grabbing his gun from his sock drawer on the way. From the window in the back bedroom he saw . . . nothing. "The motion detector light isn't on. I can't see anybody out there."

"Oh, never mind. It was probably an idle threat."

He felt his hair stand on end. "Threat? What threat?"

"You won't like it."

"I'm sure of that. I already don't like it. So tell me what's going on."

He ran back to his room, found his jeans, grabbed a shirt from the pile of clean laundry he hadn't got around to putting away, and shoved the stuff on while Chloe said, "I had a phone call an hour or so ago."

"Who from?"

"A man. He didn't give his name. He told me to close down my business or I'd be sorry. Naturally, I asked him what exactly was the trouble, but he hung up."

"What's going on now?"

"I thought I saw something in the garden. It's probably nothing."

"Stay put. I'll check it out."

He sprinted down the stairs, shoving his feet into sneakers when he hit the kitchen, then slipped quietly out of the house.

The air was warm and heavy with humidity. He stood still and silent, only his eyes moving as he scanned the area. He didn't see any movement, hear a sound. He waited another full minute, and then still seeing and hearing nothing out of the ordinary, he decided to take a walk around the perimeter of the properties before calling an overdue meeting with his neighbor and tenant.

He walked noiselessly alongside the hedge that separated the houses until he reached the bottom of the joined lot; then he edged between a mountain laurel and a pistachio tree to emerge at the bottom of his neighbor's garden.

All was quiet. He caught the scent of nighttime, and in one corner he made out the shapes of the cacti in the low-maintenance cactus garden. Matt was a big believer in the low-maintenance garden.

A rustling sound to his left had him tensing, only to see Mitzi the cat, who lived three doors down, out for a night's hunting. Pointedly, the cat ignored him and went about her business.

He'd finish walking the perimeter—because he liked to finish what he started—and then he and Chloe would be having their meeting.

Based on the temperature already, it was going to be a hot one tomorrow. And then his musings about the weather were silenced as he saw a figure run out from the alley and throw something toward the house. He caught no more than a glimpse of a thinnish man before the guy was running back the way he'd come.

Matt started to yell, "Police, freeze," but got halfway through before changing the yell to "Son of a bitch." He was already halfway to the back porch, thinking it was a bomb. A light snapped on, and he yelled, "Chloe! Get down."

By the time he got to the porch and saw that the bomb was no more than a rock that had bounced off the window without breaking it, he was furious. Nobody messed with his property, his tenant, and his night's sleep. Barely breaking stride, he pelted to where the guy had disappeared. He leapt the fence. Saw a car's lights flare and the shriek of an ignition being cranked too hard. Anybody whose pitching arm was so lame assed they couldn't throw a rock with enough force to break a window, wasn't somebody who'd run down a man standing in front of his Honda sedan.

At least he hoped not, because Matt was not going to let this punk go without a fight.

His feet hit the dirt. He landed hard, and as his brain told his legs to run, the impact of his feet hitting the gravel shuddered through him until he felt his knee pop out from under him.

"Shit!" he yelled as he crashed helplessly into the ground and watched in impotent fury as the Honda squealed past him. His eyes were clouded with pain and dirt, so all he got of the license plate was a 4 and maybe a 3.

Great. Just great.

He lay there for another minute, not sure whether he was angrier with the rock thrower, Chloe, or himself for forgetting he'd left that macho shit behind after a bullet took out half his knee.

It took him a couple of painful minutes and a lot of sweat and cursing to get himself to a sitting position with his back against the fence.

He contemplated dragging himself to his feet and hopping home, but the pain radiating from his knee all the way to his teeth made the idea of sitting here in the gravel for what remained of the night more appealing.

Rustling sounds near him heralded the arrival of Mitzi, who walked around him a couple of times, giving him a wide berth, her tail swishing. When he didn't move, the cat circled closer, and finally close enough that he could pet her. Her fur was warm and sort of dusty, and she seemed to look at him with indulgent disdain that he couldn't manage a leap she did so effortlessly several times a day.

Then he heard much louder rustling and, finally, Chloe calling him in a low voice, "Matthew? Where are you? Are you all right?"

He ignored her for a while, but she wasn't the kind of woman to give up, and he finally figured that answering her would be less aggravating than listening to her call for him all over the neighborhood as though he were a lost pet.

"Over here," he finally called, keeping his voice soft. No reason for the entire neighborhood to see him like this.

She appeared on the other side of the fence, looking over and down at him. Her face was pale in the darkness. Her hand went to her cheek.

"Oh, no. What happened?"

"Old knee injury," he said, trying to drag himself up to his one good leg, feeling like a damn fool. He forgot about the knee every time he should be most careful to remember it.

Pain twisted through him and he grunted as he almost toppled.

"Don't move," she ordered, and his mind was taken off his pain momentarily while he watched the least athletic attempt to climb a fence he'd ever witnessed. However, a lot of visible thigh was involved, which took his mind temporarily off his pain and made him happy his neighbor was no athlete.

"A gentleman wouldn't stare," she told him.

"I was wounded in the line. Give me a break."

She slid to her feet and then brushed off her palms before taking stock of the situation, which didn't take a hell of a lot of summing up.

"I can't walk." He didn't even have crutches anymore. He'd given them away the moment he was walking again.

"Right," she said. "You'll have to lean on me."

"I'm too heavy for you."

"Nonsense. I'm stronger than I look."

"Who was that asshole throwing rocks at your window?"

"We'll talk inside. You must save your strength."

She came toward his injured right side and he clenched involuntarily. But she was so smooth, she could have been trained. She slid under his arm, put her arms around his waist to anchor him, and then looked up. "All right?"

He nodded and let go of the fence. With slow, painful hops,

they started the long way around to the front of the house. It didn't take long for him to realize that she'd been right. She was stronger than she looked and also had an instinct about how and when he was going to move. He relaxed against her and the going got smoother.

"Good," she said softly. "You're beginning to trust me."

"Like a mouse trusts a bull snake."

She trilled her laugh. "I love it when you talk Texan," she said, and he found himself grinning.

"What else am I gonna talk?"

The night was so quiet but for their footsteps and his hopping shuffling the gravel. Mitzi, after rubbing past his legs, took off and he and Chloe had the night to themselves. Odd when he was full of pain and furious at his own stupidity, but he noticed the feel of her body against his, slender and elegant. Her breast was pressed against his side out of medical necessity, but still, he noticed how nice it felt.

She smelled good too. He couldn't stand perfume and he doubted Chloe wore any. But she sure smelled good.

"We've made it more than halfway. How are you holding up?"

"Better than you. You're panting."

When they got around to the front of her house he knew she didn't have it in her to get him all the way home to his place, but he thought she could make it past her car.

"Lean on the hood for a minute," she panted. "I'll run in and get my keys."

Keys? "What for?"

Even in the dark he could tell she was giving him that look again, like he was stupider than dirt. "To drive you to the hospital."

"No, I know the drill. I'll go to my doctor tomorrow. All I can do tonight is ice it and keep it elevated."

She looked as though she were going to argue, so he said a word he never uttered to a woman if he could help it. "Please."

"You're crazy. You know that, don't you?" she scolded, but she also rearranged herself under his arm and they continued walking.

The steps were tough, but he'd done this before. So, it seemed, had Chloe. She got him inside and to the big armchair in her living room where he eased himself down stifling a groan. She pulled one of the dining chairs over and lifted his foot carefully onto it. "Ice?" she asked.

"Yeah."

"I don't have an ice pack," she said from the kitchen, where he heard the sound of ice cubes being snapped out of trays. Then she came in with a lumpy looking dish towel and eased her homemade ice pack around his knee.

She took a good look at him under the light of a standard lamp she'd switched on. "All I have in the way of painkillers is Advil."

He shook his head.

"Don't be a bloody hero. You've got some heavy-duty meds at home, I'm certain. Something strong enough to ease those lines of pain." Here, she touched him, a soft stroke of her index finger down the center of his brow. It was such a dumb thing, hardly personal at all, but he felt that light touch and knew that he wanted to know more of it. He wanted to feel her hands on him. Put his hands on her. Something of his thoughts must have communicated themselves to her, for he saw heat leap into her eyes. Her lips parted slightly and she leaned closer. "If circumstances were different," she said in that soft but husky voice, "I'd kiss you all better."

He could barely breathe. Lust was pummeling him even as the fact that Brittany trusted him held him rooted to the chair like carpenter's glue.

"If your kisses can fix my knee, you're a miracle worker."

She smiled that completely female cat smile of hers. "I wouldn't cure your knee, but simply make you forget you had one."

Oh, man. He'd tried to deflect the blast of lust with his

comment, but she'd backhanded it right back to him. "The medicine cabinet in the upstairs bathroom," he said. "Prescription painkillers." He didn't need the meds as much as he needed to get Chloe out of range until he got his wits back.

He contemplated hauling Rafe out of his bed to come help him home, but he figured there weren't enough hours of night left to worry about. Besides, it was time he and Chloe had a little talk.

He placed his revolver on the table beside him, beside a biography of Coco Chanel.

She was back in less than ten minutes with his painkillers. She got him a glass of water and shook out two, offering them on her palm.

"I wouldn't have pegged you for the nursing type."

Her chuckle was low and sexy. "I was engaged to a former Italian Olympic skier who had a knee very much like yours."

"I doubt it."

She cocked her head at him. "What kind of injury was it? Football?"

"Bullet."

"Good heavens." Considering it was going on four and she hadn't had a whole lot of sleep, his neighbor looked far too good.

She wore gray U of T sweats, and with her dark hair tousled and no makeup on, she looked like a coed. "Is that why you left the force?"

"Pretty much. I was given a desk job, but I'm not cut out for a desk job." He shrugged. "I already had a couple of houses I'd fixed up and rented or sold. It worked out okay, so I kept on doing it. Keeps me busy." He paused. "Of course, I could always go into your line of work."

Her eyes widened. "My line of work?"

"Private investigation."

She recovered quickly. "Exactly. Somehow, I can't imagine you as a PI."

"A lot of people would say the same about you."

She beamed at him. "I know. That's why I'm so smashingly successful."

"Speaking of smashing." He pointed a thumb toward the window that hadn't broken. "What was that all about?"

"To tell you the truth, I don't know. I have a feeling the attack wasn't about me, but my employee." Her brow furrowed. "I can't tell you more until I've seen her."

She then took a dark purple throw off the back of the couch and laid it over him, tucking it around him with nimble fingers. She got an extra pillow out of the hall closet and tucked that behind his head. "Don't worry about it now. Get some sleep."

"I need answers, not sleep."

She patted his cheek. She actually had the nerve to pat his cheek. "And you will get them. When the time is right."

He grabbed her hand to stop her from leaving, felt the softness of her skin but remembered the underlying strength in her. "There's going to be a reckoning between us, Chloe, one of these days."

She glanced at their joined hands, then met his gaze. "We're yin and yang."

"Yeah, whenever I yin, you yang."

She sent him an enigmatic smile and gave his hand a quick squeeze before pulling free. "Good night, Matthew. Thank you for being my protector."

"I fell flat on my face," he reminded her.

"A man is no less a hero for being a wounded knight," she said, then flipped off the light. He heard her tread softly up the stairs.

A wounded knight. That woman was definitely a few ants short of a picnic. He found himself smiling in the dark. Even though he didn't think the rock-throwing punk was coming back, he kept watch until it was light.

Chapter 17

Stephanie let out a squawk of alarm and dropped her bag on the floor, which caused the man asleep in Chloe's living room to jerk awake and then swear violently, clutching his knee.

"What are you doing here?" she asked. She recognized him now that she'd gotten a good look at him. He was the man from next door. The one who owned this house. Still, it seemed kind of strange for him to be sleeping in it. "Does Chloe know you're here?"

He rubbed his eyes. "What time is it?"

"Ten of nine." She was early, but then she was usually early getting to Chloe's since, unlike her previous jobs, this was the most fun thing in her life. Or maybe that said more about how pathetic her life was than how great her new job was.

"Guess I fell asleep. And, yes, Chloe knows I'm here. She tucked me in herself."

Chloe was obviously a very sexual woman and the neighbor was seriously hot, so what they were doing on separate floors was outside Stephanie's comprehension.

They looked at each other for a few seconds. "I'm Matt," he finally said. "I live next door."

"I'm Stephanie. I work for Chloe."

"Right." He yawned. "Do your duties by any chance include making coffee?"

She smiled at him. "I'll be glad to make you a pot."

"Thanks." He dug out a cell phone. While she began making coffee, she heard Matt say, "Hey, Rafe. Need a favor." An entire tablespoon of Chloe's very expensive French coffee plopped onto the counter. Was it possible he was talking to her Rafe? Not that the man was her Rafe. Bastard.

"Need you to pick me up at Chloe's and give me a ride to my doctor. It's my knee . . . Yeah, long story. Tell you later. Thanks, man. I owe you."

She heard footsteps on the stairs, so she poured a third mug of coffee and added a dash of skim and half a teaspoon of sugar. Chloe entered the living room in what Steph thought of as her "at home" business attire. Flowing white sailor style pants and a navy and white striped T-shirt. Her sandals were red and sported tiny crystal anchors.

Steph caught the look that passed between Chloe and Matt when they first saw each other and wished someone had warned her to look away. Her eyeballs felt scorched from the heat that zapped between them, as though she'd stared right at the sun.

"Good morning, Matthew. How did you sleep?"

He cracked a grin that made him look younger. His unshaven face and crumpled shirt, even the purple woolen throw puddled in his lap didn't take away from the sheer masculinity of the guy. "Like a baby."

"Morning, Stephanie." And then, catching sight of the coffee Steph was bringing in, she said, "Oh, how lovely."

She handed Chloe her coffee first, then went to put Matt's beside him within easy reach, when she gasped. "Why is there a gun on the table?"

"Ah, yes. We had a spot of trouble last night." Chloe glanced at Stephanie standing there, and said, "Let's all sit down, then Matthew doesn't have to crane his neck to talk to us."

Stephanie had no idea why they were having social time,

but she did as she was told and sat. She sipped the coffee, which was excellent, and watched Chloe drape herself on the furniture. She'd never seen anyone who could turn such a simple act into a tiny drama.

"I rather think your ex paid me a visit last night."

Steph glanced at Matt, obviously wounded, and the gun on the table. "Did you shoot him?" she asked, half hopeful.

"No."

"Pity," said Chloe. When Matt glared at her she waved a white hand, and said, "Oh, not fatally. But a bullet some-where soft and painful in his nasty little body would not make me unhappy."

Matthew rubbed his unshaven face, then gulped his coffee. "Can someone explain what's—" He was interrupted by the doorbell.

"Would you be a darling?" Chloe asked Steph.

She supposed as receptionist it was her job to answer the door, but if the guy ringing the bell was who she thought he was, she really didn't want to answer it.

However, she got up and went into the foyer. She flicked her fingers through her hair and then opened the door.

Rafe looked at her the way a man sometimes looks at a woman he's recently seen naked and wants to see that way again soon. So why was he staying away from her then? Among all the things in her life that didn't make a lot of sense, Rafe was very near the top of the list.

"Hi," he said.

"Hi. Matthew's in the living room."

He nodded, then walked past her. He didn't even brush her, but she felt his sexuality waft around her. Powerful and intoxicating.

He nodded to Chloe and then sauntered over to where Matt reclined with his foot up. "Messed it up again, huh?"

"Yeah."

He gripped Matt's shoulder and that was it. The extent of their exchange. She'd walked in behind him and she and

Chloe exchanged a glance. They'd have been commiserating, asking for details, going over the whole dramatic story, then offering casseroles and making tea. These two macho guys managed a complete exchange in half a dozen words. Amazing.

"Would you like some coffee, Rafe?" Chloe asked him.

He glanced briefly at Stephanie. "Yeah, sure."

What was she? A waitress at Denny's? But she didn't say anything, merely got another mug out and then went around to refill the other coffees. She didn't ask Rafe how he liked his coffee. He got it black. He merely nodded thanks when she put his coffee on the table in front of the couch where he was now sitting beside Chloe.

She dragged a dining table chair over and sat, wishing Rafe didn't have to hear this.

Matthew unscrewed the cap off a prescription medicine bottle and shook out two pills, which he swallowed with his coffee. Chloe looked concerned but didn't say anything.

"Okay," he said, "tell me what happened last night."

Chloe glanced at Stephanie, and said, "I wonder if we should talk about this later? You should get that leg seen to."

"I'm not leaving here until you tell me what the hell's going on. Since Rafe is a police officer, he should hear it too."

Rafe's gaze sharpened and he glanced at Matt. "What's up?"

"I was threatened last night and my home attacked," Chloe said in a clear, theatrical tone. Stephanie liked her boss a lot, more every day, but she did manage to make even the smallest things sound like national emergencies.

Rafe was definitely a cut-through-the-crap kind of guy. "Who threatened you?" he asked.

"I think it was Stephanie's ex-fiancé."

He cut a glance her way, sharp but impassive. "This true?"

"He didn't tell me his plans. I would have warned Chloe."

"How do you know it was him?" he asked, looking between the two women.

"Stephanie told me he'd been harassing her, sending her

flowers and cards, and phoning and e-mailing her. She thought the tone was getting nastier as she refused to see him."

"Then last night when I got home there was another card. Basically blaming Chloe for breaking us up."

"Why didn't you tell me?" Rafe demanded, turning to her, his eyes hot.

She returned his look with one she hoped was cool. "When would I have done that?"

"Damn it, Stephanie . . ." But he didn't finish. What could he say? They'd slept together once and he'd made good and sure it didn't happen again.

If Matthew was surprised by the outburst, he didn't show it. He seemed like he was in a fair bit of pain. She felt guilty all over the place. She was working for this nice woman and her bad luck was following her here, affecting Chloe and her nice neighbor. It wasn't right.

"You told him where you work?" Matthew asked.

"He followed me here." She looked down at the floor. "A couple of times."

"What kind of car does he drive?" Matthew asked.

"A gray Honda Accord."

"By any chance know his license plate number?"

She rattled it off. Both men looked at her, surprised, but Chloe announced with pride, "Stephanie has a photographic memory."

"You made it to the car?" Rafe asked Matt.

"I'm pretty sure it's the same. I didn't get the whole plate number."

Chloe smiled at him. "That's all right, darling. We can't all have photographic memories."

Matt rolled his eyes, but the glance he and Chloe exchanged seemed surprisingly intimate for people who seemed as though they hadn't slept together. As opposed to her and Rafe who had slept together and didn't seem able to communicate at all.

There was silence in the room. Everyone seemed to defer

to Rafe, as the working cop. Finally, he said, "Did something happen to make him snap?"

"Yes, he told me he loved me."

"What did you say?"

She was staring at her coffee, wishing she were about a million miles away in another solar system. "I told him it was over." She glanced up. "He's been bugging me every day. I'd had it. So I lied and told him I'm seeing someone else."

Her gaze locked with Rafe's. Fire and ice warred between them leaving her hot, cold, and confused.

"That must be why he started throwing rocks," Matt said after another silence.

"Yeah."

"He certainly snapped," Chloe said, drawing the attention back to herself, for which Stephanie was grateful. "He called me and said I was nothing but a troublemaker and I'd better close up my business. I told him I'd do nothing of the kind, and then he said I'd be sorry. Naturally, I wasn't going to get into it with such a pathetic miscreant, so I politely said good-bye and rang off." She heaved a dramatic sigh. "Imagine my shock when he attacked this house."

"You make it sound like he came at you with a rocket launcher," Matthew said. He shook his head and turned to Rafe. "Stupid fuck threw a rock at her window, not even hard enough to break the glass."

As if things weren't bad enough, her ex was now an object of contempt. She couldn't even pick a guy who was a competent window breaker.

"What's the guy's address."

She shrugged. "I can't remember."

"You have a photographic memory. Think harder."

"What are you going to do to him?"

"We don't have enough to press charges. But he doesn't know that. I'm going to get my partner and we're going to go scare the shit out of this guy. I don't think he'll bother you again."

She glanced at Chloe for guidance. The other woman nodded. "I think it's for the best, Stephanie. He's caused you trouble for weeks. Let the police handle it."

Reluctantly, she nodded and reeled off her ex's address and phone number.

"I sure can pick 'em," she said, as they watched Rafe ease Matthew into the backseat of Chloe's car.

Matthew cursed as he maneuvered himself into place. "You and me both," Chloe replied.

Chapter 18

To Deborah's surprise, Rafael Escobar kept his second appointment. Deb found that she was pleased to see him. She could usually tell when somebody wasn't coming back, and she'd have guessed he would be one who would find opening up simply too difficult.

He didn't look any happier to be here, however, than he had the first time.

"Good afternoon," she said.

He glanced at her in surprise and said, "Yeah, hi." And all at once she felt pretentious for her formal greeting. Who was she, Emily Post? She was supposed to be fixing his psyche, not acting like she was serving him afternoon tea.

Maybe because he'd rattled her a bit she decided to do the same to him. "I guessed you weren't coming back," she said.

He glanced up and then sent her a half grin. "I wouldn't spend a lot of time in Vegas if I were you."

"I see you've got my book."

He had it on the table in front of him. "Yeah, I—do you really believe all this stuff you write?"

"Of course I do, or I wouldn't have written it. What is it that you find so hard to believe."

"I don't know. It feels like you're giving people rules all the time. Whatever happened to good old chemistry?"

She bridled a little at that. Was he suggesting she didn't have any chemistry? Of course, with her and Jordan lately the chemistry was more like mixing two nonexplosive substances. Like tap water with tap water.

Maybe she wasn't the last of the red-hot tango girls, but she and Jordan used to have fun in bed. It suddenly struck her that they hadn't in a while. In fact, she couldn't remember the last time they'd made love in any but the most perfunctory way.

The silence was lengthening and she realized Rafe had asked a question that she had yet to answer. "Chemistry. Yes, of course it's important. But attraction isn't always enough, is it?"

"No."

"And as I hope you have discovered from reading my book, we are often attracted to the very people who are worst for us."

"Like me with the wounded doves."

She wouldn't agree with him, of course, because therapy was about getting the patients to discover their paths for themselves. Instead, she leaned forward.

"Rafe, I'd like you to try something for me."

"What?"

"I want you to find a woman you consider attractive and ask her out on a date. But she must be someone completely confident and successful. Break your pattern and see what happens."

He looked at her steadily for a moment, so she had to force herself not to shirk that dark, dark gaze. There was the oddest expression on his face, as though he were about to perform a distasteful duty. Finally, he said, "How about you, Doc? Will you go out with me?"

She felt shocked, physically, like she'd stuck her finger in a live socket. Zapped.

"I—I, well, I'm flattered, of course." She usually saw the patient-falling-for-the-therapist attachment coming from miles away. She hadn't had a clue with Rafe. "But you must know I couldn't have a personal relationship with a patient. It wouldn't be ethical."

He leaned back. He didn't look crushed or put out, merely curious, she thought. "Okay. Let's say I stopped being your patient and we bumped into each other somewhere. If I asked you out then, would you go?"

"Why do you think you're having these feelings?"

"Why are you answering a question with a question?"

She sighed. "No, I would not go out with you."

"Why? Because there's no chemistry?"

She thought he was pretty much a full chemistry set all on his own, sitting there across from her. Every explosive, corrosive, big-bang compound on the periodical table in one dog-eared but nevertheless sexy package. She wondered if it was her. Was there a chemical anywhere that would turn into fireworks when mixed with plain old tap water?

"I am already in a steady relationship," she said.

"Okay." He grinned at her. "At least I tried. Right?"

She couldn't help herself. He might be scruffy, belligerent, and have some issues with women, but he was a charmer. "Yes, you did. And I am flattered."

He rose. "Well, thanks anyway."

"Where are you going?"

He shook his head. "I don't think this is going to work."

"But you haven't even given counseling a try."

He glanced back at her, enigmatic. His heels were so worn down on those boots she was tempted to give him the name of an excellent shoe repair service she used. He shook his head. "I'm sorry. You're a nice lady. This just isn't right."

What on earth was the man talking about? "Fine," she snapped. "Go, then. I can't help you if you won't help yourself."

He left.

She slapped a hand over her mouth, wishing she wasn't too late to stop that snappish outburst. She couldn't understand what was wrong with her. Everything in her carefully planned life felt out of kilter somehow. And Rafe had pushed her a little more off balance, she realized, with all that talk about chemistry and sizzle. The center of calmness she prided herself on, the one that existed on rules and order, felt irritable and rocky. She had a new empathy for her patients; in fact, she felt like she needed some therapy herself.

Deb sat there bemused as he carefully shut her office door behind him. She'd put his departure down to the fact that she'd refused to go out with him, but instinct and training told her that wasn't what had caused him to leave in midsession.

What a strange character he was. He was more self-aware than most of her clients and yet unwilling to do the work to fix his problem.

She tapped her pen against her paper, which suggested he didn't want to fix his problem.

As she knew well, until a person was ready to change, there wasn't much she could do.

She hoped he'd be back.

When she rose from the seating area she noticed he'd forgotten his copy of her book. Clearly he was still reading it as a business card protruded from the pages.

She picked up the book, hoping to catch him before he left the building, and as she did she noticed that the business card looked familiar.

Flipping open the book revealed a card that had filled her with irritation the first time she saw it: CHLOE FLYNT, THE BREAKUP ARTIST. She flipped over the card and there, in neat female handwriting that definitely did not belong to Rafael Escobar, was the day and time of Rafe's first appointment with her. She slammed her book shut, filled with burning rage.

It was so hot, that rage, so corrosive, she felt as though her insides were burning up. He wanted chemistry? She'd show him chemistry.

She ran for the door, bursting out into the reception area

to see a sight that sent her anger into dangerous territory. For there, in her waiting room, was Rafael Escobar, and he looked very cozy with her next client, Stephanie Baxter.

She didn't care that the waiting room was not a very private place, that Jordan, Carly, the receptionist, and a guy currently delivering coffee supplies could all hear her. She screeched, "What is going on here?"

Stephanie jumped and blushed scarlet; Rafe turned slowly to look at her. He might think he gave nothing away, but he was wrong. His body language said it for him, the way he moved protectively toward Stephanie as though he could shield her from Deb.

She flapped the business card around. "You took that job, didn't you, Stephanie? With this breakup woman?"

Guilt was written all over the little shoplifter's face. She nodded glumly.

Deb's hot gaze flipped back and forth between them like a madwoman's. "You two are lovers."

"Deborah, I didn't know—"

"Why is your appointment written on the back of The Breakup Artist's business card?" She heard her own words bouncing around the reception area like exploding bullets.

She didn't even give them time to answer. "How dare you," she yelled, feeling all those years of careful restraint incinerate around her. She flapped the card at the pair of them. "You set me up. You deliberately made a fool of me. I want to know what the hell is going on, and I want to know now!"

She'd always been terrified that someday she'd turn out to be her parents' daughter. Now she was. And spectacularly so.

Stephanie stepped forward, seeming as though she wanted to soothe the therapist. Oh, it was all so wrong. Deb's world was completely upside down. She stopped her patient with a hand gesture that was intended to mean "Stop" but looked more like a "Heil Hitler" salute. A shaky one at that. "Do you know your lover just asked me out?"

Jordan stuck his head out of his office door at that moment, stared at Deb, and then at Rafe. He came out and stood in his doorway as though uncertain whether to come forward or to dive back and retreat.

"Deborah, would you like to sit down?" he said to her in his level, compassionate therapist's voice.

"Maybe you should butt out," she snapped.

What was the matter with her? She should apologize to poor Jordan. This wasn't his fault. But screw it. She didn't feel like apologizing, everything was a mess. Suddenly, she saw that her carefully ordered life was a façade.

"Tell me what is going on this minute!" she yelled to the two of them.

"I'm sorry," Rafe said. "I can't."

She turned on Stephanie. "You brought this card into me weeks ago. You said this woman offered you a job."

Stephanie looked miserable, but she nodded.

There was a moment of potent silence. Carly, the receptionist, had stopped clacking on her keyboard; the coffee guy had abandoned the break room to stand in the doorway, staring; and Jordan could have been a stone statue for all the noise he made. She could hear the hum of the air conditioning, it was so quiet.

"Did you take that job?"

Stephanie glanced at Rafe, then at the floor. "Yeah."

"I'm asking you again, what is going on here?"

"It's nothing to do with Stephanie."

As a calming device, Rafe's interference was not successful. "Okay, if you won't tell me what's going on, I'll go and ask Ms. Chloe Flynt myself."

"Wait!" Stephanie said. "Don't you want to think about this?"

"No," she said, stalking back into her office for her purse.

Stephanie, usually so mild mannered, followed her. "But what about my appointment?"

"It's cancelled."

"You know what you always say about conflict. It's clearer

when not clouded by anger." Stephanie grabbed the book she was still holding and started flipping pages. "Look, you could read your chapter on anger."

"I'm too mad!" she yelled.

"Don't you think you should take a moment to think this through?"

"No."

She stomped past Stephanie and back through the outer office. A nervous young woman was just coming through the door. Jordan's newest client. The woman needed some backbone, was the first thing Deb noticed. She was creeping through the doorway as though she should apologize for inconveniencing it, like Stephanie used to do.

She'd reached the outer door. Stephanie stopped her with a hand on her sleeve. "Please, Deborah, let's do one of your pro and con lists."

"Fuck the pro and con list," she said, and slammed the door behind her.

Chapter 19

Stunned silence filled the reception area after Deborah's dramatic exit. "Did she just say what I think she said?" Carly asked the room in general.

"I'm going after her," Stephanie said. "I can't leave Chloe all alone to face her."

Rafe shook his head. "You ask me, Chloe's got this one coming."

"She was only doing her job."

"You interfere in people's personal lives, you're going to get into some messy stuff."

"But Deborah is never messy."

"Today she is."

Jordan suddenly came to life. He ran into his own office and emerged with his jacket on and car keys in his hand. "Carly, please reschedule all my appointments for this afternoon." He glanced at the nervous young woman who'd just walked in. "I'm really sorry, but I have an emergency."

He strode to the door and then turned back, "Oh, and you'd better cancel all of Deb's appointments too."

"I think you people need more decaf," said the coffee guy, shaking his head and dragging his now-empty delivery cart behind him.

Rafe was still standing there. He was looking at Stephanie in a way that made her want to kick him very hard and, at the same time, throw herself into his arms. Altogether a confusing mix of emotions. "I should get back to work," she said stiffly.

"You just ended up with a free hour in your day. Why don't we take a walk?"

"Chloe might need me."

"What those two gals need to do they can do better alone."

She had a strong feeling he was right. "I've never seen Deborah so angry."

"Nobody likes to get screwed around with."

"No," she said, giving him a pointed look, "they don't."

She picked up her bag and headed out. Rafe was right behind her, but there was nothing she could do about that. It was a free country.

She punched the elevator button and the doors opened almost immediately. Unfortunately, there was no one else inside. She'd thought Rafe was heading for the stairwell, but instead he followed her into the elevator car.

The doors slid shut and she concentrated all her attention on watching the floor numbers light up as they slid downward.

Five floors passed before her eyes. She felt him near her, felt his energy. She felt him shift. "I'm sorry," he suddenly blurted.

Another couple of floors dropped away. "Me too." She heard the note of sadness in her tone. She was sorry she'd ever been so stupid as to think he was different from all the rest.

Three more floors to go and they'd be out of here. Come on.

"I think about you," he said in a low voice. The intimacy in his tone felt like a caress sliding over her skin.

Floor two lit up. One more to go. "You have a funny way of showing it."

"Look. I have a problem."

"Who doesn't?".

The elevator was back on the ground and so was she. Enough of her airy pipe dreams about love. There was no one she could rely on but herself, and the sooner she accepted that the better.

She stepped out. He walked beside her. "I'm drawn to complicated women."

"Then you should find some simple ones."

"You don't understand. I always fall for wounded doves."

"So you're a part-time vet?" She had no idea why she was acting this way, so snappish and snarky. Maybe Deborah's meltdown had somehow affected her. But the truth was that Rafe made her feel snarky and rude.

They'd stepped out onto Sixth Street in the old warehouse district, which contained a lot of older buildings that had been redeveloped as offices or funky condos.

They passed a Japanese restaurant and then a coffee bar. "Would you stop snapping at me and listen?"

If Deborah, a therapist with a dozen years of training, could lose it, she really didn't see why she, a patient with problems of her own, should be polite to a man who had hurt her. "No, I don't think I will."

He took hold of her arm, not hard, but if she wanted to shake him off she'd have to make an issue of it. His fingers felt warm against her skin. She looked at him and was pulled in by the intensity of his gaze. In spite of busy traffic and pedestrians stepping around them, it felt like they were alone. "I saw you and something happened to me. I felt this electricity or something zap between us. Didn't you?"

She'd never forget that moment in all her life. She'd assumed it was because she was so emotionally screwed up that day that she hadn't been thinking straight, and that's why seeing him for the first time had given her such an emotional punch. Now he was telling her he'd felt it too?

Exasperation was building within her. Talk was easy.

"Why didn't you call? Or come by?" There it was. Out.

The implication that she'd wanted him to, that she'd been waiting for him to indicate he wanted more from her than one night rolling around on her couch.

He was so rugged and scruffy and fierce looking, but sometimes in his eyes she caught a glimpse of such vulnerability that she wanted to soothe him. Even though he was the one who'd abandoned her.

"You know what I was talking to Deborah about?"

"Yes, you were hitting on her. She told me. In fact, she was so loud I think she told all of Austin."

He smiled at that and his face softened so she wanted to lean into him and believe things could be different. "I think your boss is smarter than she comes across."

"Well, she'd have to be."

He cracked a grin. "You don't like her?"

"Not at the moment, no."

"The thing is, I do have a problem."

"Really." She said it with an edge of sarcasm, but the truth was, she was amazed to see him at counseling for whatever reason. He'd seemed like the last man who would admit to weakness.

"I'm drawn to women with problems."

"Show me a woman who doesn't have problems and I'll show you a kid who hasn't hit puberty."

He shook his head, impatient, so his hair caught the light. "To women who need rescuing. That's why I've been staying away from you. I think about you, and I want you, but—"

"But you're staying away because you think I'm needy and desperate," she finished for him.

"That's not—"

If he'd hauled off and slugged her one she couldn't have felt more flattened. "I'm going to make it easy for you. I don't need you." She shook her head. "I have a problem too. I always go for guys who use me and let me down. Looks like we both stayed true to our pattern."

"I never meant to hurt you."

She wondered how many times in her life she'd heard that line. It was the motto of most of the men in her life. She should get T-shirts made that she could hand out as parting gifts.

"Go. Have a good life." She made shooing motions with her hands. "I'm going to be fine."

He looked like there was more he wanted to say, but he didn't. He simply stood there looking tough and vulnerable at the same time.

As she walked away, she realized with a start that she'd meant the words. Maybe she'd changed in some quiet but dramatic way these last weeks. But she felt better than she had in a long time. And she liked being single and in control of her own destiny. She liked it just fine.

Deborah wanted to floor it when she got her car on the road. Wanted to gun the engine and make the brakes squeal as she rounded corners. Because she recognized how unhealthy that urge was, she held herself to the speed limit with manic determination.

Normally, when she was going anywhere new, she printed out Mapquest directions from the Internet, but today she'd been too angry to think. Fortunately, she had a street map in the car and it didn't take her long to find the address of Chloe Flynt, The Breakup Artist.

She'd expected the office to be in some horrible back alley somewhere, but the business address turned out to be in a nice residential neighborhood, not unlike Deborah's own, which only annoyed her more.

She pulled into the driveway, feeling aggressive enough to park behind the single vehicle already there. Chloe Flynt wasn't going anywhere until they'd had a good talk.

She got out of her car, locked it, and stomped up the stairs to the porch. She banged on the door and hit the doorbell at the same time. It was a technique she'd seen in movies, one she'd never, ever performed herself in real life. But she felt like a different woman, the red-hot anger coursing through her seemed to be vaporizing her usual behavior and manners. One tiny part of Deb's brain was observing her behavior with clinical interest as though she might later write a paper on the subject.

When the door didn't immediately open, she banged on it again and held her finger on the doorbell.

When the door opened, she found herself face to face with a young and very beautiful woman. She didn't realize she'd expected some bitter old harpy. "Are you Chloe Flynt? The Breakup Artist?" she demanded in a loud voice.

"Yes," the woman shouted. Then pointed to where her finger was still depressing the button. "You can stop ringing the doorbell now."

"Oh, of course." She removed her finger and the sudden quiet was mildly shocking.

"Did you have an appointment?"

The calm, easy way she spoke refueled Deb's fury. The woman wasn't even American, she was British, which seemed to add insult to injury. As though she'd flown thousands of miles for the pleasure of ruining Deb's practice. "No, I do not have an appointment. My name is Deborah Beaumont."

It was obvious that the young woman knew who she was, because she said, "Oh, are you?" and then looked her up and down with interest. Chloe looked over her shoulder as though expecting someone else to be with her. "What can I do for you?"

"I believe you know Rafael Escobar."

"Yes, I do."

"Also, Stephanie Baxter."

Chloe frowned. "How do you know Stephanie?"

"Please don't play games with me, Ms. Flynt." She tapped her foot against the porch, neatly painted taupe. "Rafe Escobar asked me out."

"Did he?" The young Brit looked quite pleased. "Are you going?"

"Of course I'm not. I want to know why you planted him in my office. I want to know how you dare take money to ruin people's lives. I want to know why you would play such a cruel trick on someone you don't even know. I want—"

"What I want is a nice cup of tea. My mother always says there's nothing like tea to make an awkward conversation easier. Well, until the drinks trolley comes out. Please come in."

"Tea? This is not a social call."

The woman looked more amused than terrified. "I had gathered that, yes."

But she walked off into the house and Deb was left with the option of standing on the porch, leaving, or following her. She followed.

The house was amazingly neat and orderly. The kitchen spotless. "I can do you a coffee if you'd prefer."

"No, thank you. Tea is fine." She felt foolish trying to hold on to her fury while this woman calmly put the kettle on to boil and drew out a teapot, some fancy-looking tea, and china cups.

"Why did you send Rafe to me? Why did you tell him to ask me out?"

There was a pause. The Englishwoman spooned tea out of a can that had a coat of arms on it and into a blue teapot, then poured boiling water over the leaves.

"I'm afraid that, just like yours, my business requires confidentiality." She brought the teapot over to the table and then carried over the two pure white cups and saucers. "However, I will just say that Rafe's asking you out is a complete surprise to me." She smiled. "I suspect he likes you."

"But when I went out to give him back my book and confront him about you—"

"I'm really rather surprised that he told you about me."

She shook her head with impatience. "He didn't. He was using your business card as a bookmark. He'd forgotten the book, so I went to return it to him. That's when I saw the card. Then when I got outside to the waiting area, he was talking to Stephanie. They had that look about them of people who know each other well."

"Yes, that surprised me too. Stephanie is my assistant, and I promise you I have no clue what she was doing in your office."

Deb felt like she'd been slapped. She, who prided herself on her professionalism, had all but blabbed that this person's employee used her services as a counselor.

"Do you take cream and sugar? Or lemon?"

"No, nothing, thank you."

Chloe poured a stream of fragrant dark tea into the cup, saying, "I'm glad to have a chance to meet you. I read your book, you know. I'm not sure we're so very different. We just work on different ends of the relationship spectrum."

No, no, no. They were nothing alike. "You scare me," she said. "You think everything's so easy. 'Breaking up is hard to do. We can help,'" she intoned in a fake British accent. "But it's not easy. I spent twelve years in university learning how to help people—and a big part of that is finding a healthy relationship."

"Do you have one yourself?"

Deb was momentarily thrown. "Do I have what?"

"A healthy relationship, as you call it."

"Yes, of course, I—" Suddenly, the headache that she'd barely kept at bay with analgesics bounced into painful, throbbing life. She saw, with the clarity that had been eluding her for months, that, in fact, her relationship was far from healthy. It was barely on life support. How had she not noticed? She and Jordan hadn't had any true intimacy in months. They barely spoke outside of work. With the publication of the book, their growing workloads—also courtesy of the book—they rarely saw each other outside of the long hours they spent at the office.

She supposed she'd fooled herself into believing that they

were spending most of their time together, but in truth, they were colleagues in business, not partners in life.

"That's not really the issue here," she managed to say.

"I don't know. I haven't been to university for twelve years." Chloe laughed lightly. "I didn't make it through the first twelve months, but I have had a lot of relationships. Most of them rotten. And I've been involved in a lot of them with my friends. I think if one person's unhappy enough to end the relationship, then it needs to end. What do you think?"

"I think I really need a painkiller. I've got a bad headache."

"Just a sec. I'll see what I can find." Chloe dropped a hand on her shoulder as she went by. "Drink up your tea."

She did as she was told. It was nice for a change to have somebody else looking after her. It seemed for so long that she'd been the one dispensing advice and comfort, tissues and support.

Chloe returned with a bottle and shook out two pills.

"Thank you," Deb said.

The doorbell rang.

"Lord, it's like Victoria Bloody Station around here today," Chloe said, and went back to the front of the house.

Deb tried to gather her wits and wondered vaguely what she'd hoped to accomplish coming here when she heard a very familiar voice from the doorway.

"Is Dr. Beaumont here?"

"Yes, in the kitchen. This way."

Jordan's voice was so dear to her, she realized as she waited for him to come and get her. How had she let herself become so distant? What must he think of her after her horrid outburst.

She saw him coming toward her with concern written all over his face. He was dear, and sweet, and the one who was always there. But she couldn't pretend anymore, not for him, not for her patients, and most certainly not for herself. "Oh, Jordan," she cried. "I'm such a mess."

He folded her in his arms. "No, you're not."

She nodded, emphatically. "I am. I made a horrible fool of myself at the office. In front of clients. I'll never be able to show my face again."

"Sure you will. You're human."

She lifted her head so she could see his face. He was smiling down at her with more intimacy than they'd shared in months. "You're not angry?"

"Frankly, I'm delighted. It makes the rest of us feel better when you show yourself to be less than perfect once in a while."

She hugged him. Hard. Like she'd never let him go. "I need to get back, I have patients."

"No, Carly cancelled them all."

"Oh, good. But you—"

"She cancelled mine too. Come on. Let's get you home."

"My car—"

"Rafe will drive it back for you," Chloe chimed in. "It's the least he can do."

She nodded. "Thank you. Please tell him the braking system can be a little touchy, and—"

"Go!" she was commanded.

She went.

Chapter 20

"**N**ow what!" Chloe said aloud as the doorbell chimed again.

She opened the door. "I rather thought you'd show up," she said to Rafe.

"I thought I should come by in case anybody needed CPR."

She held the door open so he could enter. "You didn't exactly rush over here, did you?"

"I had some other things I had to do." He looked at her from under his brow, his hands shoved in his pockets. "I feel like an asshole. I used your business card as a bookmark. That's how Deborah made the connection."

"One can only hope that the rest of your undercover work is more . . . What is the word I'm looking for?"

"Less likely to get me killed?"

"Something like that."

"I screwed up. I owe you. So if you want me to do another one of these gigs, I'll do it."

She laughed. "You really are a very sweet man, you know." Impulsively, she kissed him on the cheek. "Oddly enough, I think the slipup was the best thing that could have happened."

"Really?"

"Yes, the colleague/boyfriend, whatever she calls him, rushed to her side and I rather think the fact that for once she was the one falling apart and in a mess made him see her as someone who needs him. A lot of men like that, you know?"

He scowled at her, and when he scowled it was like a black cloud blocking the sun, so she stepped back. "Anyway, all's well that ends well, as Shakespeare says. At least, I hope it's Shakespeare. Stephanie will correct me if I got it wrong."

The thundercloud over Rafe's head seemed to darken when she mentioned Stephanie's name, and then it hit her that Deborah had seen them together earlier today. Presumably the business he had to take care of involved Stephanie, and based on the dark cloud above him, it hadn't gone well.

"I shan't need you for any more breakups, but I do have a final task for you if you'd be so good. I need you to help me return Deborah's car to her. She left her keys and the address. Jordan drove her home."

"Least I can do," he said. Since she thought the same thing, she didn't argue.

"I'll drive the car and you can follow me, then drop me back on your bike."

"I didn't bring a second helmet. Don't worry about it. I can grab a cab back."

Since she suspected a miserable Stephanie would be the next person through her door, she sent Rafe off alone and went back to the kitchen to put the kettle back on.

Deborah hadn't felt like this in years. It was like an alien had taken over her body. Needs and primal forces were coursing through her. Emotions she'd controlled for years seemed to have slipped their leashes.

Jordan drove carefully, as he always did. She watched his hands on the wheel perfectly positioned at ten to two. They were such nice hands. Steady and reliable as he was himself. He hadn't asked her where she wanted to go, he seemed to assume she wanted to go home. He didn't talk much. He appeared completely preoccupied with his thoughts. But when she reached over and touched his hand, he turned his over and gripped hers.

"I have to tell you something," she whispered in a voice she didn't even recognize as hers.

"I have to tell you something too." He glanced at her. Always the gentleman, he said, "You go first."

She licked her lips. "I am so horny, I think I'm going to explode."

The car jerked as though his foot had spasmed on the accelerator. "I beg your pardon?"

She felt smug and female. "You heard me." Of course, two therapists couldn't even get horny without some sort of analysis, so she said, "I think it's all the emotion racing around in my body. It needs an outlet." Just talking about her needs made them more immediate. She shifted her body, feeling the heavy pull of desire.

"What do you want me to do about this little problem?" He might be surprised at her behavior, almost as surprised as she was herself, but he seemed quite happy about her admission.

"I'm not going to be ladylike," she said, easing her legs apart.

"You're not?"

"No."

He slid a hand up her thigh and her skin was so sensitive there, she moaned. When he touched her she actually did moan. Then she pushed herself against his hand in the most obvious display of need she'd ever shown in her life.

"I need to tell you something else," she said.

"What?" his voice was as husky as a growl.

"I won't make it home. You need to pull over somewhere."

"Where? There's nothing around here but a convenience store, a beer parlor, and the No-Tell Motel."

"Perfect," she said.

"Are you kidding?"

"No, the motel. Hurry."

The atmosphere in the car was electric. Her skin was so sensitive, she could feel the leather of the seats against her arms and the back of her legs. She heard the traffic all around them as a low-level hum, like a sexual purr. At this time of day, businesspeople were off to meetings, parents ferried kids around, workers headed off to fix furnaces and install carpets. But inside Jordan's gray Volvo it was all about sex.

He had to take his hand away from her in order to turn the steering wheel and the loss of his hand only emphasized her need.

They turned into a bumpy asphalt parking lot that the motel shared with a convenience store offering great prices on a six pack of Bud.

She thought he might ask her if she was sure about this, but he didn't. "Wait here," he said, and she knew then that he was as desperate as she was. He was in and out of the office in no time, hopped back into the car, and drove them to their unit.

As they walked in she yanked together enough sanity to check that there was a basic level of cleanliness, which, based on the industrial cleanser smell, there was. A quick glance into the bathroom showed shiny white, if chipped, fixtures, and under the polyester flowered spread the sheets were clean.

It was all she needed to know. There was something so thrilling about being in a place like this, a place she'd never normally go to, for sex. Because she and her lover were too hot for each other to make it all the way home.

While she was checking for hygiene, Jordan went to the window and pulled the drapes shut. The clattering sound of the curtains drawing sent a shiver through her. With the drapes shut, the light in the room was muted. He snapped on the light on the closest imitation wood bedside table.

He came up behind her and ran his hand all the way down the front of her body from her neck, over her tingling breasts, her belly, just brushing her crotch so she wanted to moan, and then he was tugging at the skirt of her dress, pulling it up and over her hips. Oh, yes.

He reached around her and yanked the bedspread and top sheet down, so she was looking at the bare white sheet on top of the mattress.

He slipped her panties down and she stepped out of them. She could hear harsh breathing and knew it was hers. So much for restrained behavior.

"Get on the bed on your hands and knees," he said into her ear. He never ordered her around, but he seemed to understand that she wanted something raw and frank. No manners required.

"What about my dress?"

"Leave it." Heat was pulsing through her, pooling as excitement built. He was ordering her around. And she was loving it. Maybe after all these years of fierce control it was good to let the lid off for a while. She'd been like the tectonic plates, holding up the earth from under the sea, but steam was building, building, and one day those plates had to shift and blow. With seismic results.

A step closer to the bed, she said, "Shoes?"

"Leave them."

She climbed up onto the bed, fully dressed but for her panties, facing away from him.

"Now, pull your skirt up. All the way up and flip it over your back. Let me see what you've got for me."

She made a funny noise in the back of her throat. Part cry, part moan. Her hands were shaking as she grasped the hem of her skirt. She found that in order for it to stay up and over her hips, she had to thrust her hips up in the air and lower her front half until she was resting on her forearms.

She heard rustling and the metallic sound of his belt being unfastened. *Oh, hurry,* drummed over and over in her head.

Her most private parts, and only those, were on display for him. She knew he was looking at her there, felt his gaze like a spotlight, warming her, revealing her.

His fingers touched her sex, slippery with excitement, rubbing lightly. "Is this for me?" he asked from behind her.

"Yes." She'd never felt more sexual. Never.

He climbed up behind her and the bed rocked; then he rubbed his cock against her, back and forth until she pushed back against him, begging to be filled. He pushed inside hard, with no warning at all. Jordan, who usually was so careful with foreplay and always asked her if she was ready before penetrating her.

The sudden shock of him filling her was fantastic. "Oh," she cried.

Then taking a firm hold of her hips, he began to thrust into her in a completely fierce, unrestrained rhythm. She caught fire, combusted; pushing back, she met his thrusts with frenzied passion.

Outside she could hear the muted rumble of traffic. A car door slammed in the parking lot. And in this cheap and tawdry room, she heard mingled sighs and moans, and the soft slap of his flesh against hers.

She was climbing, climbing. He reached around and touched that needy, aching place, rubbing lightly. It was too much, and with a loud cry she slipped over the top, pulling him along with her.

He slumped on top of her, still inside her body, and kissed the back of her neck. For the oddest moment she felt emotion prick her eyelids. She knew there was a great deal they had to say, to talk about and resolve, but for once in her life she didn't want to talk about feelings. She wanted to shut up and experience them. She reached for his hand and they stayed like that for a while, deeply connected and at rest.

Her heart was banging, her breath uneven, and she didn't even want to think about what shape her dress was now in. She started to chuckle.

"What's so funny? And please tell me it's not my technique."

She turned her head, found his mouth, and gave him a quick kiss. "Your technique was outstanding. I'm laughing because my headache disappeared."

"Sometimes good sex helps heal a lot of things," he said reflectively, and she suspected he was talking about more than her aching head.

He kissed her fully, taking his time, and her undersexed body roared back to life. This time, he undressed her completely, kissing and toying with every part of her he uncovered. She took off his tie, unbuttoned his shirt and eased it off. He pulled off his socks, and she toed off her sandals so they fell to the floor with twin thuds. He kissed her breasts, teasing her nipples in the way he knew she liked. They played with each other, arousing and reconnecting, until they were once again panting with need. She opened for him and he filled her. When he entered her she thought it was a moment she'd never forget. His eyes were so serious as they stared into hers, his body so familiar and precious to her. They moved slowly, tenderly. "I love you," he said to her.

It had been such a long time since they'd been this intimate, she'd almost forgotten how wonderful it could be. "I love you too," she whispered. Then they started to move, creating heat and friction and, finally, a shared cry.

Afterward, they lay wrapped around each other with her head on his chest so she could hear the thud of his heart. "I've missed this," she said.

"I've missed you."

And so, in that cheesy motel with the noise of the highway in their ears and the faint smell of disinfectant in the air, they finally talked about things she realized they should have been talking about months ago.

"We're like the cobbler's children who have no shoes," she said with a chuckle when she realized how badly they had grown apart. "I'm so glad we're back on track."

He rolled off her and padded to the bathroom. She smiled

realizing he was still wearing his socks. How had she let herself get so distracted that she didn't give her own relationship the time and attention it deserved?

She jumped out of bed feeling energized.

"You know what I can't figure out?"

"What?" he said from the bathroom.

"I can't figure out why that woman who calls herself the breakup artist sent somebody to me. I thought at first she was some awful person who got off on destroying people's lives, but she actually seemed pretty decent when we got to talking."

There was silence from inside the bathroom. Jordan came out and she took her turn. When she emerged, thinking another round was in order, she found him fully dressed, sitting on the bed. He looked funny. Confused. Guilty. Without realizing she did it, she put a hand to her heart. "Jordan? What is it?"

"There's something I have to tell you."

"Okay." She went to sit beside him on the bed. For some reason, she felt she needed to get dressed, probably since he was. She dragged her clothes back on and then settled beside him.

"This isn't easy." He was looking down at his clasped hands.

"Okay," she said. Remaining quiet until he was ready, trying not to let her heart rate get out of control, she touched him gently on the arm.

She waited. Usually he was so verbal, so well-expressed, that to see him like this, tongue-tied and unsure where to begin, gave her a very bad feeling in her belly.

When she couldn't stand the silence another second, she cried, "Jordan, please. You're scaring me."

He let out a great sigh. "I hired Chloe Flynt to break up our relationship."

She'd been trained. For twelve years she'd studied human behavior patterns, interactive communication, and therapy of all sorts. There were a variety of models she could call from in her response. What she did was in no behavior model, textbook, or counselor's manual. It came right out of her childhood. She screamed, "You did what?"

"I'm sorry. I realize what I did was wrong—"

"But I don't understand. Why would you go to her?"

"I didn't want to hurt you. I didn't want to upset our working relationship."

She waved her hand as though batting away a fly. "No, not that. I mean, why did you want to break up?"

Silence.

"Jordan, we're therapists. Counseling people through rough patches in their relationships is what we do."

He looked down at his hands, and suddenly the obvious slapped her. "Oh, God. No. There's someone else?"

"I'm so sorry," he said.

She fell back against the hideous polyester bedspread. She stared up at the ceiling. There was a squished mosquito in the center like a tiny Rorschach test. "I'm a cliché. A joke. I wrote a book about perfect communication, perfect love, and meanwhile my supposedly perfect partner screws around behind my back."

"I didn't, in point of fact, screw her," he said in his scholarly way. "But I admit I was drawn to another woman. Seriously attracted."

"Who? Who is she?"

"An artist. A grad student at the university."

"One of your students?" He taught a class in the psych department. She wasn't the only cliché around here. Next to fancying themselves in love with their therapists, young women seemed to love falling for their teachers.

"No, I met her at a faculty function. One you were too busy to attend." She didn't miss the hint of bitterness behind his words. She wanted to hit him.

"Don't you dare try to pin that on me. You sniveling coward. Couldn't you have come to me? Talked to me? You hired a perfect stranger to break up with me?" She leapt to her feet. "I can't believe I just had sex with you."

"I'm sorry," he said. "I'll drive you home."

She wanted to snap at him and tell him to go. Just go. But she didn't think she had the energy left even to call a cab to this nasty motel.

They didn't speak at all on the way back to her house. Jordan tried a couple of times, but she shushed him. She was too angry to utter a word she wouldn't regret. Besides, she was obsessed with the fact that her entire life's work was a failure. A joke.

She was a joke.

Chapter 21

Stephanie threw her purse to the floor of her office in Chloe's house. Chloe was out and she had the place to herself, so she opened the metal filing cabinet and slammed the door shut. The noise was satisfyingly violent. Then because that had felt so good, she opened the drawer and slammed it again.

"My, someone's in a temper," that cool English voice said.

Stephanie jumped. "Oh, sorry. I thought you were out."

A flicker of amusement crossed that aristocratic face. "Is that what you do when I'm out? Slam the filing drawers? I shall have to stay home in the future."

"Not usually. But then I don't usually want to kill someone."

She nodded. "Rafe. He looked pretty grim when he arrived."

"That arrogant, moronic . . ." Beneath her anger little prickles of humiliation started to poke through. Was that all it was for him? The need to be a hero? To rescue the damsel in distress? Frankly, she was getting sick of being that damsel.

"Can I ask you something?"

"Of course."

"Do you think people can ever really change?"

"Darling girl, people change every day. Look at you. Two months ago you were working at that dreary job at the bank and engaged to that awful prig. Now you've got a fabulous job, with the best boss this side of London, and you are deciding what you want in life." Chloe smiled at her.

"Rafe says he needs to stay away from me because wounded doves are his weakness and he's determined to break that bad pattern."

Chloe's eyes got that very deep twinkly look they took on when she was thinking deeply. "Maybe he already has broken his pattern."

"What do you mean?"

"You're strong, you're vibrant, you've learned your own worth. Perhaps you frighten him."

"He said—"

"Oh, I know what he said. Darling, if men knew themselves the world would be a far simpler place. Though far less interesting, don't you think?"

She turned to walk out when Stephanie stopped her. "Wait. Did Deborah Beaumont come here?"

"Yes, she stopped by."

Stephanie took a big breath. "I see her. Professionally. That's why I need a longer lunch hour every two weeks. I should have told you, but—"

"No reason at all to tell me. It's your private business."

"I didn't know Rafe was going there."

"Well, I suppose you wouldn't. The name on the file is Jordan Errington."

"Jordan? That's Deborah's partner."

Chloe nodded, looked at her expectantly, and suddenly she put it all together. "Oh, my God. The woman who was supposed to fall for Rafe was Deborah? My Deborah?"

"Sorry. I had no idea you were a client of hers. Obviously."

Stephanie waved the words away, concentrating. "Deborah said Rafe asked her out."

"She told me that too. And Rafe admitted it."

"But—why did you tell him to ask her out? After only a couple of weeks? It doesn't make sense."

"I didn't suggest anything of the kind. I think Rafe is trying to make sense of a few things in his life right now, don't
you? If I had to guess—and why not—it's a free country—I'd
say he asked her out hoping she'd say no, so he could give up
the sessions and yet still feel he'd fulfilled his commitment to
me."

"But—"

"Is Deborah any good?"

"As a therapist? Yeah, she's great. I mean, if you'd seen me
when she first starting working with me, believe me, you
wouldn't have offered me a job. I was a mess." She made a
wry face. "A worse mess than I am now."

Chloe nodded. "I was so certain she'd be rubbish. I suspect
I gave Rafe that impression too. I wonder if she's got Rafael
facing his demons whether he wants to or not."

"All I know is, he says he can't see me anymore because he
doesn't do wounded doves anymore." She grit her teeth and
gripped her hands together.

Chloe looked at her for a moment, her purple-blue eyes
full of understanding, and said, "Stephanie, you have my full
permission to slam all the file drawers. Go around and break
some things, too, if it makes you feel better."

Then she walked with her model's walk out of the room.
Stephanie gave her time to get all the way out before opening
the file drawers one at a time and slamming them until it
sounded like her office was throwing a temper tantrum.

Rafe pulled into Deborah's driveway. She lived in a brick
townhouse in a nice area of town near the university. Lots of
trees and decent older homes. Hers wasn't grand, but it was
solid.

There were lights on inside. He knocked at the front door.
Stood there for a bit. The porch light went on and then
Deborah opened the door.

He had a moment of shock when he wondered if he'd mis-
read the address. He'd seen messed-up street women who

looked better than the woman at the door. Her dress was all crumpled, her hair was all over the place, and her eyes were red from crying. All that crying had left her skin all blotchy and none of her makeup was where she'd originally intended it. Her mascara had run and the stuff on her eyelids had seeped to her temples, her lipstick was nothing but a blurry line around the outside of her mouth, and her skin looked chapped and raw.

"I thought you were the 'Chinese,' " she said on a sniffle.

"No, I'm the Mexican."

It wasn't much of a joke and she didn't give him much of a smile, and what she did manage was pretty pathetic. "I meant Chinese food. I had a craving."

"I brought your car back." She was carrying a damp tissue in her hand, which he saw when she held out her palm for the keys. "Thanks."

"Are you okay?" he asked automatically. Stupid question, obviously.

"No, I am spectacularly not okay, as you can see." She sounded like she had a heavy cold. "Also, I am single, which makes me perfect for you. A wounded dove." She sniffed. "Ask me out now, why don't you? You're no longer my client and I'm no longer attached."

He caught the pain behind the bitterness of the words. "Deborah, I'm sorry about that. Chloe never asked me to ask you out. That was my idea."

She waved a hand grandly in the air. "All has been explained. I now know that my esteemed partner in business, life, and publishing was too much of a chickenshit to tell me he wanted out of our relationship, so he hired some English runway model to do it for him."

"Stupid prick."

"Thank you. My thoughts exactly." She sniffled and then looked behind him. "You're all alone. Do you need me to drive you back to your car?"

"No, I can call a buddy."

They stood there looking at each other. He got the feeling she didn't want to be alone.

Oddly enough, neither did he.

"Would you like to come in?"

He nodded briefly and she led him through to a kind of den area beside a small but superefficient-looking kitchen. Her house was smart somehow. As if all the highfalutin thoughts of its owner had seeped into the walls. The den was covered in bookshelves, and all the neatly ordered books seemed too heavy to interest him. Even the artwork on the walls was complex. She liked abstracts, so nothing was what it appeared to be. Like life itself, he supposed.

"Would you like something to drink?"

"No, I'm good."

He sat in a burgundy leather chair and she sat across from him, curling her legs under her and cradling a box of tissues the way another woman might hold a cat.

"I feel like such a fraud," she said, yanking a fresh tissue out of the box. "I am truly sorry for all my patients." She blew her nose. "Even you, and you were a fake patient."

"Deborah, you're not a fraud."

"I am. My own partner couldn't even talk to me. He hired a stranger to break up with me. How do you think that makes me feel?"

"Like shit, I'm guessing."

She laughed, a watery chuckle. "You guessed correctly." She glanced around the room as though the books might be judging her and finding her wanting.

"You're the shrink, not me, but don't you think maybe he's the one with the problem?"

She gestured dramatically, which caused her to drop the crumpled tissue so it bounced down her crumpled dress like a cherry blossom in the rain. "I'm canceling the television appearance, of course. I couldn't bear to share my expertise with people when all my life's work turns out to be a pack of lies." She hiccupped on a sob.

It was oddly comforting to see this normally together woman falling apart. It made her more human, and he was able to see her in a new light. "I don't like admitting it, but you helped me. That's why I had to push things, ask you out knowing you'd turn me down, so I could get out of there. But you made me face up to my problem. And that's good."

Her smile was wobbly, but she gave it her best shot. "Thank you, Rafe. That is very kind."

"And you don't believe a word of it."

"Not a syllable."

The doorbell chimed. She sniffled. "That must be the Chinese food."

He rose, knowing she would hate even a delivery guy to see her like this. "I'll get it."

"Thank you."

He dug out his wallet and opened the door. But it wasn't fast food. It was Deborah's former lover and partner standing there. They stared at each other for a second, each obviously as flummoxed as the other. Jordan's scholarly face hardened and his pale blue eyes narrowed. "What are you doing here?"

Rafe didn't like the fact that this weasel had hurt Deborah, who was a nice woman doing her best. He showed the wallet in his hands. "Getting the Chinese food."

"Deborah's in no condition to be entertaining—"

"Maybe you should leave that to her." He felt the hostility coming off the mild-mannered therapist on the doorstep and did nothing to quell it. In fact, he moved his body subtly to block more of the doorway.

He saw Jordan's face take on an enraged bull expression completely at odds with his mild-mannered exterior; then as suddenly as it appeared it was gone, and he saw gut-deep sadness. Only then did he hear the shuffling sounds behind him that indicated Deborah had come out to see what was going on.

There were a lot of things that Jordan could have said at

that moment, at least half of which would have gotten him forcibly ejected from Deborah's property, a task Rafe was more than willing to perform. What he said was, "Please."

He was looking over Rafe's shoulder. A sob, cut off in the middle so it sounded more like a snort, was his answer. He took a step closer. But Rafe wasn't making this easy. He didn't move. "Deborah, I've been such an ass. I'm sorry. I love you."

"I don't know what to do," she wailed.

"I do. Come out with me. Now."

"Out? Where?"

"I don't know. Out. We're going to stop living in our ivory tower, you and me. We're going to experience life. I'm taking you dancing, and we're going to eat Ethiopian food."

"Ethiopian food?" Rafe and Deborah echoed simultaneously.

Jordan shrugged impatiently. "I don't know. Some kind of food we've never tried. Deb, we've got to get out more and live like real people, that's all I'm saying."

Rafe turned and found Deborah looked amazingly transformed. Under the mess of makeup and blotches, she was glowing. "Okay." She touched her cheeks. "I need to fix my face." She glanced down at herself. "And change my clothes."

"I'll give you five minutes," Jordan called.

She giggled.

The two men stood there. Jordan obviously thought he'd wrestled the prize away from Rafe, and Rafe was happy to let him. Deborah was a great woman. She was worth fighting for.

Like another woman he knew.

"So," Jordan said, "do you know any good places to go dancing?"

He chuckled, pulled out his notebook, and started scrawling down a list of places. If these two wanted to experience life, there were a lot of possibilities.

When she came downstairs a few minutes later, she was

wearing jeans, high heels, and a soft, sexy shirt he bet she'd never worn before. Her makeup was fresh and her hair down. She looked hotter than any psychologist Rafe had ever seen.

Jordan obviously thought so too. He tucked the list of places in his wallet and the three left together.

Deb and Jordan headed for the latter's Volvo and Jordan opened the passenger door, but before Deb could get in he took her in his arms and planted on her a good one. They were wound around each other, their bodies pressed against the car. Yeah, Rafe thought, those two would be okay.

He waited until they'd driven off and then pulled out his cell to call a cab. Before he'd got the thing open, the delivery guy pulled in.

Rafe took the bag, which smelled amazingly good and reminded him that he was hungry. He paid the guy, added a generous tip, and said, "Any chance you could give me a lift?"

"We're not supposed to."

"I'm a cop," he said, pulling out his badge. "And I'll give you fifty bucks."

The kid couldn't have been more than seventeen and looked like he ate way too much of the merchandise. "Is it an emergency?"

"Oh, yeah."

He gave the address and they sped on their way, as fast as a 1986 Jetta could speed.

They pulled up in front of Stephanie's apartment and he took the food and paid the kid with a curt, "Thanks, man."

"Yeah, take it easy."

He didn't want to take it easy. He wanted to race to her. He buzzed her apartment, but there was no answer. She wasn't home from work yet. So he sat down on the concrete outside the front door and waited.

After a while he got bored, so he pulled out a fortune cookie and cracked it open.

People were coming home from work, but they were the

wrong ones. A few glanced his way, most ignored him. Then he saw her. She was wearing the same dress she'd worn earlier. It was blue and showed off her legs and the espadrille sandals she wore.

She did not look delighted to see him.

He scrambled to his feet with the brown bag of food.

"What do you want, Rafe?" she asked softly.

"I've had some good news. I'm going to come into a lot of money," he said, showing her the fortune he'd pulled out of the cookie. She didn't even crack a smile. She turned to unlock the outside door to the building.

"I don't need rescuing, Rafe."

"No, you don't." He reached out and touched her hair. "I do."

Chapter 22

She didn't know what to do. He was standing there, telling her he needed her, and she didn't know whether to let him in or lock him out.

He obviously felt her indecision, for he said, "I've been thinking crazy, acting crazy ever since I met you. I want to be with you."

She glanced at the bag. "Most men would have brought flowers." But there was a tiny little smile playing at the corners of her mouth if he cared to look.

He looked. In fact, he seemed mesmerized by her mouth. He pulled her to him slowly, kissing her, pulling her closer while need and want made her crazy. The bag emitted a crunching sound between them and she laughed, opening the door so they could both enter.

They sprinted up the stairs and she noticed he was a lot more fit than she was; then he took the keys from her and ran ahead to open her apartment door as though every second mattered.

Later she knew they had stuff to talk about, but right now his urgency fired hers, and as she ran through the door he held open, she dragged him with her.

"The food," he said, pausing to place the bag on her kitchen counter.

"I like it cold." Then she pulled him into her bedroom.

"You have beautiful hair," he said, pushing his hands into it.

"So do you," she replied, holding fistfuls as she pulled his mouth back to hers.

While his tongue was playing in her mouth, he found the tie to her dress and unfastened it, then pushed the fabric off her shoulders. Her breasts strained to be free of the lacy bra, but he played his fingers over the lace, teasing her a little.

This was so exciting, so unexpected, that she felt her desire building fast and furiously.

She'd thought about him so often, of all the things she'd wanted to do, to say, and now she was getting her chance.

She pulled his shirt over his head, removed his bad-boy biker boots that gave her a thrill just to put her hands on them, dragged his jeans and shorts down his legs and then his socks, so he was wearing nothing but a dangerously hot expression and a gold medallion.

She pushed him back onto the bed and with a grin, he fell onto the fluffy blue duvet. She climbed on top of him and began teasing him, running her lips down his hot skin, until she reached his cock. When she took him into her mouth he groaned and muttered something in Spanish that sounded like he was a very happy man.

She played with him, letting him know exactly who was in charge, and he seemed happy to let her take over, only going so far as to unhook her bra and remove it so he could toy with her breasts.

When she felt he'd built up a good head of steam, she slipped off her panties and, reaching for her night table, pulled a condom out of the drawer. She took care of putting it on and she knew from his groan that she'd brought him closer to the edge than either of them wanted. But he was satisfyingly hot and hard when she climbed on top of him and took him inside her body.

And when she started to move on him she found that she

was a lot closer to the edge than she'd realized. His eyes mesmerized her as they darkened to black as his passion built. Her own heat was crazy, as were her movements. She was following some primal rhythm that was like a crazy drumbeat they both heard. His hands were on her breasts, her hips, restlessly playing with her hair, and the gold medallion was tossing around on his heaving chest.

She grabbed his hands, wanted more connection, she supposed, and stretched out so his arms reached out behind him and she was low enough to kiss him, to let her breasts dance against his chest. She felt like they were linked everywhere and the final intimacy sent her over the edge, flying. He swallowed her cries into his mouth, just as she swallowed his.

It was close to morning before they got around to eating the Chinese food. She padded to the kitchen and brought the bag, paper towels, and a bottle of sparkling water back with her.

Rafe was sitting against the bunched pillows, grinning at her when she returned. "Nothing I like better than breakfast in bed."

"Are you sure you took down this name correctly?" Chloe asked, walking into Stephanie's office.

The younger woman took back the pink message slip and studied it. Stephanie was so revoltingly blissed out that Chloe almost missed the banging-of-the-file-drawers mood. "Brittany Somers. Yeah, that's the name she gave."

Chloe took back that little paper; then she began to laugh.

"What's so funny?"

"Can you keep a secret?"

"Shouldn't you have asked me that during our job interview?"

Stephanie had a sly sense of humor that was coming out the longer she worked with Chloe and was so obviously appreciated. "Good point. All right, I'll take that as a yes."

Besides, Chloe was dying to share this delightful bit of news with someone who would enjoy it. As much as she loved Nicky, her Londoner friend wouldn't appreciate the irony.

"Brittany is Matthew's girlfriend."

Stephanie's reaction was everything she'd imagined it would be. Her jaw dropped and her eyes bugged wide. "Matthew next door?"

"Yep."

"Oh, my God. What are you going to do?"

Chloe folded the paper into a perfect pink square and ran her fingers absently along the fold. "I don't quite know. This requires delicacy, tact, or does it?"

A shoulder shrug was the only response from her assistant. Unfortunately, the shrug revealed a full-on hickey that only reminded Chloe that Stephanie was getting earth-shattering sex and that she hadn't seen any in far too long.

"Tell you what. Phone Brittany back. Tell her that someone will meet her at—pick a coffee shop somewhere central, will you? Book a time. Don't tell her my name; simply get her to give you her description and tell her someone will meet her at the given time."

"Will do."

Chloe all but waltzed back into her office. Well, well, well. She'd been wrong; Matthew's reinjuring himself didn't seem to have rekindled that romance, after all. She wondered why.

She was woman enough to enjoy the frisson of excitement that danced through her body at the thought of Matthew finding himself single one day soon. She couldn't have designed a better outcome. Now she wouldn't need to worry about Brittany getting hurt.

The next day at four p.m. precisely, she walked into the coffee shop Stephanie had suggested. It was a charming place full of Italian pottery and a real barista machine gurgling and steaming. The "Three Tenors" were playing on the sound system. "Hi y'all," the young girl at the counter said. "Just sit anywheres." Chloe smiled at her. This was Tuscany, Texan style.

A quick survey of the place showed that Brittany was already here. She was seated at a table in the far corner of the room. Presumably, she'd already spotted Chloe since she had her head down and pretended to search for something in her bag.

Chloe ordered two lattes and then strolled over to Brittany and said hello.

Brittany's head jerked up. She was flushed, and she greeted Chloe with a flustered welcome: "Oh my gosh! Chloe. What are you doing here?" Her gaze flashed to the door.

Deciding to put the poor woman out of her misery, Chloe said, "I'm meeting you."

"But that's—"

Chloe took the phone message and passed it over. Brittany read it but didn't seem able to say anything. Her color deepened and she scratched at her neck as though she were developing hives.

Fortunately, the coffees arrived at that moment. In the time it took for the Texan barista to set the cups down and make sprightly chitchat about the weather, Brittany pulled herself together.

When the server was out of earshot she leaned forward. "You are The Breakup Artist?"

There was a note of awe as well as shock in the tone and Chloe enjoyed a moment of pride. "Yes, I am."

"Oh, this is terrible," she said dropping her head in her hands, so blond curls spilled over.

"Why is it so terrible?"

"Because Matthew's your friend, and I feel like a horrible person. Now you'll always know that I was so desperate to get out of the relationship that I hired someone to make it happen."

She smiled gently. "If it makes you feel any better, I don't think you two are at all suited."

"You don't?" Brittany looked genuinely surprised. "But everyone says we're perfect for each other."

"Well, in my expert opinion, everyone is wrong."

"I tried so hard."

"I know." It was obvious Brittany needed to unburden herself, and Chloe was perfectly willing to let her. "Did something happen?"

"It was the dish cloths," she said miserably.

"Dish cloths? You mean those things one uses to wash the dishes?" Chloe barely gave them a thought and couldn't imagine breaking her heart over anything so mundane.

"Yeah, Matt threw them out the window."

"Them? How many did he throw?"

"All six of 'em."

"That sounds perfectly deranged. Why would he throw six dish cloths out of a window?"

"Because they had ducks on them. He said there was no way he was going to wash dishes with a damn fowl."

In her fairly short tenure as a matchbreaker, Chloe had heard stories of theft, adultery, jealousy, meanness, and stupidity, but this was the first relationship she could think of that had hit the skids over a humble dish cloth. "I'm so sorry."

"So was I," Brittany exclaimed. "I mean, I didn't want to bring in dish cloths he didn't like. So I told him I was sorry."

She should have bought half a dozen doormats, is what Chloe thought, so she'd have some company. "You apologized?" Chloe asked. "Matt was totally unreasonable. He was the one who destroyed a gift you'd given him. He was the one who should have apologized."

Brittany's eyes narrowed. "Has Matthew already told you about this?"

"About the flying ducks? Of course not."

"Well, that is just plain weird, because that's almost exactly what he said. I think he ended up madder at me for saying I was sorry than he was for buying the wrong dish cloths."

She understood exactly how he felt. "What happened then?"

"I went home. And then you know what I did?"

"I'm guessing you baked carrot cake."

Brittany looked as though Chloe had performed a complicated magic trick. "I thought about carrot cake, but I was out of cream cheese for the icing. So I made blueberry muffins instead. It's like you can read minds or something." She sipped her coffee. "I put them in a basket and was all ready to drive them over to Matthew's the next morning so we could have a talk. But you know what I did?"

"Picked strawberries so you could make jam?"

The earnest blond curls trembled as she shook her head. "I ate three muffins. All by myself. I drank my coffee and I ate those muffins. I thought, *Matthew Tanner, you do not deserve my home baking. And you do not deserve me.* And then I wrapped up the rest of them and took them to school. I gave them to my students."

"Good for you." Backbone, she thought, sometimes had to be built slowly. One muffin at a time.

"The thing is, Matthew's a good man. I don't want to hurt him, not while his leg's still sore. I want you to break up for me. Your secretary told me your rates and I've got a check all made out." She reached down for her bag and Chloe stopped her with a hand on her wrist.

"Brittany, you need to end things with Matthew yourself."

"But I don't want to hurt him."

"People always get hurt. In my experience," Chloe smiled ruefully, "and I've got a lot. The pain is lessened when you have a frank talk."

"I wouldn't know what to say. And if he begs me not to leave him, you know I won't have the guts to resist."

"Darling, a man who throws your ducky dish cloths out the window is not a man happy in love."

"You mean he . . . ?"

"I'm not in his confidence, obviously, but it doesn't take a genius to guess that both of you are having cold feet."

"But why hasn't he said anything to me?"

"Perhaps because he doesn't want to hurt you any more than you want to hurt him."

"Oh, this is just such an awful mess." She stared down at the table for a long moment. Chloe sipped her latte, which was excellent (she'd have to buy some beans while she was here), and waited.

After a while, her companion shook her head. "I can't do it. I know I'm pathetic, but I can't do it. Please, you've got to help me."

"Well, here are my top favorite breakup techniques for someone you don't want to hurt," she said brusquely. "First, you invite Matthew out for a meal and I am the one who meets him and tells him you no longer want to see him."

The other woman's lip curled. "People hire you to do that?"

"You'd be surprised how many. It's time efficient and they salve their consciences knowing I provide a whole day's support to the former love. Ice cream, strip clubs, crying jags, whatever they want or need, I provide."

"Well, I am not interested in that option."

"I also have more creative packages. For instance, the fake relative dinner, where you take him home to meet your family. I then hire actors. You can have the Hillbilly Special, the Mental Deficiency Runs in the Family, The Crooks R Us, and one of my favorites, what I call the Hit Family, where everyone in the family separately hits up your date for a loan."

"That's terrible."

Chloe shrugged. "You could start acting strange, leave incriminating evidence that you're having an affair, you can tell him you've joined a cult, that you've decided to become a nun. The options are limited only by your imagination and budget."

"I'm not that cruel."

"I also do custom-made breakups. Why don't you tell me how you want it done."

A beat passed. Two women at the next table were discussing

riding lessons for their daughters. The barista machine hissed at regular intervals, indicating the place was getting busier. "I don't know. I thought there'd be an easy way and I wouldn't have to get involved."

"That's not what you really want. He's a decent man. He deserves honesty."

"What would you do in my place?"

"Tie the dish cloths together and strangle him with them, but that's me."

A gurgle of laughter shook her companion. "Matthew should be with someone like you. Someone as crazy as he is." She realized what she'd said and her eyes widened. "Not that I'm saying you're crazy."

"Don't give it a thought. I know exactly what you mean. I do have a suggestion. Why don't I help you write a letter?" She'd purposely gone through all the approaches she knew Brittany would never take so that this simple, straightforward method would hold appeal.

"You mean like a Dear John letter?"

"Exactly."

"And I mail it to him?"

"You could. I prefer the idea of dropping it off in person. I could have my secretary do it, or you could do it yourself."

Brittany seemed to like the letter idea. "I could bake him something nice and put that in a basket with the letter, so he'd have something pleasant to remember me by."

"I think that's an excellent idea."

"Okay," she nodded. "Okay. Let's write him a letter."

Chloe pulled out a notepad.

"You mean here? Now?"

"Why not?"

"I don't know. It seems like I should give it a lot of thought."

"Trust me, the longer you agonize over these things, the more difficult they become. You do truly want to break up with Matthew, don't you?"

She bit her lip, and nodded.

"All right. Let's get started."

"Can you write it? I'll copy it out neatly when we're done."

"If you prefer."

Brittany thought for a while and Chloe waited patiently, her gold fountain pen, which Daddy had sent her to celebrate her first month in business, poised. "Dear Matthew," Brittany said at last.

Chloe obediently wrote that down.

"I've been thinking a lot about this, and I can't go on." She stopped. "Oh, shoot. That sounds so dramatic. I don't want him to think I'm about ready to kill myself. Scratch that out."

Chloe did.

"Where are we?"

"Dear Matthew."

"Right. Dear Matthew, I am so sorry, but I don't think I can see you anymore."

"Excellent beginning," Chloe said, writing it.

"I don't know what to put next."

"What about, 'You're a wonderful man, but not the right man for me. I hope we can always be friends.'"

"Okay. I like that. It's good. Then what?"

"Sincerely, Brittany."

"But that's so short. You don't think I should put anything about the duck dish cloths in there?"

"Emphatically, no. This is simple, clear, and to the point. Matthew seems like a man who would appreciate few words in a letter like this."

"I guess you're right. But what if he writes back?"

"One step at a time."

"Okay. Thanks. You're a good friend."

Chloe passed over the pad of paper and the pen. Brittany copied the letter, dated and signed it, and then addressed the envelope Chloe also had with her.

"Did you know I was going to write a letter?"

"No, not really. I've learned to carry a few supplies. Saves time and trouble."

"I feel so bad about Matthew. I want him to be happy. Do you maybe know anyone who would be good for him?"

"I don't make matches, I'm afraid. Only break them."

"Isn't that kind of negative?"

"Not at all. I think it's much better to end something cleanly than let it drag on until the misery compounds."

She nodded, looking like a weight had been lifted. "You know, I think you're right. It's funny, but we met not too long after he was wounded, and I thought he was so brave and strong about all of that. Getting hurt and leaving the force?" White teeth gnawed a full and pretty lower lip. "This time, it was like he didn't want me helping him. And I didn't really care for the way he treated me."

She pulled out the check and tried to give it to Chloe, who shook her head again. "I like you, Brittany, and I like Matthew too. I honestly think this is the right thing for both of you." She smiled. "Be happy."

Brittany lifted that letter like it was the blade of a guillotine, but she nodded.

They hugged and Brittany headed out the door, her Dear Matthew letter clutched in her hand, while Chloe went to purchase some of the lovely Italian coffee beans. "In fact," she said, "give me two pounds. I am celebrating."

Chapter 23

Matthew sat at his dining table looking over the plans for a house. It was a renovation project a buddy had asked him to do. He'd never considered doing anybody's renovations but his own, but he had to admit, there was something satisfying about the idea of fixing up this god-awful mess of a rabbit warren and turning it back into the decent home it had once been.

His bad leg was propped on a chair, but he was off the painkillers and pretty much back to normal, or as normal as his leg would ever be.

When the doorbell rang, he got up from the dining table, frowning.

He opened the door and was surprised to see Brittany. After the way he'd treated her the other night he'd imagined she'd stay away from him until he'd done some groveling. The fact that she was here on his doorstep with one of her baskets of home-made baking and her color heightened made him feel like the biggest asshole on the planet.

He opened his mouth to apologize to her, knowing he owed her that much, when she stopped him cold. She lifted a letter out of the basket and pushed it at him. "Here," she said breathlessly, "read this."

He took it from her, his gaze narrowing on hers without

him even realizing he was doing it. She looked both guilty and resolute. "Come in."

"No, I can't." She turned away. "I'm so sorry."

She was halfway off the porch when she realized she was still carrying her Little Red Riding Hood basket. She dropped it and kept going.

He ripped open the letter and scanned the single sheet.

He felt like a death row prisoner who'd just had his sentence commuted. He read the thing again to be sure he understood the implication.

Brittany was at her car by this time, fumbling to unlock it. Only Brittany would lock her car when she was walking from the driveway to the front door to drop off a letter.

"Hey," he said. "Are you dumping me?"

She was so startled she dropped her keys. She picked them up and then nodded, her head turned away from him. "I'm so sorry," she said again.

He walked off the porch, hopping down the steps because his knee still wasn't perfect. When he got to her he put an arm around her and gave her a hug. "You know what? I am proud of you."

"Proud?" She looked at him like she might be ready to check his forehead for a raging fever.

"You finally stood up for yourself."

"You're not upset?"

Okay, play it cool, he said to himself. Jumping up and down for joy would be a bad idea, even though it's what he wanted to do. "I'm sad it didn't work out, Brit. But I am happy you had the guts to end this."

"Oh, thank goodness."

"Look, there's a whole batch of baking sitting on that porch, why don't you come inside and I'll make some coffee." He sent her a grin. "As friends."

She smiled back at him.

Over coffee, they talked about all the things they hadn't

been able to and he thought it had ended better than either of them could have imagined.

As she was leaving, he spied the letter on the hall table where he'd dropped it, and said, "Can I tell you something?"

"Sure."

"That letter impressed me. It's short, to the point, and"— he picked up the stationery and showed it to her, grinning— "there aren't any damn ducks on it."

She laughed. "Truth is, Chloe helped me write it."

His good mood dimmed faster than a flaming torch in high winds. "Chloe? You mean Chloe from next door?"

"Yes." Then she stood there biting her lip. "Oh, maybe I'm not supposed to tell you that. She didn't say anything about it being a secret."

Matthew had a bad idea he knew where this was going, and as relieved as he was about the outcome, he did not want to think that interfering princess next door had anything to do with it. She might rule Britannia, but she did not rule him.

"Why did you ask Chloe to help you? Isn't there an English teacher at your school who could have done it?" Someone who didn't annoy him and inspire him with lust in equal measures.

"Oh, Matthew, I tried to hire her."

"You tried to hire her?"

"Yes, only I didn't know it was her. I saw this flyer at my hairdresser's. The Breakup Artist. I probably wouldn't have called, but my hairdresser has a couple of clients who've used the service and they said it was great."

"Let me get this straight. You tried to hire Chloe to break up with me?"

"I didn't know how you'd take it. I didn't want you to get hurt. And I didn't know it was Chloe until I'd made the appointment."

"She must have laughed herself into a coma."

"She didn't. She wouldn't take my money, and she told me I should come and talk to you myself."

"Why didn't you?"

"I'm not great at hurting people's feelings. But she told me if I couldn't tell you myself, then I should write to you and bring you the letter. It was my idea to bring the coffee cake."

He figured that what was done was done. No point in busting Brittany's chops over something that couldn't be fixed. "It's a good cake. Thanks."

"You won't get mad at Chloe, will you?"

"Someday I will wring that woman's neck. But it won't have anything to do with you."

"You know what's weird? She talked about wringing your neck too. You two sure have some violent fantasies about each other."

"Just being neighborly."

Chapter 24

"I've been invited to the neighborhood potluck for the Fourth of July!" Chloe announced to Matthew when she went over with her monthly rent check. "I see you've got one too." She saw the identical colorful computer printout that had been slipped through her mail slot, sitting on his hall table. "What a lovely idea."

He took her envelope and tossed it on top of the printout. "You know, we're celebrating our independence from you people."

The knowledge that he was now single should have made her less attracted to him, since available men tended to bore her, but oddly enough, she was even more attracted to him now than she had been before. Especially since he showed no signs of hoping to make their relationship any warmer.

She smiled at him sweetly. "I'm not one to hold a grudge. After two-hundred-odd years, I say let bygones be bygones."

"So you're going?"

"Yes, aren't you?"

He shrugged. "Probably."

"Well, I think it will be great fun." The Carmondys, whom she understood hosted the potluck every year, had one of the grandest houses on the crescent, complete with a swimming pool.

The day of the party dawned as most days in the Texas summer seemed to: sunny, hot, and dry. She wore a red linen sundress with a scoop neck and tiny cloth-covered buttons down the bodice, lace-up white sandals, and her big straw sunhat.

Naturally, she took an appetizer to the potluck. After much mulling, she'd decided on tiny Yorkshire puddings, topped with rare roast beef and a dollop of horseradish. In case anyone missed the Britishness of the offering, she stuck tiny paper Union Jacks on toothpicks in each one. *And take that Matthew we-threw-your-people-out-of-our-country, Tanner,* she thought.

When she arrived, she noticed most of the neighbors were already there and a number of friends and relatives of the Carmondys whom she didn't know.

She loved parties and soon had a group of new friends. Matthew was already there, in his usual jeans and a navy "Don't Mess with Texas" T-shirt. Honestly.

Unable to resist, she retrieved her tray of goodies and started offering them around. When she got to Matthew, who was chatting with Chuck about football, she said, "Would you care for a British appetizer?"

Chuck chortled and grabbed one of the Yorkshire puddings, but Matthew simply looked down at her with everything carnal in his gaze without touching the food, and said, "Yeah, I would."

Chuck's attention was called away by his son looking for help in setting up a pickup baseball game in the backyard. As soon as he was out of earshot, Matthew said, "I'm hungry enough for a whole meal." It should have sounded corny and laughable except that she knew exactly what he meant. The attraction between them was like an appetite, growing more urgent the longer it went unsatisfied.

However, not even her worst enemies had ever accused Chloe of being an easy conquest. She looked up at him through her lashes and said, "It's not dinnertime yet, Matthew."

She turned and walked away.

To her shock and delight he came up behind her and said, "The hell it isn't." He then hefted her tray out of her hands and set it on the closest table.

"What are you—"

He grabbed her hand and pulled her toward the open door to the backyard. "I want to talk to you."

"About what?" They were in the garden and the hot sun beat down on them. "Really, Matthew, I haven't even got my straw hat."

He looked down at her, completely uninterested in the fact that UV rays were even now attacking her pale skin and she was defenseless but for the SPF in her Kiehl's day cream. "It's work related."

If he wanted to take the piss over her private investigation firm, she wasn't in the mood. "Matthew, I am not a private investigator. I own a company called The Breakup Artist."

"I know."

She widened her eyes as the implication sank in. "You knew?"

"Yeah, I didn't leave the force because I was a bad detective."

"Oh." Why had she never considered the possibility that she hadn't been clever at all? That he'd known all along what she was up to?

"I helped break you and Brittany up," she said, feeling for some odd reason that she needed to confess.

"I know."

Annoyance stole through her, curdling her stomach like lemon juice poured into milk. "Why didn't you say anything?"

He rocked back on his heels and appeared to contemplate some fascinating vista over her left shoulder. "I had my reasons."

"To make a fool of me, no doubt," she snapped.

"No." His gaze moved to her face, his eyes sharp and piercing. "I thought you knew."

"Knew what?" She was hot, irritable, and she'd gone to a

great deal of trouble for nothing. Suddenly, the cool, green vistas of England beckoned to her. She could be shopping in Knightsbridge at this very moment; she could be sailing off the Isle of Wight at her friend Bunny's home. She could be in Yorkshire, riding on the moors with Jeremy Kirkbride. "I missed Wimbledon," she said, following her train of thought to its station. "And the Henley Regatta."

"The Henley who?"

"It's not a who, it's a what. A rowing race. I could have worn a smashing hat and drunk Pyms and ginger," she said on a pout.

"I am not following you at all," he said, sounding as hot and irritable as she felt.

"Well, that makes a nice change. You've followed me all over Texas." She turned on her heel and stalked away from him.

She heard him call out her name behind her but ignored him, of course, as one should always ignore a man who calls after one in that particular tone. The air was hot, the grass dry, her dress felt like burlap against her skin.

"And the Chelsea flower show," she muttered to herself, thinking of the verdant lawns and exquisite flowers at the annual gardener's paradise. In point of fact, she'd gone once with her mother and sworn never to go again, but just now the idea of geraniums arranged like the milky way, and clumps of marigolds planted to resemble animals, seemed charming and she was homesick for them all.

Ahead of her a swimming pool sparkled, blue and inviting in the midst of the parched lawns and heavy air.

"Chloe! Would you hold up a minute?"

As though she were a horse. Or a convenience store during a robbery.

"I'm glad you broke us up!" he finally shouted from behind her.

Frankly, it was the last straw on the back of one camel who'd had just about enough of straw. She swung around.

"Why don't you go away and leave me alone?"

"Because I want to talk to you."

He stalked up to her until they were inches apart. His eyes blazed at her, deep, blue, endless. "I am trying to thank you."

"What for?"

"For getting me out of a relationship that wasn't working."

She snorted. It wasn't at all ladylike, and Mummy would have a fit if she heard such a thing coming from her only daughter, but this was Texas. "I shouldn't think any relationship works that has you in it."

Instead of being angry, he seemed amused. He didn't smile exactly, but the skin around his cheekbones lifted, lightening his face. "You think so?"

She felt suddenly breathless. The air was too hot, too heavy— she couldn't seem to get enough of it in her and she was becoming light-headed. "Yes. Yes, I do."

It seemed he'd moved closer, and she had no idea when or how it happened. She took a step back. Wary.

"You and I have a relationship. We seem to get on okay."

"That's because I am an extremely easygoing person," she explained. "You and Brittany weren't at all suited. She was too giving. Too nice for you."

"Uh-huh. So you're saying I need someone who isn't giving or nice?"

She wasn't going to be trapped so easily, so she gave him her snootiest expression. "I do not make matches. My expertise is in breaking unsatisfactory ones."

"So you're just going to leave me like this? Broken up and single?"

"I—" Her head felt like it was full of bees. "I'm sure you'll be—"

Before she could finish the sentence, he pulled her to him and kissed her.

It wasn't a long kiss, but it was a thorough one. She was torn between pulling away and kissing him back when he raised his head and looked down at her, as though to gauge her reaction.

"I don't, I didn't—" She was never at a loss for words. She was always the cool one, the one in control. How had one kiss from a too-tall, too-tough, too-arrogant Texan scrambled her wits? She took a step back. She heard the click of her heels on cement, but it didn't register until she started to wobble.

"Whoa," he said, reaching for her, but it was too late. With a small cry, she toppled backward, endlessly, ridiculously. In slow motion she saw his mouth open but had no idea what he said because she hit the water and the splashing noise drowned out everything else.

The shock of falling into the pool was immediate. Chloe thought about spluttering and gasping and making a wretched mess of her hair, but the water was delicious, the kiss had been delicious, and so she didn't fight the deep, blue pull of the water, but sank until her feet touched bottom. She was minus one Valentino sandal, so she kicked off the other before pushing off with her bare feet and rising smoothly to the surface.

"How's the water?" he asked carefully, clearly wondering what her reaction would be.

She laughed and floated to her back. "Delicious. Why don't you join me?"

"You are about the craziest woman . . ." he began as she closed her eyes against the sun and floated, feeling her dress billow around her like wings. Then she heard a splash and smiled up at the blue, blue sky.

She wasn't a bit surprised when she felt his hands on her, until she realized she was being towed. "What are you doing?"

"I can't float. Not enough body fat."

"Thank you very much," said Chloe, who was floating effortlessly. Even though her eyes were still closed, she knew he was grinning at her. She let herself be pushed through the water; it was wonderful, actually, the slight chill of the pool only emphasizing the sizzle that was going on just under her skin. Mmmm.

They stopped moving and the gentle lap of ripples teased her skin. She felt the way he was strong and still beside her and knew he'd reached shallow enough water that he could stand. Then the brightness of sun behind her eyelids faded and she sensed him coming closer. She waited, eyes closed, lips slightly parted, for his mouth. It came at last, warm, wet, and tasting slightly of chlorine.

He held her so she didn't float away, but she had a wonderful sense of buoyancy, loved the way the water held her up with only the slightest assistance from the man kissing her. He took his time, going slowly. They'd waited forever for each other, all frustrated burn and sizzle, and now that he was kissing her, it felt like they had endless time ahead of them and hurrying would be a crime. Yet, at the same time, she felt the building need within her.

Letting her legs sink to the bottom of the pool, she started to rise, needing to press all of her against all of him, unable to keep waiting.

He was so much taller than she that her toes didn't quite touch bottom, so she twined her arms around his neck when, to her shock, he kicked her legs out from under her and pushed her shoulder so she fell with a squeal, flailing and splashing as the water rose over her head.

She emerged spitting water and fury. "What the hell—"

"Shut up and struggle. People are coming."

Chloe didn't much mind an audience, but in view of the recent breakup and Brittany's feelings, she understood the need for discretion. So she cried "Help!" in what she hoped was a drowning female sort of voice, and tossed about artistically, until Matthew hauled her up against him and headed for the shallowest part of the pool. She imagined how they must look, like Rhett carrying Scarlett up the staircase if they'd both been caught in a rainstorm first. All wet, clinging clothes and dripping hair.

In the name of artistic integrity, she put her arms around Matthew and turned her face into his chest. The nub of his nipple brushed her cheek and, turning her head a little farther, she bit him there, through the wet shirt. He jerked and she smiled against him. That would teach him. Bully.

He was warm and wet and she could feel his heart thudding. Oh, and he was so solid. Her arms were all steely muscle and reassuring strength.

"What happened?" Stella Carmondy called out.

"Chloe? Are you all right?"

She kept her eyes shut and her face tucked against Matthew's chest. How nice that they all cared so much about her, she thought, letting the little drama play out a bit longer.

"She's not saying anything. Is she dead?"

"Of course I'm not dead," she snapped, but her words were muffled by Matthew's bulk.

"Does she need artificial respiration?"

Chloe felt the ripple against her lips as Matthew stifled a chuckle. "I don't know. Give me some space to put her down."

She opened her eyes. The grass was nasty and stubbly and brown. She did not want to lie on it. So she fluttered her lids a few times theatrically and coughed. "I'm all right. Just had a shock, that's all. You can put me down, Matthew. On my feet."

"What happened? How did you end up in the pool?"

"Don't English girls learn how to swim?"

"Of course I can swim. I tripped and fell in and . . ." And what? "And knocked the wind out of myself, that's all."

"It's a good thing Matthew was on hand to save you."

After pushing her head under so she drank half of the very unpleasant-tasting pool water, she glared at him. "Yes, it was."

"I've got all my clothes upstairs, honey. Would you like to change?"

"I think I should get Chloe right home," Matthew said before she could utter a word.

"Yes," she said in a faint voice. "I think that would be best. I've had a bit of a shock."

"Of course you have. But grab something dry first. At least let me lend you a sweatsuit." The notion of wearing a velour jogging suit filled Chloe's designer soul with horror.

"No, please. We'll soon dry off."

"Oh, honey, you're not thinking straight. At least let me get you some towels."

"All right. Thank you."

And within a minute, she was walking down the cul-de-sac, Matthew's arm around her, as she was dabbing her face and hair with a fluffy pink towel.

"Nice party."

"You're walking too quickly."

"In a hurry to get home."

The gaze he sent along with the words had lust shivering through her. She didn't reply, assuming her cat-who-got-the-cream smile would be all the answer he needed.

They arrived at his house first and, grabbing her hand, he hauled her, in a delightfully he-man way, through the back door and into his kitchen. He pushed her body against the fridge, kissing her as he did so, and she felt the heat of him through all their damp clothing.

"What are you doing?" she asked in a lazy, sexy voice, since she knew exactly what he was doing. He was undoing the three buttons that held her bodice closed. He wasn't particularly adept with the small, wet, cloth-covered buttons and his big fingers, but what he lacked in talent he made up for in determination.

She let him wrestle with the buttons, enjoying the feel of him against her, the heat they were generating and the knowledge of what was ahead. He managed one button. With more fevered kissing and some muttered swearing he got the second button open.

He grunted in exasperation and she heard the ping and

rattle as the third hit the floor and rolled. "Very good, you only broke one button."

"Your buttons are too small," he said, kissing her.

"Your hands are too big," she countered, nipping at his lower lip.

One of his big hands plunged beneath the flap of fabric and cupped her breast. She shivered.

He pulled his head back enough to look down at her. "You cold?"

"I've been dragged for miles down a public street while soaking wet, and I am currently pressed against a refrigerator."

His grin was slow and lazy, making her stomach curl. "I asked if you were cold."

One of the things she liked best about him was the way he could see right through her. She smiled back at him. "No," she said, pulling his head back down so she could kiss him again. It was true. She didn't think she'd ever been quite so hot.

As though the one-word answer had flipped a lever, Matthew went into overdrive. His big hands were everywhere, warming her where he touched.

He plunged under her skirt and dragged at her wet panties, which clung to her thighs as though trying to protect her modesty. He fought them and won, of course. She was certain he wasn't a man who gave up when he wanted something badly enough, and he wanted her. Almost as much as she wanted him.

She stepped out of the scrap of limp silk, surprised there wasn't steam coming off their damp clothing. This time when he reached under her skirt, there was nothing in his way. He touched her in that magic spot and suddenly the teasing between them was gone.

"I need to . . . I just need to . . ." he managed.

"Yes," was all she said; then he was pressing against her.

A tiny groan came from his throat. "Just a second. Don't move," he said and raced away, returning in about ten seconds with a handful of condoms.

Good. Even in the heat of passion she liked a man to be prepared.

He attacked his own belt and she stood back and watched, enjoying his frantic haste, feeling the same urge licking at her. Hurry, her body seemed to be saying. Hurry.

He had the belt undone, was unbuttoned, unzipped; then he yanked at his jeans. They stuck. He cursed. He hopped around on his good leg dragging the wet denim down and it had to be the most ungainly thing she'd ever seen.

"That's quite the striptease routine," she said. "You must have been practicing."

"Shut up or help."

She decided to shut up, it was much more interesting watching him cavort around, and the way he twisted and turned showed off the lines of his body. She loved that body.

Cursing, he finally managed to get the damn things down. He'd dragged his briefs down at the same time so she was treated to a sight that stopped her smart mouth in its tracks.

He was big, hard, and gorgeous.

She couldn't take her eyes off him. You'd think she'd never seen a naked man before.

He didn't seem at all put off by her fixed scrutiny. In fact, his lovely cock waved to her in greeting as Matthew came toward her. He hadn't taken off his shirt or she her dress, and it didn't matter. They'd waited so long, it seemed to her dimly, as she felt her skirt being lifted. She didn't want to wait one more second.

Matthew donned the condom much more smoothly than he'd divested himself of his wet jeans; then he was hot on her, his mouth so warm against hers, his tongue no longer teasing her but possessing her mouth. His hand reached for her, touching her where she was almost unbearably hot. She gasped, fearing she'd explode right then and there. But he wasn't the type to take chances, and she wasn't surprised when he explored her gently with his fingers. "You feel so good, so wet."

Her reply was an unintelligible murmur.

She felt him smile against her mouth; then he hoisted her up with such ease that she felt small and dainty. And powerful.

She wrapped her legs around his waist and slid down. He held her, easing her onto him even though, if left to her, she'd have done her usual and rushed into things. Thrown herself onto him. As it was, she felt the wonderful slow stretch as he pressed up and into her.

She felt for a moment that they were sealed together, inseparable. Wet clothing clinging to wet clothing on the top of their bodies, naked and joined below. She felt the muscles of his butt clenching under her pressing heels, felt him stroke inside her, where she was so open and wanting.

"Oh, Matthew, it's so good," she cried, and that seemed to set him off. No more restraint. No more being careful. He pounded into her, and she pounded back. She felt high off the earth, unrestrained and yet held tight. It was marvelous. Erotic. Her back banged against the fridge in a thumping rhythm that was broken when she heard a sound like shattering glass and squealed.

"We hit the ice dispenser," he panted.

Turning them, he set her on the kitchen counter, the lovely posh, dark granite counter. It was cold on her bottom, but she liked the stability and the change of angle.

She leaned back on her hands and closed her eyes. He was thrusting deeper, stroking that wonderful place deep inside her that, like the rest of her, so loved attention. She was climbing higher and higher as she felt him move in faster, more desperate thrusts.

She heard the ice maker presumably replenishing itself, their harsh breathing, and then the scrape of her fingernails on the granite as her hands clenched. As everything clenched, from her throat to her toes, and then the wonderful wave rolled over her. In the background of her own cry, she heard Matthew, felt him shudder against her and then slump forward, so his lips were against her neck, his head resting on her shoulder.

She liked to feel his breath against her neck, panting and then slowing. They didn't say anything. Didn't have to. Then she shivered as the combined cold feelings of sitting on polished rock in wet clothing got through to her.

"Darling," she said, "I'm freezing."

"Hot shower?" he said against her throat.

"Mmm. Keep me company?"

He nipped at the sensitive skin of her throat. "Oh, yeah."

Later, when they were curled up in his big, comfy bed, her body limp and satiated, she said, "I think I lost count of my orgasms."

Matthew raised his eyelids and looked at her through sleepy eyes. "You count 'em?"

"Usually it's not that difficult."

He closed his eyes again, but the skin around them remained crinkled and one side of his mouth curled.

She punched him on the shoulder. "And put that self-satisfied, smug expression away, young man."

He laughed, rolling her over and pinning her beneath him. "Just happy I did my patriotic duty."

"Patriotic—"

"Improving English/American relations."

"Oh, honestly." But since he was kissing her, and she had a feeling her mystery tally was about to go up, she let him get away with his arrogance.

For now.

Afterward, she lay with her head on his shoulder, thinking. "When did you find out what I really do?"

He was breathing so deeply, she thought he might have nodded off. He hadn't, but she could see it was a close call. He opened one eye. "Do you always talk after sex?"

"If I've got something to say."

The other eye opened, and before he could speak she said, "All right. Always."

"Me, I like to sleep after sex."

"We'll compromise. You talk to me; then I'll let you sleep."

He yawned and shook his head. She liked being here, with her head on his shoulder. His skin was warm against her cheek and she could hear the heavy thump of his heart. Then the rumble of his words. "Pretty early on."

Damn. She'd been so pleased with herself. "How early on?"

"After Rafe started spending some weird-ass hours at your place, I got curious. I followed you one day."

She rolled her eyes even though he couldn't see her. "You were always following me."

"Only the two times."

"You were jealous."

She felt him struggle, thought he'd deny it, and then was pleased when he said, "Hell, yeah. I was jealous. And crazy mad 'cause I didn't have any right to be."

"You were in torment. There I was right next door and you couldn't have me."

"Don't sound so happy about it. And I wasn't in torment."

She raised her head and looked down at him. "You weren't?"

He lifted a hand to push the tangle of her hair behind one ear. "Maybe a little."

"That's better." She put her head back down. "So, you were in terrible torment over me and you followed me. Again."

"Don't make me sound like a stalker. It was investigative research."

He sounded cross. She smiled against his chest, then turned her head and kissed him there.

"You went into a spa with a bunch of brochures and came

out a half hour later walkin' funny and with flip-flops on your feet."

"I must have had a pedicure."

"I went in after you and saw a stack of brochures for The Breakup Artist. It was easy to cross-check the phone number with your address."

"What a clever detective you are."

She didn't have to glance up to know he was rolling his eyes. "Not hardly."

"So you've known all this time?"

"Yep."

"And you didn't let on."

"Nope."

"Did you want to hire me?"

His chest rose and fell on a deep breath. "I would never have hired you. I try to do my own dirty work. Only I couldn't. Brittany's—"

His voice faded and she wondered if he was feeling awkward bringing up his ex-girlfriend while in bed with another woman. "Brittany's a darling. But you two were hopelessly mismatched. You'd only have brought each other misery."

Another gargantuan yawn. "Can I go to sleep now, or did you want to discuss world peace or global warming?"

She kissed his jaw. "Get your rest. You'll need it."

Chapter 25

Chloe walked in her own kitchen door at nine-thirty in the morning, feeling mildly guilty, and ran upstairs. "Sorry, I'm late," she said to Stephanie who was tapping away at her computer.

The younger woman said, "You don't have to apologize to me. It's your company."

"Right." Of course it was. She was mad. Utterly mad. Also annoyed with herself. She didn't like sleepovers if she could help them. It gave men ideas.

Matthew was exactly the sort of man she didn't want getting ideas. He was too—too everything. Too good-looking, too good in bed, too sure of himself. A man like that could only mean trouble.

"I should have been here in case you needed anything."

Stephanie looked at her as though she'd gone off her head. "You were only next door. I could have found you if I'd needed you."

"How do you know that? I could have been any number of places."

"Your car's out front. I assumed—"

"Forget it," she snapped. "I'm in a stupid mood. Don't mind me."

"Okay."

The day passed in a blur. Her stomach felt strange. Her

head fuzzy. She couldn't concentrate. She'd think she needed sex except she was currently having the best sex of her life. Every day. It was easy, after all, it was only next door.

When Stephanie came up beside her, where she was standing looking out the window, she jumped. "You startled me."

"Sorry. I called and you didn't answer. You okay?"

"Yes." Of course she wasn't okay. She'd been watching Matthew mow the lawn, thinking dreamily of the things he'd done to her last night. The things he'd whispered in the dark. "I was—"

"I know," Stephanie said.

"I'm not feeling right," she said, turning from the window and sitting herself firmly at her desk. "I'm sort of light-headed and woozy."

"You're not pregnant, are you?"

"No, of course not."

"Then you must be in love."

For a stunned moment Chloe stared at the woman standing on the other side of her desk; then she broke into laughter that sounded faintly hysterical. "With Matthew?"

"Unless there's another guy you're spending every spare minute with."

"Nonsense. He's convenient, attractive."

"Great in bed?"

She put a hand to her chest. "Oh, darling, don't get me started."

Stephanie nodded. "He makes you laugh."

"In his odd way."

"Have you told him things you've never told anyone else?"

She shifted in her chair. "A couple of little things, perhaps."

Stephanie nodded sagely. "When you think about the future, do you see him in it?"

"Where did you get these questions? The latest Cosmo quiz?"

Stephanie just looked at her.

"Oh, no. Not you too."

She nodded, not seeming nearly as neurotic about the idea as Chloe, but then she hadn't left quite as many men at the altar either. "Trust me, it's love."

"But I don't want to be in love with Matthew," she wailed as Stephanie walked out the door.

She turned. Looking far too knowledgeable. "Then you better figure out what you're going to do about it."

"I think I need to breathe into a paper bag."

Stephanie chuckled. "Oh, don't forget, I'm leaving early today. I'm going to be in the studio audience when Deborah and Jordan are interviewed about their new book."

"That's nice. Is Rafe going?"

She shook her head. "He didn't think it was a great idea for him to be on TV."

"Oh, right. Of course. Well, I'll watch the show and look for you."

The minute Stephanie was out the door, Matt found an excuse to come over. He looked like he'd been working hard at some sort of manual labor. He was wearing a ball cap and his shirt had flecks of sawdust on it. When she saw him on her doorstep her heart lurched. Oh God. Stephanie was right. She was in love with him.

So instead of throwing herself on his arms as she wanted to, she wrinkled her nose. "The tradesmen's entrance is around the back."

He looked as though he were thinking of shoving her bodily over his shoulder and taking her straight to bed, sweat and all, and truthfully she wouldn't have put up much of a struggle. Instead, he said, "I'm going home to shower. Then how about I take you downtown for dinner?"

"Oh, but Deborah Beaumont's on television. We have to watch it. Come on in and shower here. We can eat later."

He shook his head. "Let's go to my house?"

"Why?"

"There's a TV in the bedroom."

"Really, Matthew. Is sex all you ever think about?"

The look he sent her had her pulse rate increasing. "Only when you're around."

Naturally, they ended up watching Deborah and Jordan on television from the comfort of Matthew's big bed, curled up together naked and sharing a beer.

"She looks pretty good for a doctor," Matthew remarked when Deborah and Jordan were introduced on the television show. "Hot."

Deb did look hot. Amazing. She also seemed very different from the woman who had shown up at Chloe's house in the middle of an emotional meltdown. She seemed a lot less tense, and happier somehow.

Even dull, stuffy Jordan seemed different. More of a man and less of a geek.

The interviewer asked them the obvious questions about the book. What is the secret of lasting love? Jordan and Deborah looked at each other, and she said, "Communication is essential to a healthy relationship."

Matthew snorted. "Big surprise. It's on the title of the book."

Chloe shushed him. The interviewer asked a bit about the pair of them and how they came to write the book, then said, "I understand you two are personally involved as well as being business partners. Do you think you have a better relationship because you're both experts in love?

Jordan laughed. "No, we're like a couple of MDs who get sick but are too busy to go to the doctor." He looked at Deborah, and Chloe thought, *Wow, who knew?*

Deb picked up from there. "We love each other, but we're working at this every day."

Then the questions from the audience started. "Ooh, goodie," Chloe said. "Look for Stephanie."

But before they saw Stephanie, the camera focused on another familiar figure. Matthew shifted beside her. "What's Brittany doing there?"

"I remember she said she was going to buy the book. She

must have enjoyed it." Brittany was sitting beside a jock boy who matched her like the salt shaker matches the pepper.

"Pepper" had his hand up. He got the mic and, with a glance at a blushing Brittany, asked, "Do you believe in love at first sight?"

Deborah answered, "If it's happened to you, then I believe it."

There was laughter and clapping from the audience. Brittany's new guy said, "I'm a gym teacher and when I started at my new school I saw this woman and"—here he mimed beating on his chest—"ka-boom."

Chloe glanced up at Matthew to see how he was taking this, but if anything, he seemed mildly nauseated. He looked over at her. "Ka-boom?"

Jordan was speaking on the telly. He said, "It doesn't really matter whether it starts with shooting stars or a slow build; the important thing to remember is that every relationship is going to have problems. The really successful ones we see are where the partners talk to each other."

She pressed the MUTE button because she really didn't think either she or Matthew could take much more of this, but she left the picture on in case Stephanie was shown on camera.

She traced her finger across Matthew's collarbone, following the dip right in the middle. "Did you go ka-boom when you first saw me?"

"Honey, from the first moment I met you, I haven't been sure whether I want to make love to you or strangle you."

"Well, make sure you don't mix the two up."

He snorted. "How 'bout you? Did you go ka-boom when you saw me?"

"Certainly not." Their gazes caught and held. She thought she could stay like this forever. "There might have been a slight ping," she acknowledged.

"A ping? Like a car that needs a tune-up?"

"Well, I was jetlagged at the time. Besides, the English are a very reserved people."

"Like hell," he said, yanking the cover off and revealing her naked body, which he proceeded to devour until she was thrashing noisily and anything but reserved.

"Come on," he said when they finally got out of bed. "I want to show you something."

"What?"

"Bats."

Chapter 26

"Oh, look at them," she cried. "Aren't they wonderful?"

She was standing with Matthew and heaps of other people, loads holding cameras, to watch the nightly flying of an enormous population of fruit bats who lived under the Congress Street Bridge. All flew out at dusk to hunt insects.

At first there were only a few, like blurry birds, then suddenly the sky was dark with them. Streams of dark bats flying off. The smell was a bit rank, but the spectacle was amazing.

After perhaps half an hour, it was all over. The bridge emptied as families took the kids home and lovers walked away hand in hand, like she and Matthew, to find a restaurant.

He liked to take her to places that would surprise and delight her. He said he enjoyed her reactions, and she liked how he explained things.

One weekend he drove her down to San Antonio and they visited the Alamo, which actually brought tears to her eyes. She'd never realized how tiny and international was the force that had fought so hopelessly to save their fort.

Afterward, they ate in one of the many restaurants overlooking the river walk and spent the night in a grand old hotel that reminded her of Europe.

It was perfect. Too perfect.

On their last night after a magic, romantic walk by the river, they made love in the big, opulent bed, and while they were so intimately linked, he whispered, "I love you."

He kissed her then before she had a chance to reply, and she understood he was giving his love as a gift, not asking for an exchange.

What frightened her most was that she did reciprocate.

They were quieter than usual on the way home. A line had been crossed and she had no idea what to do about it. She knew her feelings for him were different, as well as deeper, than what she'd ever felt before.

And the knowledge terrified her.

When they reached home and unpacked the car, she headed firmly for her own home. "Thank you for a lovely weekend."

He looked at her in that way he had that told her he saw more than she wanted him to. "You coming over later?"

"I haven't slept in my own bed in over a week. I don't think so."

"You want me to come to you?"

She dropped the bag she was carrying and stomped over to him. "Matthew, I cannot go on like this. You crowd me. Control me."

"Like hell I do." He grabbed his own bag and turned for his house. "You want to sleep alone tonight, fine. All you had to do was say so."

"It's not the sleeping, it's—" She threw up her hands feeling a theatrical sense of frustration spill out of her. "Everything. I look out the window and there you are. I–I can't seem to get you out of my mind. I can't take it."

"I'll tell you your trouble, Chloe, you have to be the one calling all the shots. You've always had those Italian puppies of yours whining at your heels until you kick them a good one. But I won't be kicked around, or brought to heel so you can wipe your tiny British feet all over my backside."

"I never—"

"You're spoiled. You've got so used to having your own way, you cut and run the second a real man comes along."

"That's not true, I—"

"I told you I love you. That's what this is about."

"It's not, I—"

"I don't know why I'm crazy enough to love you, but God help me, I do. So you're scared. I get that. I'm scared too."

"You are?"

"Damn right, I am. You think I want to be stuck with a high-maintenance shrew for the rest of my life?"

"The rest of your life—" That made her crazier than the fact he'd just called her a shrew. "I can't plan that far ahead. I can barely schedule a pedicure for next week."

There was a silence, heavy with confusion and heat and close to twenty-eight years of getting her way whether she wanted it or not.

"You're fetching to break up with me."

"I am not."

He shoved a hand in his pocket and pulled out his wallet. Peeled off a couple of fifties. "I've got no idea what your going rate is, but here, I'm hiring you." He slapped the money on the top of her car. "Do it."

"Do what?"

"Break up with me."

She threw the bills back at him. Nobody ever broke up with her! Never.

She hadn't even planned to break up with him. Had she? All she wanted was for it to be easy and fun, lots of sex and laughs. No talk of love or the future, and now he'd gone and spoiled everything.

"I won't take your money," she snapped, shoving the bills back toward him. "This match I'll break up for free."

Chapter 27

Chloe walked into the restaurant and scanned the tables. It was ridiculously easy to work out which one was Alice. She could have spotted the about-to-be-dumped woman without a physical description of her at all. The woman's body language told her everything. She was tense, too eager, too hopeful. On some level she already knew it was over. Poor dear.

Chloe walked over to the table for two with only the one person sitting there, and said, "Alice?"

A puzzled glance met hers. "Yes?"

"I'm Chloe. John sent me."

Puzzle turned to quick alarm. "John? Is he okay?"

"Yes, he's fine." Apart from being a rat bastard who would pay someone else rather than do his own dirty work. She slipped into the opposite seat without asking permission, and said, "John asked me to come today on his behalf."

The woman looked at her wrist watch. Funny how people nearly always did, as though the time mattered. "Why didn't he call and cancel lunch?"

"It's complicated and I think he thought this might be easier coming from another woman. Would you like a glass of wine?"

"Usually I don't drink at lunch, but something tells me I'm going to need this."

Chloe beamed at her. Women were so smart and intuitive. "And let's order an extremely expensive lunch, on John."

"That bad?"

"I'm afraid so."

Alice took a quick breath. In and out. "Tell me one thing. Are you sleeping with him?"

Chloe blinked. What was there about her that suggested she'd have such appalling taste. "Heavens, no," she said.

"Then why are you here? Don't beat about the bush. Tell me like it is."

"John wants to break up with you and he's too much of a chicken to do it himself. So he hired me."

"He hired you to break up with me?"

"Yes."

The woman stared at her. She was in her early forties, stylish and obviously successful. She wore a smart suit and a silk Givenchy blouse. "John paid out money so he wouldn't have to break up with me himself?"

The woman didn't seem particularly hysterical, more that she wanted to be absolutely certain she understood.

"That's right."

"How much did he pay you?"

She thought about hedging, but really, in the other woman's shoes she'd have wanted to know too. "I'm very expensive," she replied, then stated the fee.

The woman across the table started to laugh.

"Order the most expensive bottle of wine on that menu. I'll call the office and tell my secretary I won't be in this afternoon."

When they were enjoying a nice bottle of wine and munching on salads, Alice said, "You know what really burns me? I'm smart, I'm successful, I'm together, I'm great at what I do. And with men?" She shook her head violently. "I'm pathetic. Why is that?"

Chloe felt like saying, "Look, they pay me to break up relationships, not to give therapy," but the truth was, she didn't know. She thought about Matthew and wanted to weep. "I'm a mess, too, in my personal life."

The woman snorted, well into her second glass of wine. "You? You're the nightmare women like me fear all our lives. You're gorgeous and sexy, and you wear the right clothes. I bet no one's ever broken up with you in your entire life."

Obviously not. However, she was beginning to realize that that wasn't necessarily because she was universally adorable. She rather thought it was because she was the bail-out queen. She always dumped men long before they had a chance to tire of her. "I'm as much a mess as the next woman," she admitted. "I have a bit of a commitment problem."

"You and John."

Over lunch they had a surprisingly good time. Alice loved art and was well traveled so they had quite a bit in common. It was an odd way to meet someone, but Chloe thought by the end of lunch she'd like to include Alice in her growing circle of friends. Besides, she was a successful stockbroker, and Chloe was beginning to realize she had to begin taking control of her life and not letting everyone else take care of her.

"May I come and see you? Professionally?" she asked when they were winding down the lunch.

Alice laughed again, it was a rich, horsey laugh, and it reminded her a bit of Nicky's. "I have to say this is the most bizarre way I've ever met a client." She dug into her bag and pulled out a business cared. "Sure. Give my office a call. Once I get through the crying jag I'm working up to, I'd be happy to help you."

"Come on. Let's get you home. I've got a bag of treats and lots of tissues."

Alice rose and straightened her skirt. "You're going to see me home?"

"Of course, it's part of the service."

"You'll come to my house and hand me tissues?"

"Tissues, brandy, lashings of tea, herbal or proper English tea, and four kinds of ice cream."

Alice started to shake her head, then paused. "What flavors of ice cream? Ah, what the hell. I'll eat 'em all."

Since Alice had walked to the restaurant from her office and Chloe had come by cab, they took a taxi to Alice's apartment. In a modern high-rise with high ceilings, and white walls covered in art. Chloe got out bowls and spoons and unpacked the ice cream while Alice changed into jeans and a ratty old blue sweater that was obviously as comforting as a security blanket.

"What am I doing with someone so pathetic he can't even break up with a woman? He hires someone to do it for him?"

"I was wondering that myself."

"Low self-esteem issues."

"But why? You're a wonderful person. John is a fool."

"Of course he is. I'm hardly ever attracted to the good men in the world. It's a sickness. I go out with men who will treat me like crap. It's like somewhere inside me I don't think I deserve any better."

"But surely you can change."

She shrugged, then put a hand to her forehead. "Ow, I'm getting brain freeze from the pecan fudge ripple. Ow, ow, ow." But she was laughing as she said it. "You know, there should be a club or a school or something for women like me where they can figure out how not to get treated this way."

"My dear," she said, "you're brilliant." She took a tiny spoonful of her own bowl of ice cream, and said, "I think I know just the person to run it. Her name is Deborah Beaumont. She's a therapist, and a good one. You might want to pop along and see her."

Maybe she also needed to see Deborah herself. Since her new friend Alice seemed like she was almost relieved to finally have getting dumped by John out of the way, she left soon after.

Something about her day with Alice made Chloe face a very unpleasant fact.

She'd messed up.

The old Chloe would have chucked a lovely, noisy, spectacular wobbly and run home to Mummy and Daddy when she and Matthew had their row. The new version, what she liked to think of as the American Chloe, had no such desire. Oh, she'd chucked a pretty decent wobbly, and sabotaged her relationship the way she always did, but this time she wasn't running away.

Going home hadn't even occurred to her. It was time to face up to who she was and what she wanted.

Perhaps Alice's words had hit a nerve. All her life she'd been drawn to men she ended up despising. Men who let her control them, who spoiled and petted her but didn't take her seriously or see that there was a good brain lodged beneath the first-class cosmetics and trendy hairstyles. Of course, she'd taken great pains to hide her intelligence until she'd come to America and started a new life. Now she had to rely on her skills, her intelligence, and herself.

She didn't even make it home.

Her cell phone rang and she answered it from her cab. "Hello?"

"Is this The Breakup Artist?" It was Matthew. The sound of his voice was so very dear and it was so unexpected that for a moment she couldn't speak. Silence hung between them.

"Ma'am? Have I got the breakup agency?"

For some reason Matthew was pretending to be a stranger. Well, she'd played plenty of bizarre games in her time like acting as though she didn't recognize a voice she knew intimately. "Yes," she managed. "Yes, it is."

"May I speak to your customer service division?"

Chloe put a hand to her chest and felt the urgent thud of her heart. "Customer service?" she echoed stupidly. What on earth was he going on about? One of them was clearly barking mad.

"I'm not happy with the service I received from your agency. I want to complain."

She sank back against the upholstery of the cab, her legs

feeling wobbly as she began to guess, and wildly hope, that she knew where he was going with his odd question.

"I am the president of The Breakup Artist. What seems to be the problem, sir?" She liked the way she'd added sir on to the end of her question. It made them sound so formal.

"One of your, ah, operatives got a little carried away and broke up my relationship by mistake. I want it put back."

Chloe felt a lump form in her throat. "You do?"

"Damn right, I do. I love that woman."

"You do?" she asked again, her voice wobbling at the end.

"Yes, ma'am. She's crazy, spoiled, a little high maintenance for my taste, but I'm nuts about her. I want you to put that match back together."

"Put a match together?" She let some of the annoyance she was feeling from the spoiled and high-maintenance nonsense leak into her tone. "But, my dear sir, this is not a matchmaking agency, it's a match-breaking agency."

"Then I suggest you branch out, or you are going to have one very unhappy customer. I want a match put back together. Oh, and I want something creative."

"Creative?"

"Yeah, surprise the hell out of me."

"I suppose you're going to order a timeline as well for your surprise," she snapped, glad he couldn't see her since the snippy tone in her voice couldn't possibly reveal the smile beginning to bloom on her face.

"By the end of next week." And he hung up on her.

Chloe sat there so stunned, she forgot to push the OFF button on her phone, holding it against her ear until an annoying buzzing sound disturbed her.

Matthew was completely insane.

She began to smile. Yes, he was. He also understood her, as perhaps no man ever had. In his shoes, she might have done something similar.

So he wanted to be surprised, did he?

She waved her feet up and down in her delight and was

momentarily distracted by the gold bows on the red strap. She'd paid a fortune for the shoes on Bond Street. Well, if all went well, she'd end up wearing tooled leather cowboy boots for the rest of her life, she supposed, and yelling "Yee-haw!"

From her cell phone in the taxi, she next called information and found out where Deborah's office was. It was almost five, but she called anyway, and was lucky enough to get put through to Deborah.

"Deborah Beaumont speaking."

"Hello, Deborah. This is Chloe Flynt."

"So my assistant said." She didn't sound happy to hear from Chloe or hostile, simply neutral. "What can I do for you?"

Chloe wondered what on earth she was doing. She'd followed instinct and not thought through the fact that the last time she'd seen Deborah the woman had been shouting at her. "I'm wondering—I know it's late—but is there any chance you could see me today?"

There was a long pause. She thought her cell phone had cut out when finally the woman said, "You mean professionally?"

"Well, I'm not asking you for a date."

Thankfully, the other woman chuckled. "I've had my last appointment for the day, but I'll be here for a while. Where are you?"

She squinted at the street signs. "About two blocks away."

"All right."

When the taxi dropped her off, she took a deep breath and then rode the elevator up.

The young receptionist was packing up when Chloe got there, and luckily, there was no sign of Jordan.

Deborah greeted her and ushered her into an office that was more like a living room. She noticed that Deborah was looking a lot more relaxed and somehow more human than the last time they'd seen each other.

"This is lovely," she said, admiring her surroundings. "Very homey. I watched you on television, by the way, and I thought you were very good."

"Thanks. Have a seat. Can I get you some tea?"

Thinking about the last time they'd had tea, Chloe smiled. "No, thank you. I just finished two bowls of ice cream. Long story, but I did recommend you to a very nice woman named Alice who may be calling here."

If Deborah thought that was strange behavior she didn't say anything, merely settled herself on one chair and motioned for Chloe to sit across from her. "So, what can I do for you?"

"I think I've made a terrible mistake. I broke it off with the man I've been seeing. We had a stupid row and I lost it."

Deborah nodded as if people did that all the time. God, they probably did. "Why do you think you did that?"

"Because I love him!"

"Why don't you tell me all about it."

So she did. Chloe wasn't one who had to be prompted. She loved to talk about herself. She'd been through all the top therapists in London, including one who wanted to throw away his practice and take her around the world on his sailboat. But most of them had been very helpful. She understood she was terrified of commitment, but she'd simply never been able to do anything about it.

When she got to the end of the recital, Deborah said, "You know, Chloe, change is terrifying. I see people all the time who, like you, understand what's holding them back, but they are so afraid of changing that they are stuck in their old patterns."

"But I do want to change."

The face Deborah showed her wasn't soft and understanding; it was tough and uncompromising. "Then what are you going to do about it?"

She opened her mouth. Closed it. "This is only my first session. Aren't you getting a bit ahead of yourself?"

"You're the expert on breaking up relationships. I'm the

one who knows about healing them. That means that in this room, I'm the boss. Okay?"

She wasn't sure she hadn't liked Deborah better when she was a ranting emotional wreck. "Okay."

"So what are you going to do about changing?"

She nibbled a corner of her thumbnail, something she hadn't done since she was a teenager.

"I'm going to get him back."

"Pardon? I didn't hear you."

Chloe sat up straight. Put her hand back in her lap. Took a deep breath. "I'm going to get him back."

If she wanted Matthew, and she knew she did—certainly for the long term—probably forever, she was going to have to work to get him back, something she'd never in her life done.

Well, she'd discovered she could run a business, she could actually help people avoid unhappiness and, therefore, hopefully, come a step closer to happiness. She could get herself a man.

"What I needed is a plan."

"You know, Chloe, most women in your position would go and knock on Matthew's door and apologize."

"I am not most women."

"No, you certainly aren't. All right. Let's talk about your plan."

"What, just the two of us?"

Deborah sat back and looked at Chloe as though in all her years she'd never come across anyone quite like her. Which, naturally, was true. "How many therapists do you think you need?"

A feeling of hope, of sneaking happiness started to seep through Chloe. "In London, I would call a summit meeting. They never fail. All my friends and I get together and they help me sort out my problems."

"It's a long way to fly to London to solve your problems."

Chloe laughed. "God, in the old days, I'd have done that, you know. Perhaps you're right. I have changed. Or I am changing. No, what I need is a Texas summit for a Texas-style plan."

"I think that's a good idea. Talking things over with friends can really help."

"Excellent. So, are you free tonight?"

"For what?"

"My summit, silly. I always say there's no time like the present."

"You think of me as a friend?" Deborah didn't sound annoyed as much as surprised. Chloe was a little surprised herself.

"I think we could be friends, yes. You've helped me a lot." She glanced up through her lashes. "And don't tell me I haven't helped you, because I heard everything from Jordan. I saved your relationship."

"You tried to break us up!"

"But it didn't work. My interference only breaks up a relationship that's already on its last legs. When two people are truly in love, all I do is make them realize it." She smiled smugly. "You and Jordan being a case in point." She shifted on the couch, curling her feet under her. "Don't you want to be my friend?"

"Strangely enough, I do."

"All right. I'll call Brittany and Stephanie, and we'll do it tonight."

"Who's Brittany?"

"Matthew's old girlfriend."

Deborah put her hand over her eyes. "Don't tell me. Don't even tell me."

They ended up at a big, noisy place with wooden floors and a live band playing bluegrass. Deborah glanced around the table and felt a wave of affection for her new friends. Brittany and Stephanie both fitted right in with this place, of course. Deborah looked as though she'd rather be home reading Freud, and Chloe had to admit that even she was a little out of her element.

Chloe said, "I asked you all to come out because I need a summit meeting of my top advisors."

Brittany and Stephanie exchanged a glance. "And we're it?"

"Absolutely." She glanced around at the three attractive women: Brittany the blonde, Deborah the redhead, and Stephanie the brunette. She laughed. "We're exactly like Charlie's Angels."

Stephanie said, "Except that we don't fight crime."

"Oh, well," she waved the objection away. "We do help people solve their problems."

"We break hearts by proxy for people who are too chicken to do it themselves. We're not Charlie's Angels, we're Chloe's Devils."

Brittany raised her glass. "To Chloe's Devils."

"Right, girls. I've got myself a problem and I'm relying on you to help me fix it."

"Chloe's Devils are on the case," Brittany said, her blond hair even bigger today than usual, which Chloe had learned indicated her level of happiness. Today, apparently, was a good day.

"I did something very stupid involving a man and I need to fix it."

Brittany hooted. "What did you do to Matthew?"

"I did what I always do. Acted like a spoiled child and made a complete fool of myself."

"And then what did you do?"

Chloe grinned. One thing about her new friends, she couldn't get much past them.

But her grin was soon wiped off her face. "I hurt him," she admitted. "I meant to hurt him at the time, but I was sorry immediately."

"Did you apologize?" Deborah's quiet words broke through her façade.

She shook her head. "No."

"Are you going to?"

"I need more than a simple apology. I need to make him understand that I want him permanently, he's not some temporary fling."

"Why would he think that?"

She ran her index finger around her margarita glass, bumpy with salt. "I don't have much of a track record. I tend to get engaged to men and then drop them. I was going to break up with him, but something stopped me; then he broke it off with me."

"Maybe he's afraid you'll run back to England."

"Right," Stephanie agreed. "He needs to understand you're going to stick."

"So you need to show him that you really are a Texan?" Deborah said, a slow smile beginning to build. She hadn't seemed like she held a grudge against Chloe for almost ruining her life, but Chloe couldn't help but be a little wary.

"I suppose."

Deborah looked around at the other women and Chloe was reminded that they were all Texans and she wasn't even close.

"We could fix your hair, make it big and Texan," Brittany offered.

"You could get a tattoo of the Lone Star in a prominent place," Stephanie offered, staring thoughtfully at Chloe's forehead so she wondered what she'd ever done to Stephanie. She'd ended up with Rafe, hadn't she? It had all worked out.

"A tattoo?" she said feebly.

"Tattoos and hair are only skin deep," Deb reminded them. "She needs to learn how to be a true Texas woman."

"They give classes for that?"

"Oh, yeah." By now, Deborah's ladylike expression was more like a python's right before it strikes. "Cowgirl University."

The other two hooted with laughter and Chloe smiled, willing to be the butt of a joke. As if.

But it soon turned out that Deborah wasn't joking at all.

"It's the National Cowgirl Museum and Hall of Fame. Check it out on the Web site. They teach Cowgirl 101, and everything from horse care to leather tooling. Honey, if you want to prove to your man that you are willing to work on this relationship, I can't think of a better way."

"Wait a minute," Brittany said. "We can have our own customized course. My aunt is Sadie Watkins Hawke."

Sadie Watkins Hawke certainly wasn't a household name in London, England, and it seemed from the momentary silence that Sadie wasn't exactly the most famous woman in all of Texas, when Deborah's puzzled expression lightened. "The rodeo star?"

"That's right. My aunt did really well in the rodeo circuit; then she went to Hollywood for a while as a stunt rider. Now she's back home and runs a ranch. I'm going to call her right now. She'd get the biggest kick out of teaching an English gal to be a cowgirl. She's likely to bust a gut laughing when I tell her our plan."

Chloe felt that now was the time to share her reservations about this excellent plan, but luckily, Deborah forestalled her. "You think your aunt would tailor a course specially for Chloe?" Her obvious feelings of doubt were shared by Chloe herself.

Brittany laughed. "No, silly. For all of us."

"All of us?" Stephanie, who had been staring vacantly into space with an annoyingly satisfied smile tilting her lips, suddenly entered the conversation.

"Yeah, we can't let Chloe go alone. She's going to need all our help. Deborah, you can give her the psychological training to be a true Texas woman, and me and Steph can give her the more practical techniques. Plus, we'll all get to ride. It'll be fun."

"When were you planning on doing this?"

"Are you kidding? After the way Chloe completely blew it with Matt, there's no time to lose. We're going this weekend."

Three voices rose in instant protest and Brittany silenced them all with a hand in the air, like the elementary school teacher she was. "I do not want to hear excuses or whining," she announced, silencing them all. "We're going this weekend. Clear your schedules."

"Where is this place?" Deborah finally asked.

"A couple hours outside San Antonio. You'll love it there. Trust me."

Chloe and Deborah traded glances. Delight was not the paramount emotion shared. However, even as Chloe opened her mouth to decline spending so much as five minutes on a dusty ranch learning to be a cowgirl, the idea began to appeal to her. Matthew wanted to be surprised?

Oh, Matthew was going to get his wish.

Chapter 28

For the first time in his life, Matthew broke the law. He told himself he wasn't really breaking the law by using his key to enter the house he owned, and that Chloe was renting. He was worried about her. He hadn't seen her in four days. Her car was gone.

Not that he really believed anything bad had happened to her. He thought something bad might have happened to him. Her rent was paid to the end of the month, but what if she'd packed up and left—without even saying good-bye?

He kept telling himself she was more of a fighter than that, but what really scared the hell out of him was the possibility that he wasn't worth fighting for. That she'd gone back to England and her regular life, leaving him behind and everything he wanted to say to her unsaid.

The second he stepped into the house next door, he wished he hadn't. It was neat. Too neat.

The fact that Chloe was a neat freak didn't register as he yelled her name—crazily when he saw her car was gone and he could sense the house was empty.

He pounded up the stairs, more than a little disappointed that she'd take off like this, even as he was thinking he could rearrange his schedule and be in England in a couple of days.

But when he burst into her bedroom, he stopped. Her stuff was still there. The girlie things on the dresser, her bedding on the bed. He could smell her. The scent of whatever she used on her skin, what he thought of as English rose.

He let out a long breath and increased his lawlessness by sitting on her bed. Wishing she were here so he could talk to her, do all the things he wanted to do to her right here on this bed. Okay, he thought, chances were he'd get another shot. She wasn't gone forever. She was coming back.

And if she wasn't coming for him, then damn it, he was coming for her.

Knowing he should leave, he lingered a little longer. He didn't touch anything, or pry. He just wanted to be in her space.

Man, he had it bad. He was a walking humiliation to every Texan male.

While he beat himself up, he held on to his cell phone, willing it to ring. Willing Chloe to tell him where she was so he could go get her. Four days was long enough to keep a man in suspense. More than long enough.

When his cell phone rang he answered before the first ring had finished. "Chloe?"

"Hey, man. It's Rafe."

"Hey. I can't talk. I'm waiting for Chloe to call." He should play it cool, make a joke, but he couldn't. He was in love with that woman and tired of playing games. He never should have pushed her.

There was a short pause. "Okay. Sorr—"

"Do you have any idea where she is?"

"You at home?"

"Yeah." Close enough.

"I'll come by later. We'll have a beer."

Of course Rafe didn't know where she was. "Sounds good."

He rose from Chloe's bed, resisting the memories of the two of them in it, when he could have sworn he heard a horse neigh.

Crazy. He was going crazy. There weren't riding stables for

miles. Still, he went to her bedroom window that overlooked the cul-de-sac. And he blinked.

Then a grin split his face.

Chloe was coming down the sidewalk on horseback, and it was the craziest damn sight he'd ever seen. She wore a blue spangled riding costume that would look more at home in Vegas than in Austin, a blue and white cowboy hat that somebody had pinned a rose onto, and a kick-in pair of boots.

She was riding a black gelding that didn't seem too happy with its rider. Easy to see why. She was holding the reins all wrong and bouncing up and down in the saddle.

"You're riding English style again, Chloe," Brittany called out. He had no idea why, or what was going on, but Chloe had a whole posse of gals with her. And he suspected they were coming for him.

It was *High Noon*—with a lot more lipstick.

He sprinted for the stairs, nearly pitching down them in his hurry, let himself out her kitchen door, and raced across the yard until he was in his own backyard. He shoved the phone back in his pocket and strode to the far end of the yard where he'd started fixing the fence earlier in the day.

He banged a nail into the fence a lot straighter than he had earlier, the grin stuck on his face.

A cowgirl. An English princess–cowgirl.

Now he'd seen everything.

Except it turned out he hadn't.

He heard the clopping of reluctant hooves and then a clipped accent saying, "Now, Raven, you don't want to make a mess of my outfit. Do not push me into this tree."

"Neck rein, Chloe. Neck rein," he heard in urgent undertones and turned.

There she came around the house. The posse must be hiding. The horse gave him a look that said, *I don't have any better idea than you what's going on, but I'd rather be back at the barn eating hay*. Chloe looked like Mattel's version of a rodeo rider—small and dainty and far too pretty to be real.

He started walking toward her to help her down, but before he'd taken two steps she'd dismounted with a flourish. She dropped the reins, but her valiant steed didn't seem like it was in a hurry to be anywhere. Probably, like Matthew, he wondered what was coming next. He watched, bemused, as she popped a coil of rope off the horn, then strode toward him spinning a lasso like a pro.

Before he'd half figured out what was coming next, the coil of white was drifting through the air like a very determined smoke ring; then he felt the thing slip over him. While she sent the rope sailing, she let out a holler, sounding like a rancher at roundup time. "Yee-haw!"

With a cry of satisfaction, she hauled the rope tight so his arms were caught to his sides. She'd roped him as neatly as a steer.

For a long moment they stood there looking at each other.

He loved this woman to his very soul, he realized, and always would. She was crazy, sweet, sexy, the last woman he would have looked for and the one he needed more than anything.

"You gonna flip me on my back and hog-tie me?"

Heat arced between them down that rope as though it were a lightning rod. "If you're very good," she said in that snooty, sexy voice that did him in every time.

Then she began pulling on the rope. Her hands were small and delicate, and the color of her nails, some kind of pale purple, flashed in the sun like drops of grape milkshake.

He didn't even think about putting up a fight; he wouldn't want her palms to get scratched. He tried very hard not to think about what her hand wrapped around the rope and pulling reminded him of as he let himself be tugged, closer and closer until their bodies were touching. His lack of mobility irked him.

"I want to put my arms around you so much I can't stand it," he said.

Her smile was both understanding and devilish. "You can't always be in control, darling."

"I love you. Which has sent me totally out of control."

"And does that bother you?" she asked, rising on her toes in those boots so their lips were inches away.

"Not one damn bit," he said, kissing her as passionately as a man can without the use of his arms.

They might have kept kissing until the sun went down, but the sound of scrambling bodies, followed by howls of glee and triumph, intruded.

"You did it!"

"Chloe, I can't believe you roped him."

"I know," she said, turning to her posse. "But it's easier when they don't try to run away." She beamed at him. "We've all been to a ranch learning to be cowgirls. It's the most wonderful place."

"What other tricks did you learn?" he asked, hoping she'd show him so he could get this rope off him.

"Are you joking? This took me four solid days of practice to get right. I had to give up leather tooling and dressage. But I'm going to go back, perhaps next year."

He didn't care whether she took up bareback bronco riding. The words *next year* sang in his veins.

However, his good mood dimmed slightly when Rafe came slouching up the path behind Brittany, Stephanie, and the shrink from TV.

"You drop by for that beer?"

Rafe had the grace not to laugh, though he could see it was a struggle. "Had to see you hog-tied with my own eyes."

"Don't be cross with Rafe, darling. He was such a help."

"I bet."

"And he and the girls are going to take the horse back for me."

"Great. How 'bout the rope? Bet that has to go back too."

Her smile was warm and intimate and so full of promise that he hoped nobody was looking at him too closely below the belt. "I bought the rope. You never know when it will come in handy."

"How 'bout the cowgirl getup? You own that?"

"Of course. I've discovered I quite like being a cowgirl."

He had a feeling he was going to like it too.

The horse sent him one last sympathetic glance, as one tethered beast to another, and then turned and headed out with the gang of g_ggling cowgirls and one lone Mexican wolf.

Then she tugged his rope and he followed his sparkling cowgirl. As they headed into his house—luckily, he'd left the back door unlocked—and up the stairs to his bedroom, he said, "I thought you'd left me."

She must have heard some of the agony he'd been through, because she stopped, right in the middle of the stairs, and said, "I wouldn't have left. Not without saying good-bye. Besides, we had unfinished business."

"You've been engaged three times. Not that I want to sound like I'm doubting your sticking power, but I had to wonder if you're the kind who takes off the minute things get rough."

She paused in front of him and turned. "Oh, Matthew." Her voice was soft. "Even at my worst I always said good-bye." She smiled a little. "Well, shouted it probably. How could you think I would leave? It's different this time."

"It's different for me. I wasn't sure how it was for you."

"Then let me show you," she said, leading him the rest of the way to his bedroom.

"Honey," he said, "there'll be lots of times when I'm happy for you to tie me up, and times I'm going to do the same for you, but right now, if you don't mind, I really need to put my hands on you."

For her answer, she loosened the ring of rope and slipped it over his head. "I need your hands on me too."

He pulled her to him, holding her tighter with his arms than that rope had held him. "I missed you so much."

"So did I. I love you." She patted her hand against her chest. "There, I said it."

"Sounded good," he said, smiling down at her. "Say it again."

She did. Then they were kissing, hungrily.

She tasted so sweet, so right, and when he felt her pushing her body against his, wriggling against him so the studs and buttons on her outfit gouged into him, he knew she'd missed him as much as he'd missed her.

"I need to get you naked more than I've ever needed anything," he said, his voice low and husky.

"But this was a very expensive outfit," she said, her pout not disguising her raging need for a second.

"Well," he said, standing back and pretending to think about it.

He stood there just a second too long, so she said "Matthew" in that dreamy, needy way that went straight to his cock like a stroking hand.

"Okay. You can leave the hat on," he said, stepping closer.

"And the boots."

His hands were on hers as they both struggled to free her from that spangling outfit.

When she stood before him in nothing but her hat, with that rose bobbing, and her tooled leather boots, shiny with newness, he thought he'd never been a happier man.

He tore out of his clothes and then, advancing on her, scooped her up into his arms.

She giggled. "Be careful of your knee."

"Don't you worry about my knee," he said, dropping her to the bed so she bounced, laughing. Then reached for him.

She climbed on top of him. "I didn't do nearly enough riding."

He put a hand behind his head and looked up at her.

"You learn to ride Texan style?"

Her nose turned up at that. "Certainly not. I ride English style. Get used to it."

And when she mounted him and he slid home so perfectly, he knew he already had.

There are more sexy shifters in
Cynthia Eden's
HOTTER AFTER MIDNIGHT,
available now from Brava . . .

"**I**'m an empath, Colin. My gift is that I sense things. I sense the *Other.* I can sense their feelings, their thoughts."

Yeah, he'd definitely tensed up on her. "You're telling me that you can read my thoughts?"

The temperature seemed to drop about ten degrees. "I'm telling you that *sometimes* I can tell the thoughts of supernaturals." She'd known he wouldn't be thrilled by this news; that was why she hadn't told him the full truth the other night. But now that they were working together, now that her talent was coming into play, well, she figured he had the right to know.

Colin grabbed her arms, jerked her forward against his chest. "So this whole time, you've been playing with me."

The sharp edge of his canines gleamed behind his lips. "No, Colin, it's not like that—"

"You've been looking into my head and seeing how much I want you?"

"Colin, no, I—" *Seeing how much I want you.* Had he really just said that?

His cheeks flushed. "While I tried to play the dumb-ass gentleman."

Since when?

"Well, screw that." His lips were right over hers, his fingers tight on her arms. "If you've been in my head, then you know what I want to do to you."

Uh, no, she didn't. Her shields had been firmly in place with him all day. Her heart was pounding so fast now, the dull drumming filled her ears. She licked her lips, tried once more to tell him the truth. "It's not like that—"

Too late. His mouth claimed hers, swallowing her words and igniting the hungry desire she'd been trying so hard to fight.

Meet the BADDEST BAD BOYS in three
wickedly irresistible stories from
Shannon McKenna, E.C. Sheedy, and Cate Noble.
Available now. Here's an excerpt from
Shannon's story, "Anytime, Anywhere."

He forced his leaden body into action. Shoved open the truck door, grabbed his grip and the bag of groceries. He made his way with heavy feet up the switchback path to the hillside cabin—and froze.

Footsteps around the corner of the cabin. Someone was passing through the foliage. The *shush-shush* of jeans legs rubbing each other. The *swish-slap* of bushes. He heard every sound like it was miked.

He let the duffel, the groceries drop. His gun materialized in his hand, though he had no memory of drawing it, or flattening his back to the weatherbeaten shingles, creeping towards the corner . . . waiting—

Grab, twist, and he had the fucker bent over in a hammerlock, wrist torqued at an agonizing angle, gun to the nape. It squawked.

Female. Long hair, swishing and tickling over his bare arm. A delicate wrist that felt like it might break in his grip. What the *hell* . . . ?

"Jon! Stop this! Let go! It's me!"

Huh? The chick knew him? His body had ascertained that she was no physical threat, so he shoved her away to take a better look.

His jaw dropped when she straightened up, rubbing her twisted wrist. He tried to drag in oxygen, but his lungs were locked. Holy shit. No way had he met this girl before. He would have remembered. *Wow.*

Long hair swung to her waist. Big dark eyes, exotically tilted, flashing with anger. High cheekbones, perfect skin, pointy chin. That full pink mouth, glossed up with lip goo, calculated to make a guy think of one thing only, and suffer the immediate physiological consequences.

And her body, Jesus. Feline grace; long legs, slim waist, round hips. High, suckable, braless tits, the nipples of which poked through a thin cotton blouse. Low-rise jeans that clung desperately to the undercurve of that perfect ass. Who the hell . . . ? This was private property, in the middle of nowhere. His dick twitched, swelled.

She did not look armed. He slipped the Glock back into the shoulder holster. "You scared me," he said. "Who the hell are you?"

Her eyes widened in outrage. "What do you mean, who the hell am I? It's me! Robin!"

Robin? His brain spun its wheels to reconcile the irreconcilable.

Danny's baby sister? He'd practically pissed himself laughing the night she'd juggled flaming torches in Danny's kitchen, although Danny hadn't been amused when the rib-eye he'd grilled got unexpectedly flambed. The steak had tasted faintly of petroleum fuel, but what the hell. She hadn't burned down the building.

Robin . . . ? Robin of the dorky glasses, the mouthful of metal? Robin who was was as cute and funny as a bouncing Labrador puppy?

The irreconcilable images slammed together, like a truck hitting his mind. Those big brown eyes, magnified behind Coke bottle lenses.

It *was* Robin. Holy shit. In his mind he'd already been nailing this girl, right and left and center. Danny would kill him if he knew Jon had entertained pornographic thoughts about his baby sister. "Ah, sorry," he muttered lamely. "I didn't recognize you. You look . . . different than I remembered. Do your brothers know you're out dressed like that?"

Her back straightened, and her eyes narrowed to gleaming brown slits. "Mac and Danny have nothing to say about my wardrobe."

"Maybe they should." He jerked his chin in the general direction of her taut brown nipples, all too evident in the chill, and averted his eyes.

"Why should they?" Her slender arms folded over her chest, propping the tits up higher for his tormented perusal. "I'm twenty-five, Jon. That's a two, and then a five."

He blinked at her. "No shit."

"Absolutely, shit. Want to see my driver's license? I wear what I please. I answer to no one."

This was surreal. He dragged his eyes away from her gleaming pink lips, and pulled himself together. "Uh, I don't mean to be rude, but what the fuck does your age have to do with anything? And what are you doing up here, anyhow?"

The gleaming lips pursed. "I could ask you the same question."

"You could," he conceded. "But it would be none of your goddamn business. Your brother gave me the keys. I'm crashing up here for a couple of weeks to do some fishing and stare at the wall with my mouth hanging open. And now, your turn. What did you come up here for?"

Her gaze fell. She started to speak. Pressed her hand to her belly.

"Um . . . you," she said.

Don't miss WHEN HE WAS BAD, a sexy
paranormal anthology from
Shelly Laurenston and Cynthia Eden,
coming next month from Brava.
Turn the page for a sneak peek at
Shelly's story "Miss Congeniality"!

A few minutes later the doorbell rang and Irene didn't move. She wasn't expecting anyone so she wouldn't answer the door. She dealt with enough people during the day, she'd be damned if her nights were filled with the idiots as well.

The doorbell went off again, followed by knocking. Irene didn't even flinch. In a few more minutes she would shut everything out but the work in front of her. A skill she'd developed over the years. Sometimes Jackie would literally have to shake her or punch her in the head to get her attention.

But Irene hadn't slipped into that "zone" yet and she could easily hear someone sniffing at her door. She looked up from her paperwork as Van Holtz snarled from the other side, "I know you're in there, Conridge. I can smell you."

Eeew.

"Go away," she called back. "I'm busy."

The knocking turned to outright banging. "Open this goddamn door!"

Annoyed but resigned the man wouldn't leave, Irene put her paperwork on the couch and walked across the room. She pulled open the door and ignored the strange feeling in the pit of her stomach at seeing the man standing there in a dark gray sweater, jeans, and sneakers. She knew few men who made casualwear look anything but.

"What?"

She watched as his eyes moved over her, from the droopy sweat socks on her feet, past the worn cotton shorts and the paint-splattered T-shirt that spoke of a horrid experience trying to paint the hallway the previous year, straight up to her hastily created ponytail. He swallowed and muttered, "Goddamnit," before pushing his way into her house.

"We need to talk," he said by way of greeting.

"Why?"

He frowned. "What?"

"I said why do we need to talk? As far as I'm concerned there's nothing that needs to be said."

"I need to kiss you."

Now Irene frowned. "Why?"

"Must you always ask why?"

"When people come to me with things that don't make sense . . . yes."

"Just let me kiss you and then I'll leave."

"Do you know how many germs are in the human mouth? I'd be better off kissing an open sewer grate."

Why did she have to make this so difficult? He hated being here. Hated having to come here at all. Yet he had something to prove and goddamnit, he'd prove it or die trying.

But how dare she look so goddamn cute! He'd never known this Irene Conridge existed. He'd only seen her in those boxy business suits or in a gown that he'd bet money she never picked out for herself. On occasion he'd even seen her in jeans but, even then, she'd always looked pulled together and professional.

Now she looked goddamn adorable, and he almost hated her for it.

"Twenty seconds of your time and I'm out of here for good. Twenty seconds and I won't bother you ever again."

"Why?"

Christ, again with the why.

"I need to prove to the universe that my marking you means absolutely nothing."

"Oh, well isn't that nice," she said with obvious sarcasm. "It's nice to know you're checking to make sure kissing me Is as revolting as necessary."

"I'm not . . . didn't . . ." He growled. "Can we just do this please?"

"Twenty seconds and you'll go away?"

"Yes."

"Forever?"

"Absolutely."

"Fine. Just get it over with quickly. I have a lot of work to do. And the fact that you're breathing my air annoys me beyond reason."

Wanting this over as badly as she did, Van marched up to her, slipped his arm around her waist and yanked her close against him. They stared at each other for a long moment and then he kissed her. Just like he did Athana earlier. Only Athana had been warm and willing in his arms. Not brittle and cold like a block of ice. Irene didn't even open her mouth.

Nope. Nothing, he thought with overwhelming relief. This had all been a horrible mistake. He could—and would—walk away from the honorable and brilliant Irene Conridge, PhD, and never look back. Van almost smiled.

Until she moved slightly in his arms and her head tilted barely a centimeter to the left. Like a raging wind, lust swept through him. Overwhelming, all-consuming. He'd never felt anything like it. Suddenly he needed to taste her more than he needed to take his next breath. He dragged his tongue against her lips, coaxing her to open to him. To his eternal surprise she did and he plunged deep inside. Her body jerked, her hand reaching up and clutching his shoulder. Probably moments from pushing him away. But he wouldn't let her. Not if she felt even a modicum of what he was feeling. So he held her tighter, kissed her deeper, let her feel his steel-hard erection held back by his jeans against her stomach.

The hand clutching his shoulder loosened a bit and then slid into his hair. Her other hand grabbed the back of his neck. And suddenly the cold, brittle block of ice in his arms turned into a raging inferno of lust. Her tongue tangled with his and she groaned into his mouth.

Before Van realized it, he was walking her back toward her stairs. He didn't stop kissing her, he wouldn't. The last thing he wanted was for her to change her mind. He managed to get her to the upstairs hallway before she pulled her mouth away.

"What are you doing?" she panted out.

"Taking you to your bed."

"Forget it." And Van, if he were a crying man, would be sobbing. Until uptight Irene Conridge added, "The wall. Use the wall."